Saviours of Sephire Trilogy

Book One-The Green Book of Spells

by
Owen Butler

Bloomington, IN Milton Keynes, UK

AuthorHouse™
1663 Liberty Drive, Suite 200
Bloomington, IN 47403
www.authorhouse.com
Phone: 1-800-839-8640

AuthorHouse™ UK Ltd.
500 Avebury Boulevard
Central Milton Keynes, MK9 2BE
www.authorhouse.co.uk
Phone: 08001974150

First published by AuthorHouse 3/6/2007

ISBN: 978-1-4259-9815-8 (sc)

Printed in the United States of America
Bloomington, Indiana

This book is printed on acid-free paper.

Dedication

In loving memory of Grandma (Kathleen Barrett)

Acknowledgments

I would like to acknowledge first of all my mother whom without the nudge in the right direction this book would not have been written. Also thank you to my agent who has been a great support and was prepared to take a risk with a new writer.

Book One

Saviours of Sephire

(The Green Book of Spells)

Welcome, to the planet that is called Sephire. This is a world that is held within a distant universe. Linking devices called portals are located on the planet's surface. Once activated they have the ability of transporting a person into an entirely different galaxy.

The inhabitants of Sephire arrived through using one of the linking devices found on Earth during the period of the cave men. When the ice age threatened mans existence, they sought refuge through the portal and began to form civilizations on the unknown planet.

Once the forever winter began to thaw on Earth, many of the people returned to their home world, but there were some who decided to remain on Sephire and became the race of humanoids. Over the coming of years humanoids populated the planet living in peace and unity. Then one day a tall dark cloaked figure appeared through an unknown portal located in the rocklands of the north. The shape of the person appeared to be human but its face was bright white and had fiery red eyes that glowed in darkness.

Those who were unfortunate to cross the strangers path were eliminated by the long sharp blade that he carried. The frightened humanoids in the north, fled for the safety of the capital. Word quickly spread amongst the scattered villages and towns of the dark menace.

Once news reached the governing council of this danger, emergency meetings were held to decide upon an appropriate course of action. The humanoids are a peaceful race had not encountered any battles before, therefore the governing council decided to send one humanoid through the portal to Earth and ask the humans for their assistance.

After several days the humanoid had failed to return and the governing council presumed that they would no longer receive help from the people from Earth, despite the rumours spoken from ancient times of how a band of humans would free Sephire from turmoil.

The majority of the governing council would have the dark danger defeated to allow the humanoids way of life to return to how it once was, but there was one humanoid who saw this as an opportunity to claim their leadership of the planet. The individual was called Peirlee, she was middle aged and delved in sorcery.

This power hungry humanoid had manipulated one of the other members with her election to the governing council.

Before the humanoids could instruct their combat forces to remove the threat, Peirlee had sought the dangerous stranger and alerted it of the forces approaching. Rather than turn against the enemy she formed an allegiance with it and they both departed through the portal from whence it came.

Their departure was only brief, for when the equivalent of three Earth years had elapsed, they returned to Sephire, only this time the dark figure had brought along the huge presence of his tribe army. Peirlee's appearance had aged due to passing through the portal but she had discovered special powers of witchcraft that provided her with longer lasting life. The humanoid had betrayed her own people and now showed all form of loyalty towards the dark master who called himself by the name of Roshtu. He traveled on a menacing dark black horse that could breath fire and fly through the air. From then onwards Roshtu was known by the scared humanoids as the dark knight.

Roshtu's army was strong in numbers and resembled the appearance of apes. They carried curved wooden weapons and used them with dangerous efficiency. The humanoid forces were overcome and many battles were lost to the tribe army. However the humanoids were able to withstand the attacks made against the capital of Sephire, called Valadreil. The town consists of tall marvelous buildings with glistening towers and is the place where the humanoids keep control of the activation to all portals that are on the planet.

With the humanoids in need of someone to lead them, it was decided to disband the governing council and instead elect the brave general to become king of Sephire.

To prevent further dangers from entering into Sephire, the portals were immediately de-activated. This allowed the humanoids to defend and re-build their resistance for the next forty years.

The present leader is King Ridley, whom had personally been involved in many victorious battles against the tribe apes. His wife is Queen Avril and together they have a daughter aged in her twenties called Princess Juliana. King Ridley holds at his disposal the royal guard forces, which are now greater in number than the tribe army apes.

In a bid to be rid of the evil threat, the king, queen and their humanoid forces ride northwards. However on their journey they are caught unawares by Peirlee the witch, and she casts a spell that places them into a trapped time vortex.

With the capital of Sephire virtually indefensible the dark knight's armies attack the depleted humanoid defenses. Roshtu can now claim overall leadership of the planet and re-activate the portals to allow further apes to enter Sephire.

Inside the control tower of Valadreil, Princess Juliana has barricaded herself with the remainder of her staff and personal guards. One of the guards anxiously turns around and faces the princess, "My lady, we must activate the portals. Perhaps we will receive aid from Earth, as spoken by the prophecy". His voice is barely heard above the sound of the constant banging of tribe army apes attempting to break through the barricade from the other side of the closed door. The princess who is dressed in her dark military garments stands still. Knowing that there is no escape from this room, she is prepared for a final battle.

Despite her young appearance, her mind is mature beyond her years. Once Juliana had not heard word from her parents she knew that this would be her decision to make but now the time for thinking is over. The princess is aware that to re-activate the portals would allow further armies belonging to Roshtu to enter Sephire and would make it impossible for the humanoids to form a resistance.

To date, the humans have ignored all previous pleas for help, Juliana wonders why should she be certain that they should suddenly come to their aid now. Yet despite this, Juliana has a feeling telling her not to give up on the prophecy. The sound of thumping against the locked doors intensifies, much louder than the sound of the heart beats in her head.

She looks to one of the control operators who sits next to a console and nods her approval to instruct the command. The controller quickly flicks several switches to open the portals but the process will only allow the activation to work for a period of three days. Once this time has passed, the portals will be closed forever more. The controller confirms that it has been completed. Juliana sighs in relief, maybe there is a slim hope that help will arrive for the future people of Sephire, but for now she feels her life will soon be over. The crashing noise subsides and the doors cave inwards, the sound of feared screams can be heard all around the princess, she looks on as her enemies approach and darkness consumes her.

Chapter One

Within the darkness the sound of terrified screaming subsides. All that can be heard is the sound of wheels moving slowly along a track of rails when bright daylight suddenly appears from the end of a dark tunnel. The hands belonging to two humans can be seen gripping onto a metal bar at the front of a boxcar on a roller coaster. The ride grinds to a halt just short of a huge drop, allowing the fear and anticipation to build within each of the passengers Robert, who is a twenty-seven year old from Glamorgan in Wales, sits alongside his energetic younger American cousin called Rachel. He looks across to her to see if she shows any signs of feeling as scared as he is but then recollects that it was her crazy suggestion, which had lead them to be here in the first place. The breeze at this height moves Rachel's blonde hair aside, showing her face full of excitement.

Although he is related to Rachel, they have spent the majority of their childhood in separate countries.

Rachel was very young when her family had moved to America but her older cousin spent the start of his academic years in England where he became good friends with a fellow student called Simon. The two friends were successful to be able to enroll at the same university as his twenty four year old cousin in San Francisco.

Robert glances to the plummet of the next part of the ride and nearly swears when he is unable to see through the clouds below and grips tightly onto the holding bar. Wishing to focus anywhere else other than downwards, Robert then feels his cousin grip hold of his knuckles as she senses that the ride is about to continue. The restless Welshman realizes that the thumping sound that he can hear is his heart pounding. Beads of sweat appear on his face but he is determined not to make a spectacle of himself, Rachel would tell the others and they would never let him hear the end of it.

Suddenly a motor kicks into gear at the back of the boxcar and it plummets to a one hundred-meter descent. A strong force of warm air brushes against Robert's face. His eyes are firmly shut as he hears the screaming once more from the other passengers behind him but it is over as quickly as it had begun.

The ride comes to a halt but the tall brown haired man feels that part of his anatomy have not yet caught up with him. His heart then begins to start beating again and a warm rush of adrenaline suddenly pumps through his veins. He is relieved that he had not made a fool of himself by screaming to stop the ride.

Once the boxcar's safety harnesses have been released, the passengers gingerly depart towards the exit.

Robert attempts to steady himself as his smaller relative begins to talk enthusiastically about the buzz from the experience. The able bodied Welshman attempts to look for the familiar face belonging to his dark haired friend called Simon from within the bustling crowd of the amusement park.

Even though Simon is the same age as Robert and they have grown up together to feel like brothers, their personalities are completely different. Robert enjoys sports and the simpler things in life, whilst his skinny companion detests physical activities and is constantly engrossed in his text books. Simon had been born and raised in Windsor and his English accent is well defined. Robert recollects the first time they had enrolled at university when the other students used to ask if Simon was related to the royal family.

The outing to the amusement park is to celebrate the end of this year's term at university. Robert has made up his mind that since his exams are now over this will be his final year in America. Once the summer break has ended he intends to return back to his homeland of Wales, where he hopes to set up a business in Industrial Technology. Simon has two more years remaining on his syllabus about studying law, whilst Rachel plans to continue learning economics. Robert knows it will be a difficult moment to break the news to his friends about his decision especially to Simon. Even though he has done well in his assessment and enjoyed his time here, he hopes that by returning home he will overcome his dilemma about trying to make something of his life and maybe he can finally begin to relax and find himself a girlfriend.

Simon had opted not to join them on the roller coaster ride, as he does not have the stomach for fast rides or for any sense of adventure, so he had decided to remain with Rachel's friend called Claire whom had been keeping a watchful eye on her younger teenage brother called Bobby. Robert groans when he thinks of the freckled face youth as he is forever finding things to moan about and is completely different to his sister. Claire is a tall brunette with a warm and friendly personality, however Bobby is small, cheeky and always used to getting his own way. Robert decides that perhaps it is a phase the boy is going through and remembers how difficult it is for a teenager to deal with the issues of growing up. Since Bobby had not been tall enough to be allowed to go on the roller coaster ride he is certain that it would have added to his constant list of complaints.

On this sweltering summer's day everyone can be seen wearing shorts and loose items of clothing.

Eventually Robert finds their companions but Simon appears to be hot and bothered and he senses that Bobby has been giving his intellectual friend a hard time during their absence. Bobby can be seen trying to kick the candy machine in an attempt to dislodge one of the bars. Claire is embarrassed with his actions, she pulls her younger brother away from the machine and warns him to behave himself.

They slowly make their way through a crowd of people. Simon sees the happy expressions on their faces, looking for the next ride or feature to gaze at whilst music can be heard playing through the public address system. Robert shields his eyes from the brightness of the hot sunshine and follows his companions as they walk wearily past stalls that are selling food, drinks and candy. On a day like today when everyone is dehydrating, Simon suspects that the drinks stall must be doing very well.

Claire decides to buy her brother an ice cream to stop him from complaining whilst Robert uses this opportunity to purchase a postcard that he intends to send back to his parents. He looks over the selection available to purchase and chooses one with a glowing red sunset of San Francisco.

Rachel clicks off her mobile phone and informs her older cousin that their other two friends have managed to hire a boat for them to use for fishing and sunbathing. Simon remarks, "I do hope the sea is not choppy, my stomach does not take well to water". Robert assures his apprehensive friend, "On a day like today, the sea should be calm". Bobby tells Simon that he is a wimp but states that he cannot wait to catch some fish and hints of the possibility that they might even see some great white sharks that are capable of eating a man in one bite. Simon's face immediately shows concern but Claire gives her trying brother a clip over the head knowing that he was trying to scare the Englishman. She tries to reassure her serious companion and tells him not to worry about Bobby's teasing. Her native New York accent is contrast to Simon's perfect English and the group makes their way out from the busy amusement park.

The five companions continue to walk in the blistering heat and arrive at the waterfront. The fresh sea breeze is welcoming but the distinctive smell of fish causes Bobby to complain and he covers his nose with his arm. His older and wiser sister decides to ignore him as do her other group of friends and they stop to look at the splendid boats and yachts that are moored behind the safety of the harbour barrier.

Claire looks up and notices dozens of seagulls flying around in search of food. Bobby however seems to be fascinated by the sight of the baseball stadium, home to the San Francisco Giants, where at the back of McCovey Cove is a huge bronze statue of a famous ball player that the youngster has modeled his own game on. The wide-eyed teenager gasps, "Wow, look at that. I'm going to make it, just like he did, then one day somebody will carve a statue of me!" Suddenly a voice remarks from behind him, "You're going to have to eat a lot of spinach to get that size". Robert and his companions whirl around and recognize that the half cast man standing in front of them is Derek. He greets them with a smile, pleased to have caught them unawares. Derek is the light-hearted member of the group, if he isn't smiling then he is joking.

Simon gestures to the row of boats and remarks, "We are fortunate that you found us otherwise we would have been wandering around for hours trying to find you". Derek smiles and warns them that Naomi has prepared some food. Naomi is Derek's girlfriend and has been for the past eight months. She is Kenyan born but had been raised in Chicago and has recently attempted her hand at trying to cook some of her native food, which has not yet been well received. Derek points towards the secured boat that they have hired and leads the way but quietly mentions to Robert and Simon, "If the food tastes horrible we can always put it on the end of the fishing hooks, I just hope the fish take it!"

They reach the boat and are welcomed by Naomi whom is a slim athletic woman with gold beads in her hair. Bobby makes a point of being the first to jump onto the boat and calls back to his companions, "Welcome aboard me hearties". They find that there is plenty of room where sun beds and chairs are along the deck. The vessel appears to be quite old and Simon points out to his horror that the floorboards creak under foot. Derek collects the fishing nets and tells him that the harbourmaster had given his assurance that the vessel was seaworthy. Simon is not so certain and as the rest of his friends place on extra sun lotion he fastens his life reserve around his waist. As Robert examines the sea charts, Bobby states excitedly, "This is going to be an adventure". Simon remarks, "I do hope not, I much prefer the peaceful life". Derek pulls back on the cord of the starter motor and it roars into life, he then proceeds to steer the boat out to sea.

Chapter Two

In the late afternoon sunshine the weather remains warm. The small party has traveled for six miles. The sea is very calm and the silent setting creates a peaceful atmosphere. The women talk amongst themselves and nibble on the food which Naomi has prepared. They are gossiping and giggling about events, which had happened during the course of the year at university. Whereas Robert and his other friends, secretly place their food onto the hooks of their fishing lines.

So far Bobby has caught the most fish and is in the process of reminding everyone about this, when suddenly two fins surface alongside the boat. "Look over there". Derek points to everyone, Simon almost falls out of his chair shrieking, "Christ, they're sharks!" Robert tries to calm him, "They're dolphins Simon, don't panic". Bobby jests, "Yeah don't swear, the dolphins will hear". The cheeky youth is beginning to aggravate Simon and a few others by now. Claire remarks, "They're gorgeous". Her voice immediately softens the tension between the two.

The fishing lines are immediately put away and everyone stands together and gazes in wonder at a male and female dolphin swimming alongside their boat. Suddenly a warning screeching sound comes from the female dolphin, then in an instant both mammals dive under water and quickly change direction on a course away from the vessel. Rachel wonders why had they done that. Claire speculates, "They must have smelt your aftershave Bobby". Upset that his sister would try to embarrass him, the teenager sits down in his chair and folds his arms to sulk.

Derek notes, "That's strange, the wind has picked up". Robert suggests it would be wise that maybe they should consider returning back to the harbour. The dark haired American footballer replies, "Okay I think you're right, it's just over an hour away from the nearest port". Rachel suspects there is something wrong because there are no other ships to be seen or any seagulls to be heard. Clouds now block out the lowering sun and it seems that all form of life has left this place. She hopes that they make it back safely.

After half an hour has elapsed, Robert and his companions find themselves in trouble. The ferocious wind causes the waves to become enormous. Rain falls heavily from the jet-black sky and the sea swirls from the storm. The boat's terrified occupants have placed on their life jackets in case they fall overboard.

Simon and Bobby have been sick from the motion of the angry sea and their muffled cries are barely heard over the deafening sound from the pounding waves that continue to crash against the light vessel.

The sea licks the ship's deck with another cold spray of water, which causes Robert and his scared companions to slip over. The anxious Welshman wipes the salt water away from his eyes and can see Derek attempting to get the starter motor working. He slides across to offer his assistance but has to shout loudly into Derek's ear to be heard, "What's wrong with the motor?" Derek replies, "I think the fuel chamber has been cracked! We should look for shelter and rough this out". Robert agrees with him but has to hold on tightly to the side of the boat to avoid being hurtled into the abyss.

Robert shouts across to Bobby and asks him to look in the box of equipment for some flares in case there are any other boats that can help them. As Simon leans out over the side of the boat to be sick, he sees the outline of some rocks in the distance and quickly warns his companions that they might have found land. Robert glances over and hopes that they can avoid crashing into the jagged rocks otherwise they will be doomed to the perils of the sea.

Claire and Rachel assist Bobby to light the flare and fire it upwards through the descending rain and scream out that they think they can see an island that is not far away. Derek yells back in disbelief, "It can't be, we shouldn't be anywhere near an island, according to these sea charts!" Naomi reasons to her boyfriend, "We don't have much choice, let's see if we can get closer and find some shelter".

Derek manages to use the last drop of fuel to point them towards the shore but suddenly the vessel then tilts upwards and it's stern disappears beneath the rising water. Robert is unable to hold on any longer and slides helplessly down the slippery deck but is fortunate to crash into some nets that prevent him from falling overboard. The boat continues to battle its way through the rising surf and gradually moves closer to the shore. When the water becomes knee height in depth, Robert and Derek each jump out and attempt to push the boat onto the beach. They fall over several times as they struggle against the dangerous current of the tide as well as the slippery seaweed that is trodden underfoot. Some of their companions lend their assistance but in order to get Simon off the boat, Robert has to pull his friend since he is too paralyzed through fear to move.

Everyone helps to combine in the final push, which is the final ounce of energy that each of them has and the marooned survivors collapse exhaustedly onto the soggy sand. The rain finally subsides but the wind continues to howl. Dark clouds have begun to clear and moonlight shines down upon them.

Derek grumbles, "I'm going to have some serious words with the weathermen tomorrow". He attempts to see if everyone else is okay. Claire is distressed and shrieks, "We had no warning of the storm!" The shock from the experience is etched on her face and she begins to cry. Rachel and Naomi are quick to console her. Bobby helps Simon up to his feet. Their previous differences are long forgotten. This is now a matter of surviving. The burning question that each of them has is where are they? And how are they going to last throughout the night?

Robert surveys the surrounding area and notices a small stream that flows into a cave. He advises his stranded companions that they could use the cave as a place of shelter. The group holds onto one another for support and walk wearily towards the direction of the cave.

Once they draw nearer they gaze upwards to the high arched entrance. Rachel manages to retrieve a flashlight, which she had recovered from the boat. They venture inside and notice that the top of the cave has an opening, allowing moonlight to shine through. Bobby says whilst shivering, "I'm cold". His sister quickly places an arm around his shoulder to offer him warmth whilst their other five companions decide to sit down on some large rocks.

Water can be heard dripping from inside the cave and the storm from outside causes a strong draught to blow through the cavern. Robert asks, "Do we have any matches, we're going to need some firewood otherwise we shall freeze to death". Derek responds miserably, "I don't know, I think the water has got to them". Naomi then asks if anyone else can hear the low humming sound. Her friends become silent as they try to hear the same noise. Simon asks to borrow Rachel's flashlight and then begins to shine the light down the end of the cave to see how far it goes. He stands up and paddles further down the stream. His companions remain where they are as they attempt to rest and come to terms with what has happened.

Simon shouts back to them excitedly, "Hey come and have a look at this". His voice echoes against the solid wall of rock. Robert is intrigued to discover what his friend has found and follows after him but as he approaches the humming sound intensifies. The curious tall brown haired Welshman notices that around the edge to this part of the cave is an archway where a blue intermittent light flashes from one end of the aperture to the other.

Simon asks, "What do you think it is?" Robert admits that he has no idea but suddenly points out to his friend, "Look there are strange markings". Simon then directs the flashlight to a panel embedded within the rock.

The rest of the group now joins them. Derek comments, "It's warmer down this end of the cave." Bobby is still shivering and remarks, "If it's warmer on the other side of this archway then I am going through".

Before he can be stopped the impatient teenager strides across only to disappear into darkness. Concern spreads quickly to his older sister and Claire calls out to him but receives no reply. Looking to one another the huddled group decides in unison to follow after the troublesome teenager.

Upon reaching the other side of the cave they are relieved to see Bobby standing in front of them, he remarks smugly, "See, I told you it was warmer this side, huh that's odd, the blue light has stopped flashing".

The others hastily turn around and are amazed to see their route back has been blocked off by solid rock.

With no other way to go other than forwards Roberts manages to find a way out of the cave and suggests they should attempt to collect what is left of their belongings from their boat.

As they prepare to enter the storm once more they are surprised to find that it has faded away. The sand is warm against their toes and the stream, which had led them into the cave has since dried out. The coldness of the air has evaporated and the temperature is now humid. Before anyone can wonder what is happening, Simon suddenly shrieks, "I can't see our boat!"

Rachel tells him not to panic and suggests that it is too dark to be able to find it now and that they should look for it in daylight. Since everyone is exhausted from their ordeal they agree with Robert's cousin and decide to rest behind some rocks where they soon fall asleep.

Rachel looks up to the blanket of stars within the red sky considering that it must soon be dawn but the blonde haired woman senses there is something different about this place. Before Rachel can pursue her thoughts any further, tiredness takes over and she too falls asleep.

Chapter Three

Claire awakens from her deep sleep and rolls over onto her side but struggles to open her firmly closed eyes. The slim brunette believes that she is in her soft bed but the smell of fresh air causes her to believe that she must have left the bedroom window open overnight and the sound of running water confuses her.

Claire is then struck with a distant memory of being in a terrible sea storm but decides that it must have been part of a dream. The young woman forces her blue eyes to open but soon becomes alarmed to find that she is on a beach but even more concerning is that the clear blue sky has changed to pale green!

Blinking several times to clear the image before her, Claire is worried that something has happed to the Earth's ozone layer or perhaps this is a nuclear fallout. Concerned that she is in danger she suddenly recollects on how she came to be here and screams, "The others, where are they?" Breathing frantically the alarmed woman stumbles to her feet in fear that her friends have become separated or that she has been abandoned but Claire then sighs in relief upon finding that her teenage brother and other companions are sleeping in a huddle behind a rock and hurries to wake them.

The members of the group awaken with the same panicked reaction and ask one another what is going on? Dazed and confused they slowly take in their surroundings. Robert shares his concerns of not being able to see their boat. Simon is horrified that they are marooned and presumes that it must have drifted out to sea when the tide had come in. Bobby panics, "We're stranded. What are we going to do now!"

Robert has no suggestion to offer but advises everyone to calm down.

As they stand bewildered Derek looks up in amazement at the pale green sky and wonders what could have caused it to change from its normal colour. Suddenly as they shield their eyes from the bright light the group of seven look open mouthed in disbelief and notice that the green sun has a glowing red-crescent shape around it. Simon speculates to his companions, "I do not think we are on Earth". Bobby retorts, "You don't say Mr. Genius". His older sister immediately tells him to be quiet. Naomi asks, "Where are we?" Nobody replies and they remain silently transfixed at the alien sky.

Robert looks further along the shore where the golden sand of the beach stretches along the coastline into the horizon. Just behind them are trees that belong to a forest. An echoed voice suddenly rings through the startled Welshman's ears, telling him, "Enter the forest". Robert asks his friends if they have also heard the voice but Simon looks at him in confusion and says that he had heard nothing. Robert wonders if his conscious is speaking to him but then the soothing voice is heard once again, "You are not safe on the beach, run to the forest". Robert continues to be puzzled by the voice that has spoken to him.

Suddenly Naomi cries out to them, "Look over there to the rocks." She points further in the distance and warns them, "I can see something walking across the sand".

Bobby stands up and begins to march off in that direction commenting, "Then let's go over to whoever it is and ask them where we are". Derek quickly holds the young teenager back to prevent him from moving.

Bobby looks up ready to give Derek a piece of his mind but before he can speak Derek tells him, "Don't go just yet lad". He squints his eyes to strengthen his vision and remarks, "Those figures are not human".

He quickly falls to the sand whilst pushing Bobby over as well. Their companions also lower to the ground to minimize the risk of being seen. Upon closer inspection the two figures in the distance now appear to resemble large monkeys that have long pointed beards and carry curved wooden objects.

As the humans lay still on the sand, Rachel whispers to her friends that she does not like the look of them, Derek remarks, "They don't appear friendly do they?" Robert's heart is beating frantically and he suggests, "I think we should go into the forest". His colleagues agree and begin to crawl cautiously up the beach towards the trees. Suddenly one of the ape creatures smells their presence and points them out to its colleague. The creature immediately launches its wooden object into the humans' direction.

Derek comments, "Don't worry that's never going to reach us, it must be at least fifty meters away."

However as soon as he has finished his sentence the weapon appears to be gathering speed, enabling it to gain further distance. Robert cries out "Boomerang!" and the others quickly dive for cover, knowing that the weapon, which has just whizzed past them, will return with deadly intentions. They remain on the sand until it passes overhead.

Bobby and Derek both gather a handful of small rocks to throw back into the direction of the hostile creatures. Simon is shaking through fear and his companions have to haul him to his feet. Robert urges them all to sprint towards the safety of the trees.

Bobby throws his large stone, which momentarily slows the apes' pursuit but they continue to loom towards the humans'. Derek decides to lead the rear of the group in case it should come to a physical confrontation. Since he is a quarterback for his American football team he intends to use his strength to fend off any attack. With his friends entering the woodlands Derek turns around and is surprised to discover that the apes are now only a few meters behind. The tough American launches his stone in the creatures' path and it hits one of them on the head that sends it tumbling to the ground. The other ape chooses to stop its pursuit to assess the threat. Derek does not wait around and continues to run, where he eventually rejoins his companions.

After what seems to be a couple miles that they have covered, the seven humans' realize they are no longer being pursued and decide to stop and recuperate. Simon asks in between gulps for oxygen, "What were those things that were chasing us?" Derek replies, "I have no idea, but one of them sure has a headache".

Scared and lost, they try to think of which direction they be should running to but the image of trees and bushes surrounding them makes their choice impossible. Naomi asks how will they ever be able to return home?

Simon is more concerned of what creatures are lurking in the forest? During this time Robert remains calm and recommends to his friends that they may discover some answers if they travel deeper into the woodlands. He then points to a dry dusty pathway and walks towards that direction. The others do not protest and hurry to catch up with him.

Bobby tells his older sister that he is hungry but she asks him to be patient and to wait until they stop again. Naomi quietly inquires to her boyfriend, "What makes Robert so certain that we are walking in the right direction?" Derek shrugs his shoulders and tries to get his colleagues attention but the Welshman fails to hear him as he is listening intently to the voice of the woman that is speaking inside his head and concentrates on the way that she is guiding him.

Green rays of sunlight shines through gaps of leaves and branches within the forest. The sound of birds and other unknown wildlife can be heard around them. Derek thinks to himself that their real danger will come from the predators of the night, whilst the others reflect on how they will ever find the way that takes them back home.

Chapter Four

Within the dark candlelit royal throne room of Valadreil, red moonlight shines against the marble floor. The room seems to be very dark, especially as Roshtu, the evil knight sits upon the grand throne. The dark lord gazes at the humanoids religious sceptre that is held within his grasp. His red eyes glow against the pale whiteness of his skeletal face as he studies the markings, which have been engraved.

Roshtu has finally conquered the humanoids and feels that at long last he has overall leadership of this planet called Sephire. He not only has control over the humanoid capital but more importantly to the dark menace he now has the power of activating the portal devices. At this very moment hundreds more of his forces are entering the planet within the Northern Rocklands of Terror. The evil leader decides not to have the humanoids killed, unless of course they threaten to rebel against him. He will instead use them as slaves of his mighty empire. The dark knight has only ever dreamt for one wish, and that is power, power to rule the universe. If anyone should get in the way of his plans for domination they will be crushed to smithereens.

Roshtu places the sceptre carefully against the grand throne. The great hall is very large and has several pillars to support its enormous ceiling. The dark cloaked knight turns around to face his audience of at least a thousand tribe army apes that obediently await the first instruction of the new leader to Sephire and he announces, "I declare ownership of this planet". His voice is loud and deep but is strained, "There is no humanoid strong enough to fight for their people. Victory is ours!" As Roshtu pauses the apes dutifully cheer and applaud their master.

The dark knight continues, "This planet is rich in minerals therefore we shall strip it for all of its worth and replenish the planets that I control through the other side of the portal. In the meantime, capture all humanoids and send them to my fortress in the north, kill any who try to resist". He raises his gigantic fist in the air and clenches it, the apes' respond again by chanting and yelling the praises of their leader. The sound is deafening as it echoes against the solid walls of the hall. The powerful leader raises his hands, which immediately silences his servants and Roshtu commands, "Go to the Northern Rocklands of Terror and use the machinery, which has been brought through from my domain".

The apes obey their order leaving just his personal servants remaining to await any further instructions.

Roshtu turns around. Flickers of candlelight protrude a tall shadow of his outline, which covers the grand throne and he picks up the sceptre once again. He wonders what significance it has to the race of people who have constructed it. The dark knight then looks across at his prize exhibit. Roshtu speaks slowly, "Princess".

In the corner of the room the humanoid Princess is helpless in being able to do anything to help her fellow people. Kept within a chamber Juliana has a slight cut to her face, which had been received during the struggle that led to her capture. Her hands and ankles are bound in chains and the king's daughter looks on nervously at the person approaching and knows it will only be a matter of time before Roshtu has her executed. She still wears her battle garments but without any weapon it would be a futile attempt to find a way of breaking free from her chamber to escape. The dark knight slowly walks across where his heavy boots echo against the marble floor. Narrowing his eyes the imposing knight looks down at her, when suddenly an unexpected ape enters the room.

The dark knight turns around and recognizes one of his loyal bodyguards called Riesk that kneels in front of him. This particular creature is much larger than the size of the tribe army apes. Riesk is armed and carries a pointed spear. He and his brother Gormosh are both responsible for controlling the ape army.

Ever since Roshtu had taken control of their planet and replenished it with precious minerals, the ape inhabitants showed their allegiance to the dark knight to build and breed his army. The conquering knight asks, "What is it?" His servant replies that a message has been received from the Northland Rocklands of Terror that the portal has become de-activated.

"What!" Roshtu shouts in disbelief. Princess Juliana cannot help but smile from her enemy's reaction. He notices her sniggering and prepares to fire a bolt of energy to kill her but then reconsiders when he realizes that she is worth keeping alive, for now. The ball of energy within his palm diminishes and the dark knight looks at Juliana knowing full well that the number of re-enforcement's that have passed though the portal will not be enough should the king and his royal guard forces break free from the witch's spell. The evil lord decides that he could use the princes as bait.

"Princess, are you going to tell me the code I need to activate the portals? The longer you take the further your people will suffer as slaves. I promise once I have all that I need, your people will be released".

Juliana retorts, "You will leave this planet bare! And will only let the humanoids live for as long as you have a purpose for us, after that you will kill us all". She waits for a bolt of energy to be shot through her as punishment for her outburst, but Roshtu smiles. He appears calm knowing that she will soon break and he begins to walk away before telling the young woman, "Give me the code Princess, in exchange for your freedom".

Juliana wishes that she could lie to fool her captor but she eventually declares, "Only one person knows of the procedure to re-activate the portals from their current status". Roshtu turns around and looks her straight in the eye and demands to know whom this person is. The defiant prisoner replies, "The king! One day my father shall return along with his guards and will defeat you".

This time Roshtu is unable to hold back his anger and sends a bolt of energy through Juliana that lasts briefly. As the princess grimaces from the pain, Roshtu declares to her, "He is not coming back". She snaps back through gritted teeth, "How can you be so sure?" The dark knight realizes this stubborn humanoid's resolve will not be easily broken and he throws the scepter on the floor in annoyance before striding out from the room. The black cape he wears is swept up by the briskness of his walk. He instructs the remaining apes within the room, "Take her to the dungeons and guard the palace". The doors are then slammed shut behind him.

Roshtu stands outside the throne room with his bodyguard and thinks about the potential threat that the king would pose if Peirlee's spell were to be broken. Suddenly two apes appear from beyond the corridor, one of the creatures has a bandage wrapped around its swollen head. "My lord one of them says".

Roshtu is irritated with the constant distractions and angrily replies, "What do you want?" Before they can answer, the evil knight proceeds to ask the wounded ape if he had been involved in a fight with some humanoids. The ape replies, "No master, the creatures we encountered on the beach two days ago did not wear the same uniforms and were not groomed in the same manner as the humanoids". Roshtu is confused and wonders whom the troublemakers are. The other ape comments that the creatures scents were different than the humanoids. Roshtu demands to know in which direction they went. The two apes reply nervously that the strangers had entered the forest. Since they are aware of the dangers of entering the woodlands they feared to follow them any further.

The bodyguard awaits his master's response. Given the hour he expects an outrage from Roshtu but the dark knight instructs him, "Riesk, ready my horse I'm going to see the witch". The loyal servant quickly departs to carry out the command. Roshtu tells the two remaining apes to return to the location where they encountered the strange beings and to follow any tracks that may have been left behind. The dark knight then walks away, hoping that Peirlee can provide him with insight as to the stranger's identity.

Chapter Five

The red glow of Sephire's moon also brings light to the forest where seven people from Earth are trying to comprehend what planet they have entered and to think of a way of returning home. The group has spent this past day walking tiredly ever deeper into the forest and are famished. Simon approaches Robert and asks him how is it that he knows where to go? Robert stops and turns around, hoping that the others will not think him crazy for what he is about to tell them. "Ever since we awoke on the beach, a voice has been talking to me, guiding me thus far". Derek interrupts, "Oh great what with being chased by monkeys throwing boomerangs and you hearing voices, I hope this planet has good psychiatrists". His joke raises a smile from the others.

Rachel walks up to her cousin and feels his forehead before asking, "You're not coming down with something are you?" Robert steps back and angrily remarks, "I am not ill". Simon attempts to believe his friend and enquires as to what the voice is saying. Robert replies, "The voice is female, it is echoed as if it is distant. She has been telling me to lead us to where the light shines along a path through the leaves and grass of the forest. However for the last half an hour she has not spoken to me".

Bobby wonders how is it that the rest of them have not also heard the voice? And for that matter whether she can be trusted? His sister agrees with him and voices her concerns, "For all we know she could be leading us into danger". These are justified questions that Claire and Bobby have asked but for now Robert does not know the answers. Suddenly a pale green light shines from behind the tree next to Bobby and out steps the figure of an angel. She looks at Bobby and speaks majestically, "It was my voice that your friend heard". The teenager looks bewildered, Robert instantly recognizes her voice and everybody steps back in amazement.

The angel walks effortlessly in front of the humans', looking at them all she smiles upon their shocked reaction. She has long flowing blond hair that falls by her side. The woman appears young and wears pale silk robes that sweep to her feet. The mysterious woman is both very wise and insightful. Although the figure of the angel is seen before them, she is not living as the light that illuminates is of her spirit.

Derek manages to ask, "Who are you?" The graceful woman calmly responds, "My name is Carmen, I am the angel of the forest and bring guidance to those in need of my assistance. My voice can be heard by the one who will bring freedom back to the humanoids of this planet". She pauses and looks to Robert, as do his human companions. He hastily objects, "Wait I am not the one, and we don't even belong here".

Carmen replies, "I know where you are from and the reason as to why you were chosen to come here".

Simon asks the mysterious angel where are they?

Carmen tells the seven companions, "You have entered the world of Sephire, its landscape is similar to your Own. The people of Sephire once lived in a time of peace, they are descendants from Earth and arrived during the time of primitive man". Simon interrupts her and remarks to his friends, "She means cave men".

Carmen looks at him to suggest that he would be wise not to interrupt her again and then continues, "In time the people developed and eventually called themselves the race of humanoids. However with the power and magic that allowed the humanoids to enter this planet, dark magic allowed cruelty and evil to enter in the form of a tall and dangerous knight. He comes from a wicked domain and seeks power and control over Sephire".

"He would have been defeated had one of the humanoids own not betrayed them. The royal kings and queens gave hope to their people and the humanoids managed to resist through control of the portals, which is the same device that managed to transport you here".

"Now you have arrived at the humanoids most darkest hour, they are on the brink of extinction, their life left spent in slavery until death. The current king and queen along with their forces have not returned past the point of the wishing well and now the dark knight has complete control over the planet".

Bobby then interrupts, "That's a shame for the humanoids' but how does all of this concern us? And how do we get back home?" Carmen replies truthfully, "For now there is no way that you can return to your home world. There are several reasons why you should help the humanoids. The portals that are now disabled can only be activated by the power of three lost magical books, if you find and rescue the king you might be able to discover the location of the lost books. The second reason to help the humanoids is that if the dark knight's army discovers you, you will be captured and killed. He will soon be alerted to your presence and knows of your threat to his plans for domination. The final reason why you should help the humanoids is that the dark knight will soon capture two of your kind. They entered this planet recently, but I was unable to guide them to safety".

Robert and Derek both say together, "We've got to rescue them!" Claire asks them how are they going to be able to do that? Carmen replies, "You have each been provided with special powers in the form of weapons. These are hidden east from here at The Monument of Stones, which is where you must go at first light. As I said you were chosen, your arrival was not by chance but an act of the gods, which is why a long time ago they constructed your weapons. The prophecy once spoken will finally come true".

"Unfortunately Peirlee, whom is the person that betrayed the humanoids was once a member of that council. Once she joined allegiance with Roshtu she then mastered her powers to become a witch. She does not know where your weapons are kept but does know of your existence and has been expecting your arrival. She is very dangerous. Even the dark is concerned of her power but fear not that is for another day".

The guiding angel then beckons the humans' towards a clearing in between the trees where a rug has been laid with berries, nuts and flasks containing spring water. Robert asks her in disbelief, "How could you do all of this when you are not real?" She tells him, "I do not just talk to humans and humanoids but to the animals of the forest as well." She then motions them all towards the food and informs them, "Here you will eat and rest tonight, for the journey ahead is both long and dangerous. Try to understand all of what I have said. Above all be careful where you go and what you say, as spies of the dark knight may be listening".

Carmen then turns and walks towards a tree, the light from her spirit fades into the night and she disappears until their next meeting. Bewildered by what they have heard, the group then hungrily tucks into their food before attempting to sleep whilst ever alert to the noises of the forest that surrounds them.

Having eventually drifted off, Robert has a dream. He pictures in his imagination that he is fighting against a tall and powerful enemy and then hears a woman scream out his name at which point he feels that his life is fading away from him. He looks down to see blood on his hands.

Suddenly the Welshman awakens in a startle with beads of sweat covering his face. He realizes to his relief that it was just a dream. Once his eyes begin to focus, Robert notices that his friends are peacefully sleeping. As Robert gently eases his head back down he ponders to himself how will they ever be able to help free the captured humans. He closes his eyes, trying not to be afraid of falling asleep once more and attempts to picture the image of the valleys in Glamorgan. Robert vows to himself that he will do whatever he can to see them once again.

Chapter Six

The dark knight rides on his black menacing horse, flying below the clouds of Sephire's red sky. On his travels he has seen many of the primitive humanoids futile attempts to flee from his tribe army.

Leaderless, the humanoids will soon surrender to his powers. Roshtu smiles on the thought. This victory had taken longer than expected but unless further of his troops have made it through the portal it will take even longer to send the iron, steel and coal back to replenish his other planets. He suddenly sees the witch's dwelling upon the horizon that is situated at the top of a steep hill. The building had once been an abbey and has spiral columns to its towers where holes in the wall allow lookouts to survey the landscape.

Roshtu brings his dark horse to the ground and canters up to the main gates. The wet conditions have made the land muddy underfoot. Roshtu recognizes the tribe army presence detached here as protection for the witch, not that she needs any but at least this way he can find out what she is up to. Even though the dark knight has Peirlee to thank for his survival and for her source of information, he suspects she posses a power even she cannot contain and might one day become a danger to his plans.

The guards obediently open the gates and tribe army apes that are on duty in the courtyard quickly manoeuvre from the horse's path. Roshtu leads the stallion towards the doors, where Gormosh, loyal servant to Roshtu and brother of Riesk is waiting for him. Roshtu can sense the servant is relieved to see his master possibly for safety from the crazy witch. Gormosh greets him and bows his head before kneeling to await his orders. Roshtu is not interested in exchanging pleasantries and asks whilst climbing down from his horse, "Where is she?" He passes his servant with the reigns. Gormosh replies, "The witch is at the top of the tower. Master she is frightening the guards with her sorcery".

The dark knight refuses to comment and walks up the spiral staircase, passing several guards that keep watch. They seem surprised to see him here. When Roshtu reaches the top of the stairs he pushes open the doors to the witch's chamber. There he sees before him Peirlee the witch, her eyes tightly shut, visibly concentrating on something whilst grasping hold of her staff. Peirlee may have found longer lasting life but her appearance is deformed with her skin stretched. She announces, "They've arrived!" Immediately opening her eyes she looks directly at Roshtu. He is unsure of what to say or do as the witch has caught him by surprise.

Roshtu looks back at Peirlee, waiting for her to add more insight to her statement. The old witch moves to the opening within the wall and peers out from the viewpoint. She remains clinging onto her staff as if it is the only thing holding her together but Roshtu is aware there is an inner power within the sorceress that many would be wise not to test.

She whispers, "I knew they would come, I knew they would arrive". Her eyes are gleaming with satisfaction that she had been right with her foresight. The dark knight questions, "Peirlee whom do you speak of?" He then predicts her response, "Not the king, Peirlee your spell, has it been broken, you withering hag why did you not speak of this sooner?"

Only Roshtu could be allowed to speak to the witch in such a manner. She immediately replies seemingly unaffected by his outburst, "It is not the royal. No, it is the group of nine humans who according to the prophecy once spoken amongst the religious sector will bring peace and order back to this planet. I talk of the warriors whom are not from these lands and come from foreign soil".

Roshtu considers of what she has said and fathoms, "Aah, so these must be the creatures the apes had seen the other day. But Peirlee these so called warriors there are only nine of them, they pose no threat to my plans. Surely I must spend all of my resources to find a way of activating the portals". The witch hastily responds, "They are a menace! And not to be underestimated, they have powers you do not know of, I have foreseen them to be a great threat".

Roshtu remains silent. In the past Peirlee had been proven to be right, so if she is correct about this he considers how will it affect his plans? Whilst Roshtu is in deep contemplation, the witch walks over to where a crystal ball is placed within the room, she gazes into the object. Staring closer she then sees a dark bird flying through the sky. Peirlee comments, "Aah raven of the night sky, what do you see? What do you tell me?" As she continues to peer into the object, Roshtu walks up and watches in amazement.

A shining light protrudes from the crystal ball. The witch's eyes become wider, as she sees the vision through the sight of the raven. She whispers to Roshtu whilst remaining fixed onto the image before her, "I see two of them, two humans, they wander near the northern borders". The dark knight suggests the humans will be caught easily, as Peirlee continues, "They have slanted eyes and carry swords!" The bright light from the crystal ball begins to fade and all that remains of the room's brightness is the flickers of candlelight. Peirlee closes her eyes to reflect on what she has seen. Roshtu declares that the humans will pose no threat to his army and he will give the order for the humans to be killed. Peirlee cries out "No!" and opens her eyes.

Roshtu looks cautiously at her to hear the scheme that she has in mind. The witch walks over to him and whispers, "Their companions will try to rescue them, you must force the two fleeing humans towards the direction of Lake Idris, for there is no escape from that place". She looks up at the tall figure of Roshtu to see if her suggestion has his seal of approval.

The dark knight nods his head and confirms with a devilish smile, "I will send a detachment of apes, the humans will be surrounded by three thousand of my army". Peirlee warns him that a long time ago, weapons had been constructed for the humans to use in battle but the place where they were hidden had been kept secret from her. Roshtu comments, "It matters not, they are outnumbered and this will finally put an end to the humanoid folk stories about their gods being able to send help to save this planet from my power".

Roshtu then whispers to Peirlee, "In the meantime I want to know exactly where the other humans' are".

The witch asks how is he going to achieve this? He replies, "Fortunately my eyes and ears made it through the portal whilst it was briefly open". Peirlee appears to be confused as Roshtu strides across to the opening within the wall and bellows down to his servant, "Gormosh, have Finch report to me immediately at Valadreil". Gormosh looks up through the pouring rain to the tower and nods to his master, where he then sends one of the apes to go to Roshtu's fortress in the north. The rider quickly departs on horseback and travels down the hillside out of sight.

Peirlee raises an eyebrow at the suggestion of Finch tracking the humans'. Roshtu says to her, "Can you think of anyone else more suited to the task?" The witch does not respond and Roshtu begins to stride towards the doors of the room announcing, "I shall introduce myself to these outlanders and see if they are worthy of the stories spoken about them. Once I have them killed, I shall encounter no further resistance. The portals will soon be activated and my conquering kingdom shall continue".

The doors of the room close behind the dark knight and he departs from the witch's dwelling on his menacing horse, where he will go to Valadreil and sit upon the grand throne of the planet that he now governs.

Within the coolness of morning, green daylight beams through the woodlands. The team of humans bound to the quest of bringing humanity and salvation back to the people of Sephire make their trek eastwards. Robert recollects of what Carmen had told him that if they were to continue along this path they should reach The Monument of Stones before the red moon rises. Bobby asks his colleagues, why had he been chosen to be a member of the group that would help the humanoids? He believes there must be others who are stronger and braver than him. Derek tells the teenager, "Hey don't put yourself down, at the beach the other day you were not afraid to stand up to those scary monkeys". Simon coughs to get his attention and corrects him, "I think the guiding angel described them as tribe army apes of the dark lord". Derek replies, "You're not going to sell many tickets to the zoo if you're going to call them that".

Rachel tells them all to keep quiet as Robert is trying to hear the path that Carmen is guiding him to follow.

Naomi asks, "How do we know the guiding angel is telling the truth?" Simon agrees with her but responds, "We have no other choice. Finding our weapons is our priority, without them we are too vulnerable from an attack from those horrid creatures". Robert finds it impossible to concentrate and sighs in frustration. He tells his companions, "I can't hear anything from Carmen, let's stop for a few minutes".

The group sips from the flasks that Carmen had provided. As they take a moment to rest, wildlife can be heard around them. Birds that are extinct back on Earth are chirping, squirrels are searching the ground for nuts to store away for the winter. Robert considers this must be the equivalent of autumn and looks at the leaves, which are a golden brown colour. The temperature is quite humid and the Welshman wonders if Sephire has seasons similar to Earth. Robert's companions chat quietly amongst themselves, discussing about their current situation and how they are all missing their home world.

Robert speculates to himself how can they survive the journey that lies ahead of them? Suddenly the soothing voice speaks inside his mind, "You will know what to do when the time arrives". Robert recognizes the guiding angels voice. "Soon you will come to a pathway that is made from stone. Remain on this route that takes you out from the woodlands until you reach fields of high grass. Continue eastwards and there you will find The Monument of Stones. Unless you reach there before the moon rises, you will be unable to discover your weapons". Then the voice of Carmen fades.

Robert rises to his feet and looks to his companions', "Come on its time to push on, another minute we loose is another minute those poor two humans have to survive". Inspired by Robert's speech Rachel and the others jog behind him with a new zest of energy. The pathway is both long and winding but eventually in the late afternoon sunshine they come out of the woodlands.

Robert hears the departing message from Carmen, "The strength of the fleeing humans is fading, find your weapons and place on the uniforms that you find, as they will disguise your scents from any unwelcome followers. You must then travel towards Lake Idris, which is located north from The Monument of Stones. There you will find your two companions".

"I can only guide you whilst you are near or within the forest, otherwise trust your instincts as they serve you well but do not underestimate the power of the dark knight and that of his witch. You leave, with the hopes of the forest, farewell until our next meeting". Her voice then disappears against the breeze.

Unaware of what lies ahead of them, the humans' enter the field with grass that reaches as high as their waists. Simon suggests these lands must have once belonged to a farmer and have been left unkempt.

Bobby asks when are they going to be stopping for their next rest. Robert informs him, "We cannot stop as time is running out and we must reach The Monument of Stones before sunset, otherwise we will not find our weapons and the two captured humans will not survive". Robert proceeds to lead his team further through the fields. Claire holds onto her brother's hand. With the teenager being the smallest, the grass reaches as high as his chin. Whilst following Robert his younger cousin looks up to the sky and can feel the warmth of the sun beginning to fade.

Chapter Seven

After an hour of continuous journey through the fields, Robert waits for his companions to catch up but they appear close behind him. The Welshman notices their clothes are now beginning to appear grubby and their faces need to be washed. Fortunately they are all wearing jeans, which has provided protection from being bitten by the insects but he notices that some of them have scratches on their exposed arms.

He realizes their clothes are probably the most valuable items that they now posses, as they are all that is left to remind them of home.

Robert begins to feel frustrated. The tall grass has severely slowed their progress and the colour of the sky now glows green, which suggests the sun is about to set. Suddenly Naomi points towards a small hill that is only a short distance away and shouts excitedly, "Look over there, I can see some rocks!" The band of humans hurries to the hill whilst still battling against the obstacle of the grass.

Eventually they scramble up the slope. From this viewpoint the humans can see the fields continuing below them for miles. In the far distance against the horizon to the north, Rachel can barely see the feint outline of tall protruding mountains. To the western horizon she notices the woodland forest from where they have come and sees a mist rapidly spreading across the fields. Rachel gazes up to the sky and alerts her companions, "The sun, it's nearly setting". They look upwards and can see that the crescent shape has almost changed colour from a glowing red to a shining green. With time quickly running out they turn to the impressive rock formation that stands before them.

Simon is bewildered with the encircling display of huge fifteen feet high stones of different shapes and texture. Bobby asks, "What fool designed this?" Claire gives him a warning look to behave himself.

Naomi speculates that their weapons are not here but her boyfriend suggests they should take a look around. The humans' feel despondent as they had hoped finding their weapons would be an easy task but it appears to be otherwise.

As the others peer behind each of the sixteen rocks, Robert looks to Simon for advice but notices his friend is in deep thought and asks, "What is it?" Simon fails to reply as his face reflects a puzzled expression. The Englishman then proceeds to walk out form the circle of stones and remarks to his friend, "Do you remember when we were back at school in Windsor, when we had to complete that assignment to do with the history of blue stones and rocks from the Marlborough downs, how they were significant for Stone Hendge?"

Robert vaguely recollects the project but urges his friend to continue with his train of thought as Simon elaborates, "We are not going to find our weapons by opportunity. We must first establish why were these stones positioned to be precisely at this location? I presume they had come from those mountains over there in the north, but I fail to understand why". Robert decides to consider of what Carmen had told him earlier and admits, "The guiding angel did not tell me anything about the significance of these rocks".

They continue to stare in silence at the rocks when suddenly Robert is struck with a thought. "Wait, Carmen did say that it was vital we reached here before sun set". His words allow Simon to establish a theory. The excited man walks briskly from one end of the circle of stones to the other. Looking up at the sky then at the lowering sun, Simon shouts out emphatically, "Sunbathers!"

Everyone looks at the skinny man, believing that his worrying state of mind has finally made him become insane, Robert asks in a quiet voice, "Sorry Simon, could you repeat what you just said?" The Englishman yells once more, "Sunbathers." He then explains, "These people are sun worshipers, do you not see? When the sun reaches its hottest temperature the position would be cast directly into the middle of this very circle". Slowly his friends realize what he is suggesting and they quickly dash towards the middle where they discover a small rock.

Derek and Robert both lift the heavy object out of the way and uncover a pile of bones. Derek looks at Simon and attempts to fake a British accent, "Maybe these people were using this place for carrying out sacrifices". Not amused with Derek's attempt of a joke, Claire hastily pulls aside the rug that is underneath the pile of bones, where underneath is a large square hole within the soil. Claire and Rachel both look down to see what lies beneath but quickly cover their noses from the musky smell. With the others wondering how deep the hole is, Derek spots a rope and attempts to pull it up, he comments, "Something is on the other end of this but it's too heavy for me to lift by myself". His colleagues assist him and together they yank and pull the thick cord. Calling on all of their strength, they slip against the grass where they continue to strain and heave but eventually drag a large wooden chest up onto the surface.

Without stopping to recover from their tiredness and fatigue the seven humans run towards the object that they have unearthed. Noticing that the chest is quite large and has strange markings etched within the wood Robert's cousin remarks, "I hope we don't need to find a key to open it". The others look at her disapprovingly, wishing that she had not tempted fate. "I was just thinking out loud," she says defensively.

Throwing caution to the wind, Derek pushes open the lid of the container. Inside the large chest are uniforms and several weapons. Naomi pulls out a wizard's hat and says in amazement, "This has a tag on it, it reads, to be worn by the human called Rachel". The others look on in disbelief. They discover that each weapon and item of clothing has already been marked with their names. Claire asks, "This is too spooky, how did the people that made these know of our names?"

Robert tells them, "The guiding angel did say they were made a long time ago, perhaps it has been our destiny to be here on this planet". Remembering of what had Carman had told him the Welshman suggests that they each change into their uniforms.

Deciding to use individual rocks as shelter, Robert begins to take off his jacket and finds the postcard he had intended to send onto his parents. The Welshman looks at the picture of San Francisco. With its sun setting over the skyline, it looks picturesque. He decides to keep it safe somewhere to remind himself of the planet of where he comes from and then changes into his grey trousers and thick green jacket.

Noticing that the jacket has gold studs on it, he then places his boots on and is surprised that they fit perfectly. He then walks towards the middle of the circle to rejoin his companions. There he finds Rachel already waiting. His cousin wears dark clothes, and a purple cloak that hangs down to her shoes. On her head is a pointed hat with a silver star, resembling a druid. Naomi, whom is dressed in a similar costume, accompanies her. Claire also steps out but her outfit has a shawl around her neck.

Bobby then appears but the teenager continues to wear the same clothes that he was previously wearing and argues, "I'm not changing into that outfit it will make me look silly". Robert warns him that unless he changes into his uniform his scent will not be disguised and will give their position away to the apes.

Claire issues a threat to her brother that unless he obeys Robert then she will drag him behind the rock and change him into his new clothes. Knowing that he has run out of excuses, Bobby grudgingly obeys his sister.

Derek joins his friends, wearing black trousers, boots and a jacket he comments that the outfit feels warm and comfortable.

Bobby finally appears, he wears a uniform similar to Derek's except that his has knee length socks and a red jacket but it does not prevent him from complaining that it is too baggy. Derek remarks, "Don't worry kid, you'll grow into it one day".

The group walks over to collect their weapons but Bobby asks, "Wait a minute, where's Simon?" Slowly the remaining human steps out from the shadows of the stones, wearing a gold outfit of a legionnaire resembling a Roman soldier.

Derek and Bobby are unable to prevent themselves from laughing and fall to the floor in fits of giggles, leaving everyone else slightly shocked at the sight of Simon's appearance. Derek questions, "Are you sure the humanoids have the right person for the uniform?" Bobby comments, "I don't feel so bad about my outfit now". Simon politely remarks, "You do not have to be a giant to fill these boots, sorry I mean sandals". He looks back at his friends sheepishly and cannot help but laugh at himself. Claire tells him that he looks quite handsome, which causes the legionnaire to blush.

Remembering that elsewhere on this planet the pursued humans are in danger, the seven companions realize they cannot dwell here for very long. One by one they collect their weapons and place their old clothes into the chest, which is lowered back down through the opening within the ground. Naomi reflects, "I hope we come back to collect them one day and return to Earth". Her friends share her thoughts.

Robert looks at his bow and a satchel containing many arrows. With the sky now a glowing red colour of night, he attempts to take a practice shot with his arrow. Robert is surprised to find that when he pulls back on the string, the arrow begins to glow in flames. Once released, he watches it travel for some distance before the arrow falls into darkness. He picks up the bag but is surprised to discover the satchel has barely any weight to it. Simon looks closely at his shield, which protrudes an energy beam that surrounds him. Establishing how strong it is Robert gently throws a small stone towards

Simon only to see it bounce back from the light of energy. He suggests to his friend that it must be a force field. However Simon nearly demolishes one of the ancient rocks when he accidentally presses a button on his spear, which triggers a laser to fire from its point. This causes everyone to duck for cover. Derek pleads, "Hey that joke earlier, I didn't mean it, just don't kill me". The strong American then curiously fastens on some gloves and taps it against a small rock, only to see it crack into pieces.

Meanwhile Bobby is happy to receive a cave mans club as his weapon, which is very light to hold but he is certain that it posses exceptional power. The teenager wishes that he could use it back on Earth to play baseball with, as he believes it would help him score many home runs.

Naomi holds onto a bow, which seems to be taller than Robert's, aiding her with a stronger torque to fire her arrows to cover a greater distance.

As the group begins to descend from the hillside, Naomi asks Robert in which direction should they be heading to? Robert answers that Lake Idris is situated north from here. Rachel picks up a book and the moonlight shows her that its cover is titled, 'The Magic Book'. The first page appears to show a map of Sephire. Her companions gather around and look at the drawing to see how far they have to travel.

Naomi glances across the fields, she has placed some glasses on, enabling her vision to become magnified. She notices something trudging through the fields below and quickly warns her friends. They instantly lower to the ground in case the figures are creatures belonging to the tribe army.

Derek asks her, "What do you see?" Naomi looks again and replies, "There are a group of fifteen people but these must be humanoids as their skin is similar to ours but they resemble the appearance of peasants and beggars with their clothes torn and hair kept long". Simon asks Robert if they should use this opportunity to introduce themselves to the humanoids? Robert responds, "We can't, we don't have time".

Claire inquisitively places on the headband, which she had collected from the chest but then suddenly clutches her head in pain, as a strong vision flashes before her eyes. The pain subsides but leaves her laying on the floor in shock. Her friends are concerned and ask her what is wrong? She informs her companions, "I saw an image of apes that are close and are waiting to ambush the travelling humanoids".

Rachel presumes that Claire's headband must warn her of potential dangers. Robert suggests that if it causes her pain perhaps she should not use it. Claire replies, "The pain has subsided I think I am okay".

Naomi points out the group of apes who wait to ambush the unsuspected humanoids. Robert whispers, "If we can't introduce ourselves to the humanoids, the least we can do is to be certain that they pass through these fields safely". He then crawls down the hillside to the field below. The others wonder what he intends to do and as they hold onto small laser weapons that form as part of their arsenal and they follow the Welshman.

Chapter Eight

With their first confrontation against the tribe army apes looming, Robert contemplates a course of action to take. Bobby comments enthusiastically, "Great I get to use my club". Robert orders the teenager to calm down, as their attack must not allow further apes to know of their existence, otherwise the captured humans will be killed. The commanding Welshman informs everyone that they must catch the apes by surprise and discusses his strategy of attack, "Simon and myself will go in as close as possible towards the approaching pack". At which point Simon grimaces. Robert then instructs Bobby, Derek and Claire to arrive as backup and indicates for them to appear from the side of the battle. "Finally, Naomi you cover us with your bow, Rachel you can support Naomi in case any of the apes try to escape".

Simon asks Robert what are they to do with the apes once they find them? His friend replies, "We have to kill them, otherwise the apes will destroy the humanoids. If they escape they will warn the dark knight of our presence". The others acknowledge their individual tasks and move to get into position. Unsure about killing a creature Simon hastily crawls through the grass with Robert.

The humans wait nervously for the enemy to arrive, they are uncertain if they will successfully be able to use their new weapons efficiently to defeat the apes. Claire senses that the enemy patrol is very close whilst further ahead of her, Robert waits in silence. He is desperate to know of the apes' location and is tempted to stand up and see for himself but common sense prevails. Robert continues to remain flat on the grass, he turns to his friend whom seems to appear petrified and whispers, "Simon, as soon a I fire a couple of arrows, activate your energy shield to protect us until Bobby and Derek arrive". Simon nervously nods back in agreement, wishing he could be anywhere else other than here.

Robert grows impatient to get on with the attack and places his ear to the ground hoping the sound of the apes movement will indicate their direction. At first he is unable to hear anything. The waiting seems to be taking forever as the tension continues to build inside each of the humans. Suddenly Robert can hear a pounding sound, after realizing it is not his heart he considers that the thumping must be the movement of the apes but the pounding then begins to fade. Robert looks back in horror at Simon and gasps, "The apes have changed direction, they must have spotted the humanoids!" Robert crawls quickly in pursuit of the apes within the shorter grass leaving Simon to whistle for his companions to follow. All thoughts of fear have been cast aside as he realizes that Robert needs his protection. He catches up with him to find him already engaging the enemy in battle. The legionnaire hurriedly activates his energy shield and notices that his Welsh friend has caught the apes unawares.

His companion continues to fire his arrows to good affect in the direction of the creatures. By the time the apes realize where the shots are being fired from, Bobby and Derek commence with their attack. The human teenager strikes his weapon to the ground so hard that it causes the creatures to fall over. A large crack appears in the earth and two apes plummet into darkness. Naomi brings two other apes crashing down with her arrows whilst Claire and Derek finish the remaining threat with laser shots. After the brief battle is over, the humans quickly look to one another to be certain that nobody is hurt or wounded. They are relieved to have not alerted any further apes or the travelling humanoids with their presence. Having initially congratulated one another upon a successful mission the humans begin to feel remorse for killing another living being, Simon kneels down to be sick from the experience but Robert explains that had they not killed the apes then the creatures would have certainly attacked the defenceless humanoids.

The cold reality of battle hits home to each of them and they decide to hide the remaining bodies of the dead apes within the tall grass. Robert quickly helps his friend back to his feet. With the adrenaline of battle now abated, Robert again looks at the map from Rachel's book and announces, "Lake Idris should be less than two days ahead of us". He passes the book back to his cousin and determinedly leads the group towards the northern horizon. Each of the humans' remains silent, ever watchful to the dangers that Claire might be sensing.

Chapter Nine

The tall buildings of Valadreil glisten in the brightness of daylight. Where once lived a peaceful and idealistic society now contains eight thousand of Roshtu's tribe army. Their duty is to control the town, the humanoid prisoners and the room that operates the portals. The royal palace can be seen, monumental by its splendor. Within the courtyard, one of Roshtu's loyal bodyguards called Riesk, escorts a creature up the steps leading towards the palace.

Meanwhile the humanoid princess is held captive within the dungeons located below the royal throne room, her cell is cold, dark and unforgiving. Tired and left alone in isolation she lays on the uncomfortable bed, unaware of what time or day it is. She almost wishes that the evil dark knight would decide to have her executed sooner rather than later as she can no longer abide waiting for the inevitable to happen.

Juliana senses that Roshtu takes great pleasure in watching her fall from grace. The princess wonders why has her father not returned? Something must have happened to him, he could not have been killed otherwise Roshtu would have no reason for keeping her alive. Juliana is unable to prevent herself from crying, but then realizes the sentry guard located on the other side of the locked door might hear. She decides not to give her captures the satisfaction and holds back the tears to remain strong, if not for herself then for her people.

Princess Juliana sighs and rolls over to her side. She wearily peers into the darkness of her confinement and hears a dripping sound within the corner of the room. Unable to rest any longer, she decides to walk towards the door to see if there is an ape guard situated outside. When she approaches the distinct sound of snoring can be heard through the open grating. Suddenly Juliana can distinguish the sound of muffled voices coming through the ceiling from the throne room above.

The determined brown haired woman creeps over to the bed and cautiously stands on top of the mattress to eavesdrop on what is being discussed. As she holds her breath she is able to distinguish the booming voice of Roshtu. "Finch, I have a duty for you alone, unless you keep me informed of their whereabouts your race will suffer, succeed and your family's life will be spared".

Juliana wonders what Roshtu is scheming, she concludes that the dark knight has brought in a tracker, but who does he want followed? Before she can continue to question Roshtu's requirements, she hears the evil knight speak a word that causes her heart to beat hope through her soul once more. "The witch tells me they are special, I think her mind is failing, she overestimates them they've been here for some time and have done nothing to hinder my plans. However should you catch any of the humans', kill them, one by one. In the meantime track them and keep me informed of your progress".

The princess cannot believe what she has heard, "Did he say humans?" she asks herself and whispers in disbelief, "This means they have managed to make it through one of the portals, whilst they were briefly open". She then realizes the snoring has stopped from outside her prison door. The humanoid quickly sits down onto the bed and is relieved the guard has not noticed her eavesdropping.

Inside the royal throne room, Roshtu talks to his tracker, "Finch my servant Riesk, will meet you at Lake Idris, where the humans will attempt to rescue their colleagues. My army of three thousand will be waiting to ambush them". The dark knight finishes and dismisses Finch, who retreats from the darkness of the great hall. The shadow of Finch suggests the creature is cat shaped and has a long tail. The princess held captive in the dungeons below, had not heard the last part of the conversation between Roshtu and Finch, if she had then hope would have not returned to her.

The dark knight sits on the seat of the grand throne, alone in the darkness of the room. A wicked smile begins to develop on his face, as he senses the humans' end is nearing.

Elsewhere, in the northern borders of Sephire, a patrol of sixty-tribe army apes charge in pursuit of two humans'. The huddle of creatures suddenly halts when they reach the top of a hillside. The commanding ape searches the southward fields before turning around and instructing the captain of his patrol, "Take half of the troops and charge from that direction". The ape points towards a route that he wants them to take. The patrol leader informs his second in command that his group will continue to follow the humans on their current path. The other ape questions his superior's decision and asks, "Would we not kill them easier if we attack as one?" The leader looks back and replies, "We will not attack as I have orders directly from Gormosh that we need only to drive the fleeing humans' towards Lake Idris, apparently Roshtu has some surprise waiting for them".

The second in command obeys his orders and leads half of the section towards a southwest direction.

The ape commander remains still and squints its eyes upon two far away figures before issuing the order for his troop to charge down the hillside and continue their pursuit.

Four miles away from the chasing tribe army, a dark cloaked man turns around to his companion and asks, "Yoshi, do you still see them?" The other man wears white robes. Both men carry swords as their weapons. Yoshi the skilled Samurai warrior from Japan answers, "The apes have now formed into two separate packs, if we remain on this path the apes pursuing from the side, shall catch up with us. I fear we can no longer out run them".

The dark cloaked man is Hideki, a well-trained Japanese Ninja. They had encountered the tribe army apes two days ago, on this strange and mysterious planet and have barely managed to fight their way past the hostile creatures. Hideki is aware they have little time to waste. Whilst pointing to the eastern horizon he suggests, "Maybe we can gain some ground by taking the path which leads towards those mountains over there". Yoshi nods in agreement and they run towards that direction.

At Lake Idris it has become twilight, the lake itself spans for miles. The edge of the lake leads to shallow streams where rocks have risen from the ground. Mountains surround the water that stretch high into the sky. Daylight rarely reaches this part of Sephire due to the mountains blocking out the sun. The temperature at Lake Idris is freezing. Despite it being picturesque this is a place where nobody would wish to remain for very long.

The two Japanese warriors have now encountered a gigantic squid that runs terror in these parts.

Deciding they stand no chance in fighting against the creature they continue to run away and jump from rock to rock whilst being careful not to fall into the ice cold water. Along the riverbank of the lake, the pursuing tribe army apes have now caught up. Holding onto torches of fire, the apes watch enthusiastically as the horrible squid closes in on the two helpless humans.

Hideki carries a long thin pointed sword with ancient markings engraved into the metal. He keeps the weapon poised ever ready to swing it towards the dangerous tentacles of the squid. Yoshi carries a smaller curved sword. His breath is visible in the cold temperature as the chanting of the watching apes intensifies.

The two humans now reach the end of the lake, where they find a small waterfall. Should they fall into the water they would not survive. The large squid approaches and squeals in delight, knowing that they are trapped. The tribe army apes gather to watch the finale. The squid attacks Hideki with its tentacles but he manages to successfully fight off the attack, cutting away at some of the tentacles in the process. The ghastly lake monster decides to then strike at Yoshi, who barely manages to defend himself from the first attack, but during the next assault it manages to prize the sword away from the Japanese warrior, leaving him completely defenceless.

Hideki sees this and runs to aid his friend but does not notice a stray tentacle, which strikes the Ninja on the side of the head and sends him crashing to the ground. The coldness of the water momentarily stops Hideki's heart from beating. He watches helplessly as the squid prepares to crush his colleague. The monster wraps a huge tentacle around Yoshi, when suddenly a whooshing sound can be heard coming from the direction of the pine trees.

The squid moves its huge eyes across to the sound, where a single flamed object is seen to be lowering from the sky. The object falls too quickly for the lake monster to react and the glowing flame of an arrow hits the squid directly in between its eyes. The squid squeals in pain, causing it to let go of Yoshi and it charges towards the tribe army apes that are along the riverbank believing them to be responsible. The apes' try to avoid its destruction. With the arrow still lodged in its head, tentacles of the ferocious squid mortally strikes several of them.

With the tribe army in retreat, Robert and his companions run to the Japanese warriors and help them to their feet. Before they can be properly introduced, Claire grasps her headband and warns, "There's an army of apes that are approaching from all directions!" Simon yells, "It's a trap!"

Looking for a way out from here Hideki notices a gap from inside the rock of the mountain, "There is a cave over there". His voice is powerful despite his mouth being concealed behind the hood. He retrieves his weapon, as does Yoshi and the nine humans' dash towards the opening within the mountain.

The tribe army apes continue to battle against the squid. With the humans nearing the entrance of the cave the apes launch their spears from a large catapult and the weapons fly through the air from the other side of the lake towards the direction of the squid. The rest of the ape army marches across the shallow water where the lake monster is left for dead and the apes begin to converge in front of the cave. The humans' bolt inside the darkness of the mountain for protection and have their weapons poised and ready for use.

The apes gather closer towards the entrance and suddenly halt. They do not wish to go inside for they know that those who have previously entered have never been seen again. The sound of a horse is then heard from above. The ape army looks up and sees Roshtu has arrived. The dark knight orders his servants to enter the cave. One of them reasons to Roshtu, "But master it is haunted, not even the witch would go in there". Without any hesitation, Roshtu fires an electric bolt of energy from his gloved hand at the ape, killing it immediately. He looks to the rest of his tribe army apes who stand to attention below him and tells them in a booming voice, "We fear nothing on this planet, everything on this planet fears us!"

The apes reluctantly obey their master and begin their approach but before they can enter, an arrow is struck from inside the darkness of the cave to the top of the entrance and the ground begins to shake.

Suddenly rocks from the mountainside come crashing down and covers the entrance to the cave, thus preventing the apes from pursuing the humans. Roshtu screams out in anxiety, as it appears that the menacing humans have eluded him. Deciding to seek the witch's council, the dark knight flies on his horse through the sky, leaving the apes to physically remove the rocks that block the cave.

Chapter Ten

As light vanishes from the rubble of rocks, the humans are surrounded in complete darkness. Whilst they are coughing and brushing the dust away from their uniforms, the light from Claire's headband begins to shine and shows that each of their faces are also covered in grime.

"Why did you block our exit for?" Bobby asks annoyingly at Robert, who replies, "We are not yet ready to take on an army of that size". Naomi inquires on what they are to do now? Before anyone can speculate, Claire informs her companions that she can feel a breeze coming from a dark passageway behind them, which leads further inside the mountain. Simon mutters, "I wish I was back home". Robert tells him, "Everyone wishes they were home, but we're not. We must try to find a way out from this mountain, I suggest we follow the passageway that Claire has mentioned".

As the humans make their first steps towards the passage, Simon trips over something on the floor, causing a small object to be sent crashing into the wall. Claire directs the light from her headband towards the ground to see what Simon has stumbled into. Each of them gasps in shock and remain frozen to the spot as they see before them a pile of bones and some carcasses of what used to be several tribe army apes. Derek whispers, "I have a bad feeling about this". Bobby thinks they were wrong to have ever considered entering the cave and suggests they go back to remove the stones that block their exit.

Robert responds, "We are not going back. There will be thousands of apes on the other side of those rocks that are trying to get in. We must continue along this path". Simon attempts to calm his nerves and remains close to Claire to provide her with protection from his energy shield, whilst she uses the light from her headband to show them the route forwards.

The humans commence slowly into the huge mountain, ever watchful of the dangers that might jump out on them. Robert remains at the back of the group, with his bow and arrow poised and ready for use in case anything should attack them from behind. The pathway is narrow, winding and constantly varies in gradient. Tired and dejected, the humans decide to rest after what seems to have been a day of endless struggle. Drinking the few remaining drops of spring water from the flasks that Carmen had provided, they attempt to breathe in what precious little air is available. Each of them desperately needs to sleep but the fear of what dangers may be lurking in the darkness prevents them from closing their eyelids.

Rachel uses this opportunity to properly introduce her companions to the two Japanese humans they had rescued earlier. Yoshi tells her that Hideki and himself are trained in the skills of martial arts. Hideki comes from the school of Ninja and he studies the way of the Samurai. Whilst offering them her flask of spring water she asks, "How did you come to be on this planet?" Yoshi explains to her that the Japanese government had picked up a mysterious signal on their long-range sensors. Once they had discovered the source of the signal, the military commanders gave clearance for the special operation to be carried out to establish what was through the other side of the device.

Derek questions if the Japanese government would have sent re-enforcements through, Hideki responds, "No one else knows of our existence. Our operation was kept strictly confidential with the military commanders. If we failed to return within a certain time line, our superiors were going to destroy the device, in case it could be used as a weapon against our country".

Wishing they had found a better circumstance to introduce themselves to their oriental companions Claire and her friends briefly explain how they arrived on this planet. Robert is silently relieved to be in the company of two brave warriors. As everyone attempts to gather their strength to continue, Derek asks Robert what is their next objective once they find a way out of the mountain? Robert informs everyone of what Carmen had told him about finding a lost book to be able to free the humanoid's king and queen along with their forces. Naomi wonders, "How do we use this book to get home?" Robert has no answer for now as that remains to be a mystery.

Rachel explains to the Japanese warriors, everything that they have learnt from the guiding angel but at this moment Bobby stands up and brushes some of the dust away from his jacket when his nose begins to twitch. Hideki and Yoshi are listening to Rachel, when Bobby suddenly sneezes very loudly. The sound echoes against the walls of solid rock above and below the passageway. If there was anything skulking in the darkness it would almost certainly now be aware of the humans' presence.

Bobby apologizes sheepishly, as everyone glares angrily at him. Naomi and her companions stand and look nervously around them, expecting an attack. Robert urges them to continue along the dark path and tells them, "Come on we've lingered here long enough". However when they begin to move a loud growling sound is heard from a distance behind them. "Run!" Derek shouts and they quickly dash behind the golden legionnaire outfit of Simon. Claire runs alongside him and together they lead the group along the path. Robert glances anxiously behind him and can see a large shadow reflecting against the rocks, which glow from his drawn arrow.

The rumbling sound intensifies as the pursing creature draws nearer. The humans reach a corner of the long passageway as Robert spins around and releases two of his arrows into the direction of the ceiling.

He watches the flamed arrows whiz down the tunnel and strike the ceiling that causes rocks to come crashing down and blocks the path behind them. Not waiting to see the outcome,

Robert hurries to join his colleagues and runs past the corner of the passageway only to bump into his friends who have suddenly stopped. The nine humans stare in amazement as they look across the huge opening that they have reached within the very centre of the mountain.

Darkness of space stretches for miles inside the cavernous mountain, where only a bridge leads across to the other side. "Wow!" Bobby gasps in disbelief. His older sister attempts to see how far the opening reaches. However, Claire and her friends are unaware of the eyes that are currently looking down on them from above.

As she directs her light towards the ceiling of the mountain, thousands of bats suddenly swoop down upon the group. Fortunately Simon is quick to activate his energy shield and protects them from the onslaught.

Robert yells, "Lead the way across the bridge!" His voice is barely heard over the loud squawking sound of the bats.

The winged creatures see the humans attempt to cross over and begin to try and knock into them from the side. Robert and Naomi use their arrows efficiently but the impact from the bats', forces the humans' to hold onto the ropes of the bridge for protection. Simon grips on for dear life and they make slow progress for what seems to be an endless attack. Claire shouts in his ear, "I can see a doorway on the other side".

She continues to hold onto him whilst the others remain huddled behind them. Simon composes himself and proceeds to slowly struggle across. During this time Rachel attempts to sift through her manual of spells.

The humans eventually make it across to the other side of the mountain. Derek holds firmly onto his girlfriend's hand but they become separated when the bats continue to swoop down on all of them. Knowing the door will be their only means of an escape from this terror, Derek uses the power of his gloves to punch his way through the creatures that block his route. He reaches the handle to the door and pulls it back only to be sent tumbling to the floor as further bats fly through from the other side.

Simon's energy shield begins to flicker and shows signs of its power being drained, as does the energy from each of the humans'. The bats' see this and commence to charge once more, causing Robert and his companions to step backwards, ever closer to the edge of the cliff to the mountain. With only centimetres to spare from falling into the abyss, Rachel removes her hat and rubs its rim before shouting at the top of her voice, "Magic hat we need your keep make these bats fall asleep!"

Suddenly a power surges from Rachel's pointed hat and in an instant the winged creatures fly to the top of the mountain, cling onto the rocks within the darkness and begin to fall asleep. There is an eerie silence, which surrounds the humans and they use this opportunity to bolt towards the open doorway. Once everyone is safely through, Derek firmly closes the door and they each draw a sigh of relief. Rachel's companions pat her on the back as they are amazed by the power of her hat. She can scarcely believe it herself and cautiously places the hat back onto her head.

The Saviours of Sephire continue their journey and walk up steps that lead to the top of the mountain without encountering any further incidents and finally discover a way out where they reach the snowy mountainside. Robert and his eight colleagues are pleased to be able to breathe in fresh air once again.

Chapter Eleven

Roshtu flies on his horse within the western skies of Sephire, seeking the witch's advice. The dark knight recognizes the frail figure waiting for him at the main gates of her dwelling. The horse lowers from the sky and Roshtu rides towards Peirlee. She asks sarcastically, "You arrive for my counsel, are the humans still alive?" Roshtu replies, "Enough Peirlee, next time I will not leave the task in the paws of those bungling apes and will deal with the humans myself".

As he descends from his horse the witch retorts, "That is, if you have another opportunity, I have sensed a royal arrival". Roshtu replies in shock, "The king!" Peirlee nods her head and informs him, "The humans will now try to release him". She then begins to walk with the aid of her staff, as Roshtu follows closely alongside she tells him, "Do not concern yourself, if the humans' find The Book of Spells they will not understand the language of the text".

Roshtu asks if her spell is impossible to break. She does not reply but instead provides Roshtu with a small circular orange ball and a note of paper. The dark knight reads the contents of the note and smiles of her scheme before tearing the paper into pieces.

Part of the sentence can be read from a shred of the torn paper. "Through a special gateway, then Princess Juliana..."

Gormosh the loyal servant of Roshtu then approaches. The ape commander informs his master, "Finch has found the humans and is keeping us informed of their location". Roshtu smiles and then orders Gormosh to prepare his army to begin marching towards the Argian Waterfall where they will battle against the humans.

Once the ape departs, Roshtu informs Peirlee, "Go to Valadreil and carry out your plan". The witch smiles and returns inside her dwelling as Roshtu then saddles onto his horse to follow the army of apes.

Elsewhere on the snowy mountainside, the small team of humans' begin their climb downwards unsure of how to reach the location of the wishing well that the guiding angel had previously spoken of. Below them are white clouds. The temperature at this height is numbingly cold but they continue to trudge through the snow. Once through the mist Robert can see the distant green trees of woodlands when suddenly he can scarcely hear a familiar voice of someone speaking to him. He stops to alert his companions that Carmen is trying to tell him something.

Whilst Robert attempts to concentrate the others stop and rest. Bobby feels bored and decides to roll some of the snow into a ball where he pushes it back along the route from where they have come from.

The temptation to build a snowman is too strong for the young teenager. After a couple of minutes, he completes the finishing touches and settles the snow into a round head shape. Bobby steps backward and admires his masterpiece. Derek, Naomi and his sister pat him on the back for his efforts.

Suddenly Robert turns around to them and shouts, "Come on we must hurry". Simon asks, "What did Carmen tell you?" But his friend has no time to answer and walks hastily down the mountain leaving the others to catch up.

Bobby picks up his club and glances back at the snowman one last time but could have sworn that he had seen the snowman's eyes blink at him. Deciding that his mind is playing tricks on him the confused teenager turns around and follows his companions.

Once Robert and his friends are out of sight, the snowman's head begins to move and looks towards the direction of where the group of humans have left. Suddenly it's eyes blink and two pointed ears appear from the snowman's head with a tail breaking free from the snow. Slowly, the snowman begins to shake from the inside and then disintegrates in all directions. Coughing and spluttering the snow out from its mouth is Finch, a feline creature that has the ability to become camouflaged within its surroundings.

The secretive creature had crept too close to the humans and had almost been caught out by Bobby. An irritated Finch shakes the rest of the snow from its fur and follows the humans' footprints.

Chapter Twelve

The journey down the mountainside eventually leads the humans' southwards of the planet where they find themselves surrounded by green valleys. They are relieved to have not discovered any further outposts of the tribe army. Simon remains concerned that Robert has not yet told them of what Carmen had informed him. This is the first time he can ever recall seeing his good friend to be this tense.

Robert turns around and continues to hurry his companions along, warning them that time is running out. Derek notices that Bobby is lagging behind and attempts to quicken the teenagers walking pace. The grass from the hillside is slippery from the earlier rainfall. The looming clouds overhead threatens another downpour.

After an hour of further trekking across the hillside the group abruptly stops in their tracks as a distant thunderous noise can be heard. Rachel comments, "Sounds like rain". Claire tries to gain some insight from her powerful headband and remarks, "No, it's not rain, it is something else that I'm sensing".

Derek continues to walk forwards. The others look to see where he is going and become troubled when they watch him fall to his knees and motioning for them to approach cautiously. They crawl along the damp grass and look into the distance where they gaze upon the wondrous sight of the Argian Waterfall.

Claire whispers, "It's impossible to describe something so beautiful yet terrifying". The astounded team can see that at least three miles away is a gigantic waterfall, where a river plummets into a large lake below. The sound of the noise is very loud and clouds of mist rise from the spray.

The humans' remember that they have to strategize a way to enter the tunnel. Naomi places her special powered glasses on and informs her companions that her enhanced vision shows there are several tribe army apes stationed on a platform leading behind the waterfall. Robert notifies the others of what Carmen had told him, "We need to get to that platform and enter a tunnel which is behind the waterfall". Simon feared that was where they have to go and his stomach begins to feel queasy once again. Robert explains on what they need to do, "The tunnel will lead us to the Green Book of Spells, where we need to speak the magic phrase from the book's contents to allow the humanoid leaders and their forces to be freed from the spell that holds them captive".

His friends look afraid with their objectives, as they know the tunnel will be heavily guarded. Robert warns them, "There is more that I need to tell you. Unless we act quickly we will be hopelessly outnumbered, as Roshtu is marching his army towards us and will be here before nightfall".

After a moments pause to digest all that they must accomplish, Rachel asks her cousin if he knows of the magic phrase that they have to say? He informs her that Carmen could not tell him of this and that she will have to attempt to understand the book.

Robert discusses his intended battle strategy and suggests they should split up into two separate teams and approach the platform from either side to confuse the apes. Naomi and himself will fire their arrows from distance providing cover for the others to attack. The two groups will then re-join at the entrance to the tunnel. "Derek, Claire, Naomi and Bobby you will be the team that attacks the platform from the left, the others will accompany me and approach from the right". He indicates to them the route he wishes for them to take before asking if they understand their tasks. His colleagues acknowledge that they do, and after everyone wishes one another good luck. With a determined look in their eyes the two teams begin to crawl cautiously towards the thunderous Argian Waterfall.

The attack on the apes guarding the platform goes according to plan. Robert and Naomi manage to remove some of the apes from distance with their bows. Claire uses her laser efficiently, sending the last ape to fall down into the abyss of the waterfall. Accustomed to the feeling of combat, the humans are able to control their fear and adrenaline. Each of them is well aware that the battle ahead through the tunnel will be their toughest yet.

Rejoining into one team at the mouth of the tunnel, Robert decides it is useless to attempt speaking and be overheard above the deafening noise of the waterfall. He places an arrow to his bow and they enter the darkness of the tunnel. Dozens of apes instantly jump out and surge towards them, brandishing their curved wooden weapons. Simon's energy shield protects the humans from the weapons that are thrown at them.

Derek and Bobby force their way through the blockade and send the creatures crashing to the floor. The struggle further down the tunnel seems to be lasting forever as they continue to battle through an endless barricade of apes. With time and energy fading, the humans eventually clear the tunnel from any further danger and reach an area where they discover a large hole. Around the perimeter are huge rocks, where at the side they notice a bucket, which is connected to a rope with pulleys attached.

Recovering their breath from the fight, they realize the bucket is quite deep and appears big enough to take them all down to the level below. Yoshi suggests they all get into the bucket. Suddenly Robert spins around and fires an arrow at a charging ape causing it to tumble to the ground. The humans enter the device and wonder where it will take them. Naomi shoots one of her arrows at a lever within the wall and the bucket begins to descend.

With the bucket touching the surface of the bottom level, the apes guarding this narrow corridor look perplexed because they are unable to see anyone inside. Robert and his companions suddenly rise to their feet and release a volley of shots, which removes the ape threat. Hideki and Yoshi both somersault out from the bucket with their swords poised for action. The others climb out where they discover a dark candlelit tunnel that has several closed wooden doors on either side.

Claire is surprised not to be able to hear the sound of the waterfall. Derek asks Robert which door does he think the lost book is behind? He replies that he has no idea but quickly suggests they try all of them.

Bobby walks up the corridor with a gleam in his eyes and proceeds to bring his club crashing against the entrances. Unfortunately his actions enable several more tribe army guards to enter the corridor.

Watching her friends fight against the enemy, Rachel looks to her manual of spells to help find a solution to their problem. Closing the magic book, Rachel takes off her wizard's hat and attempts to shut out the noise of mayhem, which is happening around her.

Naomi fires an arrow into one of the last remaining apes when she suddenly notices Rachel rubbing the rim of her hat and watches her placing it back onto her head. Before Naomi can call out to her, Rachel vanishes from sight. Standing open-mouthed Naomi taps her boyfriend's shoulder to get his attention.

Derek looks at Naomi wondering what she wants but he notices that she does not speak, instead the African woman points towards the doors on the other side of the corridor. The humans watch in amazement and witness the doors being opened in succession. Appearing from the last room of the corridor is Rachel. The wizard walks towards them clutching onto an old dusty green book with a beaming smile on her face and exclaims excitedly, "I've found the book we are looking for!"

With everyone congratulating his cousin, Robert fathoms that the magic hat had enabled Rachel to become invisible and had allowed her to walk through solid objects. With time running out before the evil knight arrives here with his armed forces the humans quickly enter the device that had brought them down and Yoshi cuts the rope with his sword, which causes the bucket to rise.

Coming to a halt, the humans reach the top level and hear the dim sound of the waterfall but are surprised not to see any daylight coming from the exit of the tunnel. Simon asks everyone, "Is this the right level?"

Robert whispers, "There was only one level upwards". Remaining inside the bucket they each squint at the tunnel but now realize that a tall dark silhouette is blocking out the daylight. Robert believes the figure to be at least seven foot in height. Slowly the stranger turns around, its face is bright white with bony features and has eyes red with fire that glows within the darkness. The humans gasp in terror with the realization that this is Roshtu and being trapped inside the bucket they are easy prey.

Roshtu notices that the woman wearing a purple pointed hat is clutching onto the Green Book of Spells.

Claire immediately senses that something is about to happen. The dark knight booms out in a powerful voice, "Welcome to your deaths!" The human female quickly urges her companions to jump out onto the floor and they land onto the concrete with a thud, just before Roshtu sends a bolt of fire from his gloved hands towards the pulleys within the ceiling that sends the bucket plummeting downwards to the lower level where it smashes into smithereens.

Realizing that his attack has been foiled, Roshtu yells in annoyance. The humans scramble to retrieve their weapons. Frightened to be up against a terrible foe and with no plan of attacking the dark knight they each slowly rise to prepare against another assault.

Roshtu looks at them one by one, sizing them up individually and taking his time to decide which to attack first. He then raises his hands of power towards Rachel but fails to notice Bobby approaching him. The adolescent's sister yells out in despair when she senses what her brother is about to attempt. The dark knight pauses and wonders what the female is screaming at when he suddenly detects a small human with blonde hair that raises an object into the air. Bobby then brings his caveman club crashing down with all of his strength, directly onto the foot of the dark knight.

Roshtu cries out a terrifying scream of pain that rattles the wall of the mountain. He pushes Bobby aside and the teenager is sent flying through the air, where he lands hard onto the floor. Bobby is momentarily winded, although he still manages to hold onto his weapon.

Roshtu pulls back his gloved hand, where a fiery ball of energy builds with power. He releases it into the direction of Bobby who can only watch helplessly, when suddenly a flamed arrow diverts the ball of energy away from its intended target and sends it exploding into the rocky wall. The impact creates an opening for the humans to use as an escape. Robert, who has saved Bobby from certain doom, then shouts for his companions to run. Derek being the quickest picks the brave teenager up from the floor and leads his friends towards the created gap within the wall. Robert and Simon support the back of the departing group and use the protective energy shield from Simon to deflect further shots that Roshtu fires.

Chapter Thirteen

Robert and Simon follow their colleagues across the platform and reach the top of the hillside where they find themselves within a large open field. Rachel frantically searches through the pages of the recovered book only to discover it is written in an incomprehensible text. She warns her companions, "I don't know where the phrase is".

Before they can offer their assistance, a deafening sound of marching causes the ground to tremor. The humans decide to form a protective circle around Rachel who continues to attempt to find the phrase that will release Sephire's king along with his forces. Naomi tells Robert's cousin not to give in and suggests she uses her magic hat for help. "I never thought of that". She replies and takes it off her head but then struggles to know what instruction to give it. "Don't take too long," Derek shouts, as he looks aghast at the large army of apes that covers the entire width of the hillside. Robert asks his friends to remain vigilant but as he says this Simon's grip of his energy shield begins to shake through fear.

From across the field, Finch informs Riesk, "They're over there". He then points in the direction of the humans. The powerful ape marches his army towards the humans and commands them to halt once they are within meters away. Naomi has two arrows ready to release as she anxiously waits along with the rest of her companions for the inevitable to happen.

Suddenly within the sky, a dark figure flying on a black menacing horse arrives. Robert announces, "Roshtu". Everyone except Rachel looks upward. The dark knight holds his position and speaks out to the humans, "You have no chance of escaping. Give me the book and I will let you go". Robert calls back, "We will never listen to you". A ray of green sunlight breaks through the clouds and shines against Robert's silver ring of the Welsh dragon. The brightness of the reflection momentarily blinds Roshtu, his eyes glow in anger and he bellows out the order for the apes to attack.

Suddenly Rachel yells from within the circle of protection, "Magic hat serve me well, find the page to break the spell". Within an instant, pages from within the Green Book of Spells begin to automatically turn over.

The apes' charge and attack with their weapons raised. Robert and Naomi release continuous arrows into the mass of creatures, whilst Hideki and Yoshi cut through apes with their sharp swords. Bobby uses his club to knock the enemy over and Claire fires her laser. The humans almost succumb to the shear number of apes' when the book in Rachel's hands stops on a particular page. She sees the sentence is written in gold leaf writing and calls out the phrase, "Arsh marsh tin be tuke, arsh marsh lin be douke".

In an instant a large circle of flame appears next to the humans' and the sound of a rider's horn can be heard. The apes stop their attack and appear stunned when they witness the humanoid king, queen and their royal guard forces of at least eight thousand, ride out from the vortex. The sound causes Roshtu's horse to panic and loose control.

The humanoid at the front of the attack is dressed in battle clothes but wears a crown on his aged head.

With a fearsome expression on his battle scarred face King Ridley looks at the events before him and orders his guards to attack the apes' who surround the small group of humans.

The ape army retreats to the Northern Rocklands of Terror hoping to re-group. Before any introductions can be made the humanoids and humans look up to the sky and await Roshtu's wrath. The dark knight manages to regain control of his horse and shouts out powerfully, "You humans' will regret the day you ever entered this planet". The royal guard forces raise their spears ready to fire at the dark knight but before they can do this Roshtu warns the humanoid leader, "I shall return King Ridley, one day this planet will be mine!" He then fires a large bolt of lightening that the humanoids have to block with their shields.

The menacing horse blows a fiery flame out from its nostrils, causing the people below to dive for cover.

Using the diversion as a means for his escape, Roshtu releases the small circular orange ball that Peirlee had given to him.

Robert looks up from the trembling ground and notices that Roshtu has created a gateway of his own, which is linked to a planet that is both dark and terrifying. The dark knight rides his horse into the open gateway before it closes immediately behind him.

Once everyone manages to get to their feet, the surprised royal leader jumps down from his horse, walks towards the group of humans and introduces himself as King Ridley, "So I have you to thank for our freedom, who would have thought the old alliance of humans and humanoids would exist once again, these are strange times we live in".

The king shakes each of them by the hand. When he greets Bobby, the teenager looks up at the royal that has a brown beard and asks, "Can we go home now?" His sister who stands next to him gives Bobby a nudge to behave, although she knows it is a question that they are all considering asking the king whom is left frowning by the request. Robert steps forward and states, "Your highness, we have successfully completed the tasks put before us. We were told you could activate the portals, enabling our return to our home world".

As soon as Robert has finished speaking, the elegant queen of Sephire looks nervously to her husband when she notices him staring at the Green Book of Spells that one of the humans is holding. King Ridley asks the woman with the pointed hat to give him the book. Rachel looks across to her older cousin for instruction but the strong Welshman nods his head in approval at which point Rachel gives the book to the humanoid leader.

King Ridley addresses everyone; "We must depart and make haste to Valadreil and free our people from slavery". He then whispers to Robert, "We shall speak about the portals another time, for now you are to accompany us to Valadreil". The humans are then helped up by humanoids that ride on horseback before the king's commander, issues the order to charge. The hillside is covered with three thousand riders as their horses gallop southwards to the humanoid capital

Chapter Fourteen

The journey to Valadreil takes the royal guard forces some considerable time as they continue to ride throughout the night. King Ridley looks over to his wife, both of them fear of what has happened to their daughter. Without stopping for food or water the middle-aged royals are frantic to get back to the capital to save their child before it is too late. The humans are tired from their clash with Roshtu and his army but they manage to grip onto their riders. Hideki tries to look at the scenery but the darkness of night only provides a feint outline of trees and fields.

After several hours the humanoids approach the tall wooden gates of Valadreil. They arrive expecting to have to battle their way through an army of apes but are instead greeted by thousands of relieved humanoids that have somehow managed to be freed from captivity. King Ridley looks pleasantly surprised at the people who welcome his return but he does not stop to find out what has happened because he desperately wishes to find Juliana. Claire and her human companions try to absorb their surroundings but everything is happening too quickly for them to notice the size and splendor of Valadreil.

Upon reaching the courtyard of the royal palace, the royal guard forces are brought to a halt, where King Ridley and Queen Avril are relieved to find their daughter waiting for them. The ordeal of being held in captivity has not taken away her beauty as she is seen to be wearing a white elegant dress. The people of Valadreil cheer and applaud the return of the king and queen of Sephire. The race of humanoids are relieved that freedom has been restored to this magnificent town.

The king jumps down from his horse and is immediately cuddled by his daughter whom had feared that she would never see her parents again. She cries both tears of joy and relief and says, "Father I can't believe it! It's so good to see you and mother again. What had happened to you?" Her father replies, "Juliana the time for answers will come later, all you need to know is that we have these humans' to thank for our safe return".

Everybody who is within earshot becomes silent by the word, humans. Some humanoids are resentful of humans because they have not previously heeded their call for aid, whilst others are in disbelief that this is the sign of the ancient prophecy becoming more than just a myth.

As the queen cuddles her daughter, Robert and his companions are helped down from their horses. The awestruck Welshman gazes at the humanoids that stand around him and senses that the people have discovered a new hope.

King Ridley asks Juliana, "How did you escape? I thought the town would have been controlled by thousands of Roshtu's army". His daughter replies, "There were many apes here father, far too many for us to fight against and our people were kept in confinement. I was held prisoner in the dungeons below the palace, when this woman, whom now stands next to me, aided my escape. Together we began to free other prisoners to struggle some resistance, then the apes must have been alerted to your return and they fled to the north".

The royal leader then asks the woman standing alongside his daughter, "You rescued my daughter?" A petite woman steps forward and speaks softly, "Yes your majesty". The king rewards the humanoid for her bravery and announces, "You are to become one of our royal handmaidens". This is an honour given to those who are trusted by the royals to become their servants. He then asks for the person's name, to which she replies calmly, "I am called Gwelyn".

King Ridley rejoins his wife and daughter, before standing in front of his people who have gathered around the courtyard and beyond on the cobbled streets. The king addresses his audience with a boisterous voice, "Tonight we celebrate our return and victory over the dark knight and that of his army.

This night we celebrate our freedom!" The humanoids roar and applaud with such delight. So much relief and elation can be seen on their faces.

That evening, the people of Valadreil spend their time eating, drinking and dancing to merry tunes that washes away all of their previous fears and troubles. The nine people that have arrived from a distant planet called Earth are happy to be part of the celebrations but they desperately wish to return home.

During the full swing of the festivities King Ridley sends a request to Robert for them to have a private discussion within the royal throne room. Robert manages to sneak away from his friends without them noticing and makes his way towards the palace. He does not wish to tell his companions of where he is going because he does not wish to give them a false sense of belief.

Inside the throne room the powerful majesty sits on the throne that he governs and talks quietly with his daughter, "Juliana I am very proud of the strength and resilience you have showed. I believe you are ready to become the future leader to Sephire". Princess Juliana replies, "It's been my duty both to Sephire and to you father that I remained strong, but I sense you wish to talk about something else". Her guardian cannot hide the admiration of how his daughter has the ability to read his mind and confesses to her, "I was hoping that since we have restored a small element of freedom, you would take the opportunity to decide upon your future husband". Juliana looks at him in aghast and replies, "Father we must continue to press on with our attacks against the tribe army, I cannot consider my future plans for happiness until we have secured the freedom to all of our people".

The king reluctantly accepts her reasons but asks, "Please, give it your consideration". The king then allows his daughter to leave and rejoin the celebrations outside. He watches her walk out from the room, silently hoping that he will live to see the future generation of his bloodline continue.

As soon as Princess Juliana opens the doors of the throne room, she bumps into one of the humans whose appearance is clean cut and well dressed. Robert can sense that he has startled the beautiful princess and apologizes for making her jump. She glances at him and notices he has a sparkle within his eyes that instantly captures her attention. Robert cannot help but blush with embarrassment when the young woman fails to take her eyes away from him. King Ridley is concerned that he cannot overhear what is being spoken and asks Robert to enter the room. The brown haired man politely excuses himself from Princess Juliana and she calmly walks away.

King Ridley continues to be seated upon the grand throne and grasps hold of the humanoids religious scepter. As the Welshman walks closer towards the majesty, two guards within the room obey their orders to leave and close the doors behind them. Robert and the humanoid leader are now alone. King Ridley regretfully announces to Robert, "You and your companions cannot go home". Robert is dumbfounded and asks, "I thought you knew how to reactivate the portals?"

Despite his years, King Ridley still posses an enormous amount of strength and provides an expression, which suggests that he will not be spoken down to. King Ridley informs Robert, "Our knowledge about the portals is minimal. We merely stumbled across them and have only the ability of controlling access to them but thanks to the dark knight that has now been taken away from us. There were rumours spoken long ago about the portals being linked to three books containing magic powers".

"You have managed to retrieve the Green Book of Spells the other two books are the Black Book of Barmothenue and the Blue Book of Wisdom. Where they can be found, I do not know. You must understand that I cannot allow you to leave until I have restored freedom to all of our people. If the stories about your kind are true I would not dare allow you leave, besides I need every able man, boy, woman and child to fight against our enemies. If Roshtu returns we must be ready to defend the capital and so far his witch has not yet shown herself. Due to her sorcery we have had to endure many dark days".

Suddenly a knock is heard at the door. The king orders the person to enter the grand hall and one of the royal handmaidens dressed in the uniform of yellow robes steps inside. Robert instantly recognizes the face of Gwelyn behind the partially concealed hood. She passes a note to the king. He reads it and then allows her to leave but on her way out the handmaiden glance across to Robert but he fails to notice since he is looking down dejectedly at his boots.

The king looks up and can sense that his human guest is upset and explains to him, "I remain grateful for your help. You and your friends shall remain under my protection where you can each help to rebuild our defenses against an attack. In return for your assistance you will be allowed to search for the lost books. Maybe we will be able to find a way of sending you all home".

Robert remains silent but looks back at him with a slight glimmer of hope to hold onto. He then accompanies the king out from the throne room to join in with the celebrations that will carry on until the early hours of the next morning.

As the morning sun begins to rise, a mist surrounds the sleeping town of Valadreil. At the steps of the royal palace, Robert places some bread inside his holdall. He then picks up his bow and creeps quietly through the empty streets and moves towards the exit of the gates. Suddenly he becomes aware of someone running up to him. Wondering if it is an attack from a spy, Robert grabs hold of an arrow ready to be drawn to his bow, when he then recognizes that the person approaching is Simon.

His best friend walks up and asks, "Where do you think you are sneaking off to?" Robert tells him to go back to the palace and look after their companions. Simon questions,

"You are not attempting to find the lost books by yourself are you?" Robert responds, "No Simon, I'm going into the woodlands to seek Carmen's guidance as I don't know what we're supposed to do".

The English legionnaire objects and tells Robert, "If you are going, then I am coming with you". Robert notices that look of defiance on his face and knows full well that he will not be able to prevent Simon to remain behind. He grudgingly nods his head in approval for the legionnaire to accompany him on his travels.

The two humans slip past the guards who continue to sleep off the celebrations from the previous night before joining the dusty pathway that leads away from the town of Valadreil and towards the direction of the woodland forest.

With the image of Robert and Simon disappearing within the morning mist, their voices can be heard as the two human companions chat quietly amongst themselves about happier times they had experienced back home. One of the carved statues that they have long since passed, suddenly takes the shape of a feline and the figure of Finch begins to materialize. The creature assigned by Roshtu to track the humans then chooses to jump down and follows Robert and Simon, where he too fades into the morning mist.

The fate of the humanoids and the nine humans, for now remains to be uncertain.

Book Two
The Struggle for Freedom
(The Blue Book of Wisdom)

Chapter One

Robert and Simon walk quietly along a dry dusty pathway. The mist from the morning has long since cleared and it is now a warm sunny day. The two friends have been walking for several hours, their destination is to the woodland forest where they hope to seek guidance from Carmen, the humans' spiritual angel. Robert suggests they both stop to rest and points towards an area of dry grass where they both sit down.

The sound of birds chirping in the distance almost brings the two humans to forget the circumstances that have brought them to this planet, for now they both feel at ease. Robert recollects the time back on Earth whilst they were on the boat. Before the dark clouds had gathered that led to the ferocious storm and had caused them to seek refuge on the unknown island, where they discovered the portal that transported them to this strange and magical planet.

Feeling hungry the two friends decide to eat some of the bread they had found earlier from Valadreil.

Simon drinks the last drops of spring water from his flask and comments, "We will need to fill these up for the return journey". Robert replies, "I think there is a river that flows through the forest, where we can fill our flasks".

The sun makes them both feel sleepy, their thoughts dwell upon the dramatic experiences they have encountered during their adventure, as well as the terrifying sensation of fighting in battle, where they have had to kill a living being and learn how to control their feelings of emotion. Simon asks, "Do you think Roshtu will ever be defeated?" Robert fears the dark knight will return, ending this peaceful atmosphere and replacing it with a frightening terror, one that no person on this planet can easily destroy.

He comments, "We will have to face him again. I can only hope that the witch will be defeated and the humanoid forces will be able to capture the dark knight's fortress in the Northern Rocklands of Terror".

Simon wonders when will they encounter the witch, as she has not yet showed herself. The legionnaire then asks Robert if he had seen the look on the humanoids faces when King Ridley had returned back to his people. His Welsh friend remarks, "The humanoids need someone to lead them, this is what keeps them going and builds their resilience to fight for their freedom. Unfortunately for us King Ridley will be preoccupied in restoring strength and protection to Valadreil that I doubt he will spare any time or resource in aiding our return to Earth". Simon thinks about their human companions who remain at Valadreil. Robert reassures him, "They have probably wondered where we have gone but I am certain they are quite safe under the protection of the humanoids".

As they sit in silence, Robert allows his mind to dwell on a woman he had recently seen. He asks Simon if he believes in fate and destiny in meeting the perfect woman whom he would intend to marry. Simon is momentarily surprised by the question and gives his answer some consideration before replying, "To be honest that is something I would like to do once I am older, although" he pauses. Robert sees him hesitate and urges him to continue, "Well I'm not sure if I should be saying this but I like Claire. I cannot describe the feeling but it is there, I can see it within her eyes when she looks at me. If it was not for the dedication required to pass those dreadful law exams I would have asked her out".

Simon proceeds to ask Robert if he has his eye on any women back home. His friend replies that he has never felt completely secure in any of the previous relationships he has been involved in but if he were to return to Wales he would like to settle down and begin the search of finding his perfect partner.

Before Robert can elaborate any further the two companions suddenly hear a rustling sound coming from several meters behind them. Concerned, they look to one another. Simon whispers, "Could just be an animal". Robert remarks, "To make that sort of noise it would have to be quite large, do you wish to wait around to find out?" He then considers that it could be a spy sent by Roshtu to follow them.

Simon looks anxiously back to his colleague but fails to reply. They quickly gather their holdalls and run further along the pathway.

The two humans continue running to the best of their ability whilst trying not to alert any further spies that may be lurking within the facility. Simon glances over his shoulder and informs Robert that he cannot see anything pursuing them. Robert tells him to keep running until they reach the safety of the trees, which are now only a short distance away.

Having reached the entrance of the forest, where beyond lies shadows of darkness, Robert suggests they should both climb one of the trees to be certain they are not being followed. Once they reach a stable branch to support their weight, they patiently wait for something to appear below them. After several minutes have elapsed Simon motions to Robert that there is no threat and indicates that he is going to climb down to solid ground. Robert gestures at him to remain still for a little while longer.

Continuing to wait, Simon rests his head against the bark of the branch as his neck has begun to ache.

Robert is about to concede to Simon's request, when all of a sudden something dashes out from the tall grass. It inspects the path beneath them. Robert cannot see the body of the person and can only notice its shadow against the dusty surface of the pathway. As the figure crouches, Robert realizes they do not have much time before the suspicious character concludes they have not gone forwards but upwards.

Simon looks nervously to Robert for instructions, where he motions to his friend that upon the silent count of three he will give a signal for them both to jump down onto their pursuer. The Welshman then gives the command and the two humans' fall down and hold onto the assailant with all of their strength, it is apparent that they have managed to catch the stranger unawares.

In the midst of yelling, the dark cloaked figure manages to push them back, causing Simon to fall over.

Robert continues to wrestle with the attacker and manages to place an arrow to his bow. The figure realizes it is defeated and stops struggling.

Once the dust from the skirmish subsides, the cloaked stranger rolls over to face its captures. Robert and Simon are both surprised to realize that they had just been wrestling with Hideki, dressed in his black Ninja uniform. Robert demands to know what he is doing here, as he is annoyed that he has wasted his energy on him.

Hideki replies, "I saw you both leaving Valadreil this morning, I thought you were going to abandon us and find the lost books for yourselves". Simon helps Hideki back to his feet, where the Ninja brushes the dust away from his uniform. The Englishman then informs him they are here to seek guidance from the spiritual angel of the forest. Hideki says nothing but looks skeptical of Simon's answer. They follow the pathway, which takes them deeper into the forest.

Shortly after the three humans have left, another figure approaches from the grass and stops to inspect the tracks left behind. The feline creature is the elusive tracker named Finch. He also enters the forest whilst cautiously looking around in case he is spotted.

Meanwhile further ahead, Simon asks Hideki when had he learnt his skills of tracking. The Japanese warrior replies, "I started when I was very young, tracking was included within the first discipline of our training. I was considered to be the best in my class". Robert mutters under his breath, "That's a comfort". He is frustrated and wonders why Carmen does not talk to him, "Where is she?" he asks out loud.

Hideki questions how much further must they go until the spiritual person magically appears? Simon then hears the sound of running water coming from nearby and remembers that they need to fill their flasks up with water. He then asks Robert to give him his container, which he does whilst Hideki continues to suspect the angel is all but a figment of their imaginations. This triggers a frosty reaction from Robert and sensing that an argument is about to take place, Simon walks hastily away. Relieved to be leaving the debate the legionnaire mutters, "If those two argue like this, they will awaken everything within the forest".

Robert is irritated with Hideki's accusations and cannot withhold his response any longer, "Maybe you should go back to the others and ask them about the angel, they all saw her". Hideki comments, "And leave you two alone? You would soon find yourselves in trouble". Robert retorts, "We surprised you perfectly well".

A short distance away, Simon reaches the edge of a riverbank and kneels against the soft surface of the grass, although he does not notice several leaves scattering from beside him. The human fills each container with water and begins humming to himself. However just away from the Englishman's sight, the first flask of water rises slowly into the air by itself. The lid opens and when it is slightly tilted back, tiny droplets of water begins to fall to the ground.

The skinny Englishman finally manages to unscrew the tightly fitted lid and lowers his flask into the river.

He gazes into the river and sees his own reflection. Pausing from his humming Simon comments to himself that he needs to wash his hair and face.

Behind the legionnaire a log rises into the air by its own accord and increases in height. The legionnaire attempts to screw the cap back onto one of the flasks but fumbles it out from his fingers. "Blast" he remarks and looks to the ground to retrieve it. As Simon directs his sight away from the river, the waters reflection shows the log just above his head. Holding onto the log ready to strike it against Simon is the image of

Finch, the creature's teeth are clenched as he prepares for the moment to knock the unsuspecting human into the river. The feline pulls the log back, ready to bring it crashing against his target, when all of a sudden an alarm beeps from Simon's wrist. The loud sound causes Finch to loose his balance from the branch that he perches on. The reflection in the water now shows a panicked and horrified expression on Finch's face, as he cannot prevent himself from plunging into the river.

When Simon finds the button on his watch to stop the beeping, he is startled when he hears a sound from the impact of a log falling into the river and witnesses an impressive effect of splashes around it. The young man continues to watch the object until it drifts further downstream to a shallow waterfall. The legionnaire then hears a distant blood curdling sound from a creature within the forest, he fears that it might be a predator and quickly returns to his human companions, where he finds them still arguing.

Robert speaks in an irritated voice, "Look Hideki, Rachel is my cousin, why would I wish to leave my relative abandoned as well as my friends?" Hideki apologizes and realizes that he might have been wrong with his suspicions. Much to Simon's relief he watches them shake hands and Robert accepts the flask that his friend offers. Robert now thinks that he will not hear anything from the guiding angel today and suggests they should remain in the forest for the evening and return to Valadreil at first daylight. The three humans begin gathering some wood and attempt to start a campfire to keep warm.

Elsewhere in the forest the soaking image of Finch is seen, he clings desperately onto reeds of the riverbank. The creature uses all of his strength to pull himself back onto the wet grass and lands exhausted onto the surface while spitting water out from its mouth. His fur is very greasy from the water and resembles a bird that has just taken a bath. Cold and shivering, Finch departs the forest to find somewhere warm to spend the night whilst cursing the humans under his breath for continuously bringing him to grief.

Chapter Two

That evening the red sky is clear and the three companions, with the comfort of a campfire are settled under a blanket of stars. Simon is struggling to fall asleep when he suddenly hears something coming from only a short distance away. Thinking it may be a spy waiting to catch them unawares, he retrieves his spear and decides to inspect the area himself. He attempts to waken both his colleagues but they are fast asleep. Simon proceeds to tip toe away. The sound of Hideki's snoring muffles his movements.

The English legionnaire mutters under his breath, "I wonder if Ninjas are taught about hearing enemies approaching in their training". Having heard a rustling noise once again, Simon prepares himself mentally for an attack and creeps ever closer towards the sound. He knows he should not be wandering this far alone but there is a light coming from behind a nearby tree that draws him closer.

Suddenly Carmen steps out from behind the tree, which startles the human. The guiding angel motions the legionnaire to remain silent and beckons him to come closer and thus leading him further away from the others. Simon whispers to her that he should awaken Robert, as his close friend wishes to speak with her. The humanoid angel responds, "He must not know that I am here and you cannot inform him of our discussion". Simon appears to be confused with Carmen's request and asks, "Can you no longer guide Robert?" She informs him, "I can still guide him but I fear that by speaking to your companion will place him in further danger than he is already about to face. Soon the dark knight's evil magic will haunt your friend and will turn his loyalty towards the witch".

Simon reacts angrily, "You are wrong, Robert would never betray us, besides we would not allow it to happen". He realizes that his outburst might have been too loud and ponders what has made Carmen to suggest this. The notion of Robert turning against them does not sit well with him and he wonders how does Carmen knows of this?

The guiding angel continues to talk to Simon, "Your friend's transformation will happen over time, a spell already surrounds him. I can only sense the events that are about to take place, in time actions may take place to prevent those events from ever happening. Unfortunately I do not know how or when the witch will carry out her plans".

The skinny Englishman pleads with her as to why they cannot warn Robert that he will be placed in danger? Carmen responds, "You must not tell your colleague or anyone else of what is about to happen, the consequences would be severe to you all. In order for the witch to continue her spell she will need to remain close to your companion. If Robert is alerted to her presence he may attempt to defeat her on his own, which will be a terrible mistake because she is too powerful to be taken single handedly. To beat her will require your combined strength. If the witch suspects that we know of her plans she will not place herself in the position to be caught and would strategize a more dangerous attack on the humanoids and yourselves".

"Once the witch takes the physical form of her true self, only then will you be able to make your attack. Your companions must be with you but you must make certain that she is killed for Peirlee is too dangerous to simply be locked away behind doors. If you tell the humanoids or your companions, spies of Roshtu might overhear you and warn the witch".

Simon reluctantly nods his head and accepts the burden of carrying the secret alone. He then asks Carmen if she knows anything about the other two magical books that they need to find. Carmen suggests that he and his companions should search the archives from the governing council that are contained in the underground passageways of Valadreil. She reminds Simon to remain close to Robert and wishes him good luck. Then the illuminating green sparkling light from her spirit fades into the night of the forest and she is gone.

The well-spoken human is stunned by what he has just been discussing with Carmen. Questions and thoughts swirl around his mind, causing his eyes to feel heavy. Simon decides to make his way towards the last of the flickering flames of the campfire where he rejoins his two sleeping companions.

The legionnaire sits down to where he had previously tried to rest and looks at Robert sleeping. He considers about the strong friendship that they have and wonders what could possibly turn Robert against them to aid the witch. The Welshman suddenly awakens with a startle. Robert's eyes adjust to the darkness and he notices his dark haired friend staring at him. Robert asks, "What is wrong?" Simon considers long and hard on his response, wishing that was able to warn his friend about the possibility of future events but he eventually decides to remain true to his pledge of secrecy and replies that nothing is wrong.

Feeling tired, they both rest their heads back to the ground of leaves to sleep. The campfire has now burnt out and the sound of Hideki's snoring is heard around them.

Elsewhere on Sephire, the hunched figure of Peirlee the witch gazes into a small crystal ball within a darkened room. The image of her wrinkled face is more terrifying against the flickers of candlelight.

Around her are long flowing curtains and carved furniture, it is evident that she is not within her dwelling in the west. Gazing closer into the small circular object she mutters a strange dialect. The image of clouds appear from within the globe. Peirlee cackles, "The clouds of Sephire, what do they see? What do they tell me?" The clouds swirl around and gather into a dark black storm where the picture of the Northern Rocklands of Terror takes shape from within her crystal ball.

"Aahh, events that are current and events soon to take place". Peirlee says as before her eyes she sees a vision of Roshtu standing in front of his fortress, surrounded by sharp jagged rocks within rain and lightening.

The witch senses an army that Roshtu will bring with him, an army so large that it would render any humanoid attack to be hopeless. The image within the crystal ball then changes to the face of King Ridley. "The King, yes your time will soon come. With you out of the way and the books to be found, I can open the portals, allowing Roshtu's return. However there is one more obstacle in my way", she pauses to remember what it is.

The face of King Ridley is then replaced with Robert's face and she exclaims, "The human, the one who stands to get in the way of my plans, he will fall easily under my spell. Soon he will be mine, first his heart then his soul and finally his spirit. None of his friends will be able to guide him out from the darkness. My presence will haunt his dreams, his thoughts. Yes I can see you now more clearly I can smell you and hear your heart pounding inside my head. I am watching you, stalking you, waiting for my moment then, you shall be mine!" She shrieks and clenches her withered fist, showing an expression full of glee with the power she possesses.

The image of Robert disappears from within the crystal ball and it immediately stops shinning, causing the candles to blow out and fills the room in complete darkness.

Chapter Three

The next morning suggests it will be another hot and sunny day. Green rays of sunlight beams down onto Valadreil with the crescent shape around the sun glowing brightly. The forces of the royal guard would prefer a much cooler climate as the strengthening to the town's defenses continue. They have been working non-stop through fear of an imminent attack from the witch and the remaining tribe army apes.

Since the dark lord had fled, King Ridley has expected the witch to make a swift retribution, he wonders why she has not yet attacked. From the balcony of the watchtower the king looks across the tall splendid buildings of Valadreil and sees far below where his people work tirelessly to carry out his orders. The king picks up a viewing mechanism that enables his vision to become magnified. Scanning the horizon he almost expects to see a huge army of apes to be gathering beyond the distant hills. He draws his vision back along the main pathway leading to Valadreil, where he sees three humans returning to the capital.

King Ridley reflects of the myths spoken in the folk tales, of how a group of humans would free the people of Sephire from a dark and terrible threat. Should they find a way back to Earth he fears this will trigger Roshtu's return. In his mind, King Ridley knows that he cannot allow Robert and his colleagues to leave for it would place his people into danger. The king must be certain that Sephire's capital is safe, only then can he prepare his forces to march northwards and strike the dark knight's fortress.

Commander Teltris then emerges at the top of the watchtower. His appearance in the military uniform is imposing. King Ridley informs him that the three missing humans have returned. The battle-scarred face of Commander Teltris clearly shows he is still annoyed they had crept out of the town. He suggests to his king, "My Lord I think we should have them confined and placed under surveillance, until we know of their reasons for leaving".

King Ridley responds, "Commander, would you treat the Saviours of Sephire in such a manner?" The commander appears flustered in trying to defend his reasoning and to not offend the king but his leader informs him, "Relax commander, I am as skeptical about them as you are, but they do posses great power, that we must use to our advantage. So in the meantime we shall treat them as our guests".

Commander Teltris automatically nods his head and assists his leader to place his cape back on and follows the king down the staircase to inspect the town's defenses.

In the royal gardens, Queen Avril and Princess Juliana are busy picking daffodils. The grass has been cut short and boasts a variety of summer flowers that are in full bloom. Bees are buzzing around collecting pollen, whilst birds chirping provides this place with a relaxing atmosphere. In the middle of the grounds is a fountain, carved from marble. The mother and daughter are sitting on some wooden benches.

Princess Juliana has missed her mother since she had been trapped within the witch's time vortex. They are being observed by several of the designated protectors from the courtyard above. Even in these hot temperatures the guards must endure to wear their long cloaks and steel helmets.

Juliana asks her mother if she knows whether the humans have returned, her diamond necklace sparkles against the sunlight. Queen Avril replies, "I am sure they will appear soon do not fret". The queen wears a silk orange gown with veil and golden earring's dangle from her ear lobes. The young princess asks, "Should we not send out a search party?" Her mother responds, "That will be for your father to decide, now come it is time for us to eat". They both stand and begin to walk away from the fountain.

Walking through the gardens, Juliana comments to her mother, "I spoke briefly with Rachel, the blonde haired human with the pointed hat. She seems quite pleasant not at all what I expected after the stories that father had told me when he spoke about the Saviours to Sephire". The queen looks at her daughter knowing the reasons why the king had tried to dismiss the importance of the humans, for she knows her husband is the true leader of the humanoids not these outlanders. It will be the humanoid planet at stake should the dark knight's armies' attack. If these people from Earth manage to find a way back to their own planet she is certain they will leave the humanoids to face their enemy alone.

Queen Avril is concerned that the people of Sephire believe their problems are over by the presence of mere humans. The queen does not respond to her daughter. They reach the top of the marble steps leading away from the gardens and pass some hand picked flowers to an awaiting handmaiden, before walking inside the palace under the protection of their bodyguards.

From the opposite side of the courtyard, Bobby sits on a wall along with Rachel and Yoshi where they bask in the sunshine. His special powered club rests at his feet. The young teenager throws a stone into the air and attempts to catch it whilst trying to imagine that the stone is a baseball.

Yoshi is sharpening his curved sword and Rachel is busy searching through her manual to learn some magic spells. Claire suddenly approaches and informs them that their missing companions have come back. "That's a relief". Rachel sighs, thankful to hear the news. Yoshi asks how does she know of that they have retuned? Bobby's sister explains that the headband she wears provides her with the power of intuition.

Naomi then appears with Derek and she informs her companions that by using her special powers of stronger vision she has seen their friends approaching from a mile away. They decide to make their way towards the gates of Valadreil to be certain that their three colleagues have not come to any harm.

Robert enters the town and passes through the tall wooden gates. The guards stationed at the entrance of Valadreil allow Robert, Simon and Hideki to walk through without hindrance. "It's about time you lot showed your faces". Robert looks up, recognizing the familiar voice. He knows this is as much of a welcome that they will receive from Bobby.

The others greet their arrival, despite their concerns. Naomi asks where had they gone? Hideki replies, "These two were headed for the woodland forest, I tracked them in case they were ambushed".

Suddenly a voice comes from above their heads, "And were they?" The group is startled and looks up only to recognize it is King Ridley.

The guards around them instantly bow their heads. Simon replies, "We saw no threat from here to the forest". The king responds, "Good, you were fortunate, it was foolish to have left without protection, you are not to leave again without my grace for it is not save outside of this town".

As the humans acknowledge the king's wishes, Robert notices Commander Teltris giving them a suspicious look. King Ridley then announces to the humans, "Those who have returned I will send food and water to your chambers, I would like to invite you all for diner in the throne room at sunset. There are things that need to be discussed". The king finishes speaking and walks away whilst being accompanied by his servants. The guards around the humans return to their duties leaving Robert and his friends to ponder of what the king had said.

The noise from humanoid workers bringing wood into the town causes Robert and his companions to regain their senses. The broad shouldered Welshman slowly leads them through the streets of Valadreil.

The appearance of the humanoid people comes across as poor. They wear tatty garments and do not seem to have jobs to attend. Rachel had earlier found out from Princess

Juliana that the humanoids have so far managed to survive by controlling certain areas of land where farming continues, thus allowing enough food to be provided but only in the supply of rations. The town shows signs of wear and tear due to the constant battles. For now this is a period of rebuilding for the humanoids.

Rachel asks, "I wonder what the king want to talk about?" Derek fears, "Probably to requisition our weapons". Claire is certain that their weapons cannot be used in the humanoid hands. The tall woman turns to Simon and asks, "On your travels, did Robert see the guiding angel?" Robert hears the question but does not reply. Simon regrettably answers, "No he did not". The legionnaire wants to confide with them all of what he had discussed with Carmen but manages to contain his secret.

Wood being used to reinforce outposts along the town's outer structure causes dust and wood chipping to drift in the air. The nine humans together again, wander into the housing section where the common humanoids live, there they can see young children playing in cobbled streets. The youths jump out of the way from the horses path whenever a royal guard rides past them. Robert is amazed by the size of the town and the activity of the guards, King Ridley has his forces working hard.

Making their way further into the humanoid capital a young girl suddenly dashes towards Robert and kisses the ring of the dragon that he wears upon his finger. The young girl's mother picks her up to carry her away. Robert places a hand on the mother's shoulder and asks why had her child done that?

The female humanoid fails to respond but instead points to the ring that he wears before hurrying away.

The other humans gather around Robert and look at his jewelry. Simon snorts, "They are under the impression that you have slayed a dragon, I wish I had purchased the same ring when we were shopping in Windsor". Bobby remarks, "It would be cool if there were real dragons here". Robert looks nervous with the prospect of what would be required of him should the teenager be correct.

The band of humans' gaze upon the tall glistening towers of the royal palace. Naomi asks her boyfriend, "What do you make of King Ridley?" Derek whispers to her, "I think he should show more gratitude to us for having freed him and his army from the witches spell". Simon tells them they should consider themselves fortunate. If the majesties were anything like the ancient kings back on Earth, they would have them thrown into dungeons and left to be forgotten. Claire remarks, "I doubt he has invited us over for our company".

Rachel mentions that the king's daughter seems friendly as well as one of her handmaidens' named Gwelyn. Upon reaching the royal courtyard that name rings inside Robert's head, Gwelyn, echoing through his ears. His mind drifts to the image of the handmaiden and the group walks towards their chambers to refresh.

Chapter Four

As twilight arrives to Valadreil, the nine people from planet Earth approaches the royal palace. Even though the banquet is supposed to be a social gathering, Robert has suspected otherwise and has brought his weapon with him. Naomi gazes through the tall magnificent windows, where in the sky she can see thousands of birds searching for a place to settle for the night. Her thoughts reflect on the wildlife she has seen so far on this strange planet. The wildlife remains one of the reasons why she wishes to return to Kenya should they ever find a way back to Earth. Her thoughts then return to the predicament that they are facing. None of them has asked to be on this planet, a chain of uncontrollable circumstances has forced all of their hands and placed them into this dire situation.

The humans assemble in front of the closed wooden doors of the throne room and they await the guards approval before they can enter. During this moment Naomi considers that one of her friends may even die in battle for a faith that they have been forced to believe in, all for the sake of returning home. She then feels Derek hold onto her hand and smiles at him, in an attempt to hide her anxiety. The guards eventually allow the humans to proceed into the throne room.

Once inside they are escorted to a marvelous carved wooden table, large enough to host an army.

Suddenly the doors behind them open and King Ridley walks in accompanied with the queen to the sound of trumpets playing. The humans are amazed with the majesties ceremonial clothes and bow before them. King Ridley suggests the humans can place their weapons in the corner of the room under the supervision of his guards. The Saviours of Sephire accept his offer and sit down to dinner. The middle-aged brown haired king realizes that not everyone is present, he turns to his wife and asks, "Where is our daughter?" Queen Avril replies, "She should be on her way". The royal is embarrassed by his daughter's lateness and comments, "That girl can never be punctual". He casts his hazel eyes around the table with the uncertainty of whether they should proceed without her.

Suddenly the princess walks into the room. With the glow of Sephires sunset beaming through the glass paned windows her appearance seems heavenly.

Juliana wears a green ceremonial dress and holds a single white flower. She reaches the table and glances across at Robert. She had already heard about him from her earlier discussions with Rachel.

King Ridley then allows everybody to commence with the meal. The royal glances across to his daughter with an expression to suggest that he is not best pleased with her but when Juliana meets his gaze her father's scowl lightens by the softness of his daughters crystal clear blue eyes.

During the main course of duck, everyone attempts to make polite conversation, Queen Avril talks about the different seasons of Sephire, whilst Bobby feels it necessary to describe the details of the latest baseball world series to the high ranking humanoid officers at the table.

Once the last course has been served the king dismisses his food servants and the doors of the room are closed. The humans, sense that the real talking is about to begin.

The humanoid leader announces, "I trust you have enjoyed our hospitality. In order for you to find the location of the two remaining magical books you will need to read through the archives written and documented many years ago, long before the days of the royal family. I will grant three of you access to the archives, although you will need to find a translator since the books would have been written in the ancient text".

A woman dressed in the yellow handmaiden's uniform, steps out from the shadow of a pillar within the grand hall and speaks, "My lord". The king looks around to see who has spoken. The handmaiden pulls back her hood and the majesty recognizes it is Gwelyn. She announces to the royal,

"A relative I once knew taught me of the ancient text when I was a young child, if you are able to temporarily spare me from your services I can try to assist the humans with some of the translation".

The humanoid majesty ponders over her request before accepting her offer to help the humans. King Ridley then asks that in return, Rachel and the boy are to help with keeping the children of the town away from hindrance to the royal guards. He then requests for the others to work alongside his forces to maintain the defenses of the town and scattered villages up to the northern borders.

Naomi is less than impressed with the king's request and voices her disapproval, "This is not our war to fight." Her outburst immediately silences the room. The majesty responds to her that it became their fight once they entered Sephire.

Queen Avril gives her husband a look to request that he keeps his patience. He looks across at her and attempts to reason with the humans, "Your weapons were crafted many years ago specifically so that when you entered our world you would be able to help us". Robert motions to Naomi to calm down, and agrees to the king's conditions.

The food servants are then called back into the room to clear the table and everybody departs to their chambers to retire for the evening. On their way out from the throne room King Ridley asks Robert to accompany him with the morning inspection along the perimeter walls of the town.

Once the new day arrives, Simon knocks onto the door of Robert's quarters. After a while Robert pulls back the door to greet him. The skinny Englishman notices that his friend is still wearing his sleeping garments and reminds him that the king will soon be waiting. Robert apologizes whilst in between yawns, "I'm sorry, I must have overslept, although for some reason I still feel tired". He closes the door and quickly gets changed before dashing downstairs to meet his companion.

As Robert reaches his friend the humanoid leader arrives with the protection of his guards. Robert asks the royal if Simon can also join them on the inspection. The king has no objections and the rest of the morning is spent walking along the outpost walls surrounding Valadreil. Robert advises the guards to position archers around the perimeter of the walls as well as any high advantage points that they can find.

The brown haired man informs King Ridley that Simon, Claire and himself will search through the library of ancient books, leaving the others available for the king's services. The majesty notifies Roberts that Gwelyn will arrive mid afternoon to collect his team to be shown to the underground passages of the palace.

Chapter Five

When Robert gathers his human companions, he provides them with news of their individual tasks whilst remarking that his group will be working tirelessly to find the location of the missing books but fears it may take months for them to search through all of the records. Claire warns her younger brother to behave himself whilst they are apart. She knows that she is going to miss him. Rachel senses this and assures her that she will be keeping a close eye on the teenager.

Robert gives his best wishes to all concerned and instructs them not to take any unnecessary risks. They hug one another, uncertain of the next time that they will see each other again and depart into their separate teams.

A knock is then heard at the door and Gwelyn enters the room. The polite handmaiden greets them with a smile. She carries on her possession a bunch of keys and a candle. The handmaiden then asks Robert if his team is ready. Robert nods his head but deep down he is upset to be separated from some of his friends. "Come on." Simon tells him and sympathetically pats him on the back. Before Claire leaves the room she gives Bobby a peck on his forehead, much to the teenagers annoyance.

Gwelyn leads Robert's group to the opposite section of the palace, where steps lead down to the cellars.

The young handmaiden lights her candle with a match and they walk through the cellars that are stacked with many bottles of wine. The group approaches a locked cast iron gate but the flickers of candlelight do not carry beyond. Gwelyn informs the humans, "Nobody has walked along these corridors for many years". She attempts to find the correct key that will release the lock and the gate opens with a high pitched squeak. Robert places a fiery arrow to his bow and steps alongside Gwelyn, if there is anything lurking within the darkness he will protect her. They lead the way closely followed by a frightened Simon and Claire. Her headband provides them with light to help guide them forwards.

The group continues to walk along the dark passages for some time but eventually reach another set of locked gates. As Gwelyn attempts to open it, Robert asks her about the original governing council and of what she knows of them. Gwelyn explains that the members of the governing council had never previously encountered any battles before, so when the humanoids were attacked by the dark knight and his ape army the council made severe errors with their battle strategies.

"Many humanoids died as a consequence of the governing counselors' failures. Over time, the people of Sephire held the members responsible for placing them into the hopeless situation and it was decided to disband the committee. The people elected the general in charge of the defenses to become king. From then onwards the royal family became the governing power of Sephire and that of its people. The books that had been written by the governing council could not be destroyed for religious reasons. Therefore the king at that time decided to conceal the books deep underground, hoping that no one would bring them up to the surface because the reputation and trust of the governing council could not be relied upon".

Gwelyn then opens the gate in front of them. Robert is amazed with the handmaiden. He considers her not only to have been brave in rescuing the princess from capture but is fascinated by her beauty and knowledge. Simon asks, "How is it that you know so much of what had taken place, these events that you speak of would have happened way before you were born?" Gwelyn replies that when she was younger her grandfather had told her about the humanoid's history.

Once through the other side of the gate, flights of stairs beckon them down to the next part of their journey. Upon reaching the bottom of the stairs, Simon is surprised to find that the air is plentiful, he had previous concerns that being so far below the surface would mean oxygen would be in short supply. He assumes there must be another passage that leads to the surface. Gwelyn directs them to where they find a room containing wooden shelves reaching as high as the ceiling that holds thousands of books and manuscripts, which date back to long ago.

Claire gasps, "This will take years to get through!" Shocked by the volume of work that they face, the team walks into the room and uses Gwelyn's matches to light the candles. In the middle of the archive room is a large wooden table and a set of chairs. Robert suggests they should try to think calmly and logically on how to approach the search for information and recommends they each start from one stack of shelves.

Simon considers that all of the governing council members must have documented a set of books. The quiet Englishman then remembers what Carmen had told him about one of the governing council members betraying their people and wonders if he can find the books written by that individual. As he begins his search Gwelyn provides him with a suspicious glance.

The research is long and tiring, each book removed and each page turned creates an increasing amount of dust within the room. The wooden seats are becoming uncomfortable and space is found to be lacking on the table. Most of the pages they have seen so far contain an incomprehensible text, fortunately some of the books have drawings, providing the humans with some indication about events which had happened during the humanoids past.

After several hours the group is tired and decides to rest. Claire remarks, "The sketches in the books resemble carvings from our planet of cavemen and Egyptians".

Robert asks Gwelyn if she needs any refreshment and hastily asks the others once he remembers they may also need some nourishment. She informs Robert that if he asks one of the handmaidens they will prepare some food to bring down to them. Claire offers to assist Robert, leaving Simon and Gwelyn alone.

Several minutes elapse and Simon is struggling to find a conversational topic to discuss with Gwelyn, eventually the skinny Englishman asks her what has she been looking at since they have been down here and he stands up to see what she is holding. In doing so, he startles the handmaiden and Gwelyn reacts by picking up a book that is closest to her. She replies that she has found nothing of particular interest.

Simon then asks her how had she been successful in freeing the princess. She quickly answers, "Oh it was nothing".

Simon had thought the dungeon where the princess was held prisoner would have been heavily guarded.

Gwelyn tells him that it was and explains that she had been fortunate to arrive when the guards were sleeping and shot them easily with her laser. Once she had rescued Princess Juliana they then began to free other prisoners and had found the tribe army apes were already in retreat from hearing of the kings release from the spell.

Simon considers her tale to be slightly unbelievable but decides to sit back down in his chair, when he suddenly notices that underneath the book that Gwelyn is holding are detailed drawings of the palace. He almost questions her about this when Robert and Claire both return. The Welshman carries a jug of water and Simon hastily assists Claire with the tray of food that she has brought but completely forgets what his question to Gwelyn is about. He decides that it was probably not important and continues to assist Claire to distribute the food to the others.

Chapter Six

A month has now passed since the humans were separated into their individual teams. Rachel and Bobby remain in the town of Valadreil and try their best to keep some of the young humanoid children busy with games and drawings. Derek and Naomi accompany the royal guards patrolling the eastern shores, whilst Hideki and Yoshi ride with the patrols up to the northern borders. Both groups have been involved in brief skirmishes with outposts of the tribe army but have managed to bring food and aid to the humanoid villages. Each of the humans now fight for restoring freedom to the people of Sephire but wait as the inevitable battle between the humanoids and the dark forces of Roshtu slowly approaches. Only those searching through the archives can rescue the humans away from the certainty of war.

Inside the archive room, directly below the palace of Valadreil, the search for valuable information continues. On this particular evening Simon and Claire are looking through ancient manuscripts. Claire asks Simon if he knows whether Robert and Gwelyn are returning. He assumes they have departed for the evening. Simon is tired and frustrated with his friend's forgetfulness of his duties. He asks Claire what her opinion is of Gwelyn. Claire sees no cause for concern that Robert should like her and comments that the handmaiden has been helpful. Simon considers Gwelyn to be a distraction to their colleague and has observed that Robert's concentration is not where it should be whenever the handmaiden is close by.

Claire suggests that perhaps they have all been working too hard and should rest for the evening.

Defeated, they blow out the candles within the room, lock the gates behind them and make their way back towards the stairs that lead up to the palace.

Reaching the last steps from the cellars, Simon senses how deeply Claire misses her younger brother and suggests that she should go and see him. Although Simon hates to admit to himself that he is relieved not to have the little nuisance around. Claire thanks him for his support and wishes him goodnight. The Englishman watches her leave when he suddenly realizes he needs to return back to Gwelyn, the bunch of keys which he holds within his grasp.

As the legionnaire walks past some royal guards whom stand to attention by the throne room he moves towards the handmaiden's chambers and gazes through the palace windows that overlook the gardens.

Under the red moonlit sky, Simon recognizes Robert taking a stroll but he is appalled to realize that he is accompanying Gwelyn and is holding hands with the handmaiden.

Simon is livid that Robert should choose to forget the importance of finding the lost books. Everyone is working extremely hard, some are probably in battle with tribe army apes and here he is neglecting his responsibilities and holding hands with a woman he hardly even knows!

Simon attempts to calm down, but the anger within him will not subside and he decides to march outside to demand an explanation from his colleague.

Robert and Gwelyn both see the golden legionnaire's uniform of Simon approaching. Robert mutters, "What does he want?" Simon stands before them embarrassed but very angry with his friend. He cannot find the words to say in asking Robert to justify his actions and blurts out, "So, do you know what time it is?"

Gwelyn replies in a soft voice, "You two seem to have things to discuss, so I'll bid goodnight to you both".

She walks past Simon and recovers the bunch of keys, which he dangles. Once she is out from earshot Roberts asks the legionnaire why is he checking up on him? Simon attempts to explain that he only saw them by chance, but Robert is enraged, "Why can you not give me a moment of peace to do as I please?"

Simon cannot believe what has happened to his old friend and attempts to bring Robert back to reality.

Robert snaps back, "I know that Simon, you don't have to remind me". This time the Welshman has raised his voice, which is something that he has never done previously to his friend. Simon can only attempt to point out to Robert that he knows nothing about Gwelyn but Robert has heard enough and storms off, whilst slightly knocking into the distressed Englishman as he walks past.

Simon stands alone in the gardens' and realizes that his friendship with Robert now hangs by a thread.

He is annoyed that Robert will not listen to reason and feels frustrated that despite Carmen's prior warning of the witches spell he has been powerless to prevent her dark magic from influencing his friend. Simon cannot help but allow a single tear of anger to escape from his eye.

During the early hours of the next morning, whilst it remains dark and everybody except for the guards at the main gates of Valadreil are sleeping, a slender cloaked figure walks across the courtyard. There is no sound of the person's footsteps as the individual has removed its footwear. The hooded figure stops and looks around to be certain that it has not been seen before standing in front of one of the statues against the wall of the courtyard. The figure waits in silence and then quickly slips a note next to a statue before departing quietly towards the direction of the palace. Ten minutes pass by and the note is barely visible against the statue. Then within an instant, a furry paw from a creature quickly gathers the note, taking it out of sight and into the darkness.

The next few days become awkward for Robert and Simon and ever since their argument Claire has sensed the tension between the two has been rising. On this particular afternoon in the archive room, Robert complains of a headache, Claire and Gwelyn tell him to rest and to only return once he feels better. As soon as he has left, Claire proceeds to ask Simon what is wrong between himself and Robert.

Simon desperately wants to confide with her about the witches spell but decides not to as Gwelyn is present. Simon is suspicious of Gwelyn's motives but has so far been unable to find any evidence to suggest that she is trying to deceive them. Simon does not reply to Claire and leaves the room. He is desperate to mend the rift with Robert but in order to achieve this he must first find the identity of the witch.

Claire looks concerned and attempts to find out from Gwelyn if Robert has mentioned anything to her about his arguments with Simon. Gwelyn hesitates to respond but eventually decides to tell her that Robert believes Simon to be jealous of their relationship. The human female is aghast by what Gwelyn has said, although she does not confess but she carries her own feelings for Simon and thought he had felt the same. Should Gwelyn be correct this would mean that she has been mistaken. Claire begins to panic, her emotions torment her. The handmaiden asks her if anything is wrong as she appears to look faint. The human excuses herself from the archives leaving Gwelyn alone in the room. The handmaiden picks up a book, which she had previously concealed and begins to examine its' contents.

In the courtyard, several children stand in a diamond formation waiting to catch an object, a young child carries a wooden stick and attempts to make contact with a small stone in the air. The swing misses the target, "Strike three you're out!" yells Bobby from behind the boy. The teenager has decided to pass the time by introducing baseball to twenty of the humanoid children aged between eight and thirteen. The young humanoids seem to be enjoying themselves even if they are slightly apprehensive of Bobby's excited approach to the game. Sitting on a wall out from harms way Princess Juliana and Rachel keep a watchful eye. The weather is pleasant although there are clouds in the sky that would cause everyone to dash for cover should it begin to rain.

Over the past few weeks the princess has become good friends with Rachel and holds her opinion to be valued. Despite them coming from different planets they are both the same age and have shared the same problems brought upon them whilst growing up. The princess is intrigued with the information that Rachel tells her about her colleagues. The human female explains of what she knows of their individual backgrounds. Juliana is fascinated with the culture and world that they come from. Rachel then asks Princess Juliana how close is she to her parents? The princess admits it is very difficult to always be seen to be doing everything correctly and explains that she gets on very well with her parents but over the last ten years it has been difficult to be a proper family because of the continuing threat of the dark knight.

They both smile when they see Bobby get struck out and listen to him protesting the decision, when suddenly one of the royal handmaidens' dashes towards them. Her face appears shocked beneath her yellow hood of the uniform. "Princess, princess". She says in between breaths for air. Juliana asks, "What is it Ishma?" Concern now begins to show on her face.

Ishma pauses to find the words, "Come quickly it's the queen she has been taken ill!" Juliana looks worryingly to Rachel and they both dash towards the palace. The young royal has a terrible feeling on the health of her mother.

Chapter Seven

Eastwards of the planet, within the misty fields, a small assembly of tribe army guards gathers. The second in command looks up to the sky and turns to the leader of the group, commenting, "Where is he?

We can't stay here for long". Their leader is clearly seen as the ape, whose beard has begun to turn white, identifying it as the eldest. The ape turns around to the others and informs them their visitor will be here soon. After several moments have elapsed they slowly become impatient. The second in command suggests, "Come on lets go, he's not going to show and we cannot risk being seen this close to Valadreil". The leader hastily retorts, "If we return empty handed Gormosh will not be pleased".

The group of apes move closer towards some rocks to hide from any humanoid scouts that may be lurking within the facility. The second in command now shouts out the visitors name, "Finch, where are you? Show yourself, you dirty creature". Suddenly the ape jumps up and down in pain, clutching its hairy shin and yells, "Something kicked me". The other apes suspect it is an attack but then the image of Finch becomes visible. "I'm right under your nose". Sneers the elusive feline.

"Enough games Finch, where is the note?" The leader demands. Finch argues, "First my money". The gusty wind causes his fur to be swept to one side and he adds, "A tracker needs to survive in these conditions".

The commanding ape opens a pocket from its belt and tosses two coins towards the tracker. He quickly gathers them up from the grass and hands a white note to the ape who then inspects it and informs the others that the witch has sent word from Valadreil.

The commanding ape stares at a small but detailed drawing on the note and comments, "Good it won't be long until the witch will instruct us to attack, I will take this to Gormosh in the north". The commanding ape then orders his second in charge to meet with Finch at the same place tomorrow. Finch is then told to retrieve another note from the witch tonight at Valadreil.

Finch accepts the task and snarls at the second in command for calling him a dirty creature. The tracker makes his return journey to the humanoids capital of Sephire.

Princess Juliana arrives at the entrance to the royal chambers. She is surprised to find so many royal guards positioned in front of the closed doors. Before she can ask one of them what is going on, the king steps out from the room along with Commander Teltris. Princess Juliana immediately sees the grimaced expression on each of their faces. Her father attempts to conceal it when he recognizes her.

She asks him what is wrong with her mother? The king speaks quietly, suggesting that his inner strength is faltering and informs his daughter, "Your mother had fainted earlier. Once she regained consciousness she became delirious and unaware of her surroundings".

Mortified, Juliana cries out, "I must see her!" And moves towards the door, but her father blocks the route, explaining that the queen is sleeping and needs to rebuild her strength. The princess turns around and throws herself into the arms of Rachel, who is there to comfort her. The king instructs his guards to send Gwelyn up here, as he now requires her services to tend to his sick wife. Rachel helps Juliana along the corridor, leaving King Ridley in deep contemplation.

When Robert arrives to the archive room he cannot see Gwelyn. He asks Simon and Claire as to her whereabouts. They inform him of the king's instructions for Gwelyn to help the queen recover from her fainting. Robert is less than sympathetic and is annoyed with the royal leader for removing Gwelyn given the first opportunity, believing the majesty to be overreacting. Robert then orders Simon and Claire to continue searching through the books as he is going to find out the severity of the situation and walks out from the room. After a while Simon picks up a book that Gwelyn had been looking through earlier and notices that the writing on the spine of the book is in gold lettering. Simon asks, "Do you not think it strange that Gwelyn would be interested with the building plans of Valadreil?"

His companion does not answer, instead she asks Simon a question of her own. "The other day I was talking with Gwelyn, she told me of what you and Robert had been arguing about". Simon tells her that he does not wish to discuss it.

Less than convinced, Claire shakes her head and departs from the room, annoyed with Simon that he continues to conceal information from her. Simon is left alone in the room to wonder what he has done to upset her.

During the evening, a hooded figure small and slender again leaves a note by a statue unnoticed in the courtyard. The note is later retrieved by Finch who mutters upon the handsome reward he expects to receive for passing the information onto the tribe army. The creature crawls through the deserted streets of Valadreil, darting from one hiding place to the next, remaining unnoticed he departs the town as the pale green sun begins to rise. He cautiously makes his way eastwards, using the tall grass as cover.

Finch constantly checks that the recovered note remains safely concealed under his fur.

Chapter Eight

Later that same day, a tribe army outpost assigned to rendezvous with Finch, arrives at the designated meeting place to retrieve further instructions that the witch might have sent. The apes wait impatiently when suddenly Finch approaches. "You took long enough getting here", the commanding ape says, clearly annoyed with the delay. Finch responds, "The journey is long".

Unsatisfied with Finch's response the ape demands the tracker to give him the note. Finch bargains for his food and money, reasoning that was the agreed deal. The ape tells him that was the agreement, which he had yesterday but today he decides what happens.

Finch is disappointed and explains that he has gone without food to be here in time. The ape reluctantly throws some dead mice for Finch to eat. "There, and that's only because I'm feeling generous, now hand me the note!" The commander shouts and then two other apes grab hold of Finch's arms. They pull his head back to prevent him from struggling. The ape leader sees the note under the felines fur and snatches it from his possession.

The ape looks at the contents of the note and immediately alerts the others that the witch has already given instructions to infiltrate Valadreil. He tells them they must join with the other strike team that is currently heading this way from the north. The apes jump onto their horses. The threatening leader provides Finch with a menacing look as he considers this his revenge for kicking him in the shins the previous day.

An upset Finch kneels against some rocks within the grass to shelter away from the strong winds. Feeling hungry, he nibbles on the scarce amount of flesh on the dead mice when he suddenly hears the bellowing sound of a horn from nearby. The departing apes are confused and stop to look at one another but realize when it is too late that they are being attacked by several humanoids who now appear from distance, and fire laser shots from their spears.

Most of the apes are hit and fall from their horses. The ape leader looks on in horror as his colleagues are now dead on the grass. He calls out desperately for Finch to help him but cannot see where the creature has gone to. He shouts out once more, when suddenly an arrow pierces through his body. The strike instantly kills him and he falls from his saddle.

Derek soon appears at the scene, arriving with his girlfriend who rides on horseback under the protection of the humanoid guards that ride with them. Skirmishes such as these have become common of late.

The humanoids inspect each of the dead apes in case they carry any important information. However unknown to them, Finch remains trapped behind some rocks, which leads away from the battle.

Derek praises Naomi, "That was a nice shot". He then falls silent when he notices a white piece of paper grasped within the paws of a dead ape. "What's this?" He wonders and picks the note up. The humanoids gather around Derek to see what he has discovered. The muscular American examines the note and then states in disbelief, "Oh my god".

Naomi looks concerned at her boyfriend, before she can ask him what he has read, Derek urges her to fire the warning arrow, which is a specially constructed rocket that can be seen for miles.

"Fire it quick! Hideki and Yoshi might see it". Naomi lights the rocket with a match and releases it high into the sky. The object explodes fiercely and shakes the ground they stand on. Finch has to cover his ears from the deafening sound.

Naomi asks, "What is it?" Derek tells her and those around him that they must quickly return to Valadreil, because the tribe army attack is imminent. They quickly saddle back onto their horses and Derek points to a nearby hill where he instructs two of the guards to remain and notify Hideki and

Yoshi's patrol, to ride to Valadreil with haste. The two guards accept their instructions. Derek and Naomi, along with the remaining riders, gallop towards the capital, hoping that they are not too late to save their friends.

Once the guards have departed away from the corpses of tribe army apes, Finch quietly crawls along the ground and rummages through the uniform of the dead leader. The feline is delighted to discover a pouch that is full of coins. He then decides there might be a reward, should he venture north and alert Gormosh that the humanoids are aware of the attack. The tracker rubs his paws together, believing he will become rich. He creeps through the grass, remaining to be unseen from the two humanoids stationed on the hill.

With the setting of the green sun, word has spread throughout the town of Valadreil that the queen's health as worsened. King Ridley can sense that his wife is slowly dying and feels helpless in being able to bring her back to recovery. The king has become bad tempered, bickering with his guards, the humans and with his daughter. Those who obey the majesty have quietly begun to question the commandership of their leader believing that he has become affected by the queen's decline in health.

Later that evening Derek and Naomi burst past the entrance of Valadreil along with the other humanoids of their patrol. Without stopping for the guards at the gate, they rush towards the palace. When they arrive at the courtyard the larger presence of armed guards brings them abruptly to a halt. Derek jumps down from his horse and demands to see the king. The dark haired American footballer then tells Naomi to find their other human companions.

Derek is escorted to King Ridley. After several minutes the majesty arrives and demands an explanation for the human's return. At this moment Naomi, Rachel, Claire, Bobby and Simon appear with Princess Juliana. Derek hands King Ridley the note he had found from the skirmish with the apes earlier that day.

The humanoid leader examines it and grimaces, before announcing, "We have a spy in the palace!"

The people around him gasp in shock. The king explains, "I have here a note, its intention is to alert the tribe army forces in the north that the attack on Valadreil will take place soon. The note is written on paper found only from within the palace". Derek asks the royal if he suspects anyone for betraying the humanoids vulnerability. King Ridley voices his suspicious of Robert especially since he is not present.

Rachel interrupts him, immediately informing the royal leader that his suggestion is madness, as they would never betray the humanoids. Princess Juliana voices her agreement of what Rachel has said. King Ridley fails to listen to his daughter and immediately assigns members of his guards to remain in constant contact with all of the humans in case they are plotting something. He then instructs the other guards to gather all forces away from the palace in order to protect the entrance of Valadreil, for that is the only way the tribe army can enter the town. The king leaves the humans bewildered by his accusation. Princess Juliana apologizes and tries to explain that she will reason with her father. Rachel suggests to the king's daughter that she should remain with her ill mother.

Hideki, Yoshi and Robert suddenly appear and inquire to know what is happening? Claire updates them with news of the situation and suggests that in order to clear their names from any wrongdoing they will need to find the spy.

Bobby asks his sister if her group has found anything useful in the archives, she informs her friends that it is becoming impossible to translate the vocabulary. Robert attempts to order the royal guards to leave but the sentry will only take orders from the king. The princess advises the humans to rest and recuperate before any attack should arise. The humans reluctantly agree and are escorted away to their chambers by the royal guards.

Chapter Nine

The next day brings a heavy downpour of rain, the royal guards protecting the entrance to Valadreil remain vigilant. They have not slept during the previous night as King Ridley suspects an attack from the apes will soon take place. The lookouts on the defensive walls complain that they are unable to see for a great distance because of the driving rain. Their leader instructs them to remain firm and to hold their positions.

Elsewhere, the nine humans have been confined to their chambers under the supervision of the guards.

Claire comments to her companions that the clouds will not clear today. Hideki and Derek both share their different adventures whilst they had been on their separate patrols. Hideki mentions they did not venture north because they had been hindered by the appalling weather conditions. Yoshi adds that he had never seen rain, fall so heavily before. Derek talks about the small-scattered villages that he and Naomi had seen during their travels, where they witnessed much poverty as the humanoids lived in fear of the tribe army forces.

Robert appears tired and troubled with the situation and departs to his quarters to rest. The others are concerned with Robert's state of mind and wonder if there is anything they can do to help him recover.

Simon excuses himself from the room. He needs to be alone as the temptation increases to confess his secret with the group about the witch being responsible for Robert's illness. He wishes he knew of a way to find her identity for this all to be over. After closing the door behind him Simon is immediately confronted by Commander Teltris. The startled Englishman attempts to explain that he needs some fresh air. The commander can see that the human appears to be pale and tells Simon that he will escort him to an open doorway further along the corridor but takes possession of Simon's shield and spear.

The rain continues to fall heavily and causes most of the streets in Valadreil to become muddy. The uniforms of the royal guards minding the outposts to the town, stick to their soaked bodies whilst the humanoid townsfolk remain locked inside their homes for protection.

Inside the palace, Princess Juliana sits nervously outside her mother's chambers, praying that she can recover from her illness. Juliana becomes concerned when a handmaiden dashes out from the room, screaming at the guard to bring the king. Juliana enters her mother's room fearing that the worst has happened.

At the opposite end of the palace, Rachel tells her companions, "I am going to see the princess". Bobby asks her, "Why do you want to do that?" The blonde haired wizard replies, "I just want to see if she is okay".

The others decide to join her to find out if the king has yet to come to his senses. Claire knocks on Robert's door but receives no response and assumes that he has fallen asleep. Under the escort of the guards, the group walks along the corridor.

Once they have left the room, Robert wakes up but feels groggy. He opens his door and wonders where everybody has gone to. He then looks outside their chambers and notices the guards have also disappeared. "Where are they?" he asks himself. Robert retrieves his magic weapon and walks away from the room, hoping to solve the mystery.

Commander Teltris, who is observing Simon, coughs purposely as he can see that Simon is day dreaming. Simon turns around, "Sorry, am I boring you?" He asks sarcastically. The tall commander suggests, "I think you should return to your chambers". Simon acknowledges his request and they begin to walk back along the corridor. As they turn around the corner they are surprised to bump into Robert.

The commander immediately points his spear at Robert. The Welshman is alarmed that he will be shot down and yells, "What do you think you're doing!"

Commander Teltris stands firm and demands Robert to explain why he is wandering without a guard watching him. The human innocently tells him, "They'd left the chambers I had fallen asleep only to awaken and find that everyone had vanished!" The commander is suspicious but Simon convinces him to lower his weapon. Suddenly a high-pitched scream echoes from a distant corridor.

Raising his spear one more, Commander Teltris is in two minds of knowing what to do. Robert and Simon tell him they want to help but the commander is apprehensive in allowing the humans to have their weapons back as they might use them against him. Robert yells out in frustration, "When are you going to start trusting us!" With the sound of further screams and raised voices, Commander Teltris hands the two humans their weapons and the trio run towards the direction of the commotion.

The humanoid sent to collect King Ridley eventually finds him pacing in the royal throne room, upon seeing the guard, King Ridley stops and turns to look at him "What is it?" he asks. The guard replies, whilst still in shock, "My lord, the queen, she is dead!"

The king instantly falls to his knees. The words have sliced his legs away from him. Humanoids within the throne room hurry to console him when suddenly a gigantic boom explodes from outside the palace.

King Ridley rises back to his feet, suspecting it to be a warning signal coming from the front of the palace to alert of an attack at the entrance of Valadreil.

He is surprised to be informed that the alarm came from the back of the palace. This would suggest the attack is elsewhere. The king is then struck with the realization as to the whereabouts of the attack, he screams, "Juliana!" The sound echoes loudly against the pillars and stonewalls of the throne room. He quickly picks up the royal scepter and makes haste to rescue his daughter whilst being accompanied with his guards.

Rachel walks down the stairs leading to the queen's chambers. As she nears the bottom of the steps, a loud ear-piercing scream comes from beyond the corner. The group of humans and royal guards hurry to find out what is wrong. Rachel reaches the last step and sees Juliana, fallen on her knees whilst looking bewildered. Rachel calls out her name, the princess turns to face her and stares blankly back at Rachel.

Suddenly Claire senses a warning from her special powers and gasps, "Apes!"

Derek instantly pulls Robert's cousin back from the last step as royal guards push past her to aid the kings daughter but the guards are immediately sent crashing to the floor by wooden weapons belonging to tribe army apes. Derek cannot believe the apes have somehow managed to penetrate the inner walls of the palace. King Ridley had been wrong in believing that the attack would be to claim the town, it was actually to kidnap the princess.

Realizing they need assistance, Derek instructs his girlfriend to hurry outside to the gardens at the back of the palace and fire the warning arrow. Naomi sprints quickly back up the steps, knowing that any hesitation could result in the princess being killed or captured.

The humans attempt as best they can to defend their position by using their magic weapons, which the humanoid guards have allowed to be placed back into their possession. However there are too many tribe army apes to battle against as they have now managed to take control of the corridor. Yoshi receives a cut to his arm that wounds him and Derek instantly yells out for his companions to retreat to the top of the staircase until help arrives. They reach the top of the stairs, still defending themselves when a loud explosion is then heard from outside. The apes attacking the humans realize that royal guard forces will arrive shortly and they hurry back down the stairs to complete their task of capturing the princess.

King Ridley arrives at the corridor where mayhem is happening before his eyes, there in front of him are members of the royal guard hopelessly outnumbered by thirty tribe army apes. He intends to help save his daughter but the guards who remain at his side warn him it is suicide until help arrives. The king defiantly speaks, "I will not let them take my daughter whilst there is still breath left within me". He then runs to rescue his daughter whilst stepping over unconscious and dead members of the royal guard who have fallen. Those following him into battle expect that they will also fall to their deaths. However unaware to them and the apes, the scepter King Ridley carries, possesses great powers. The end of the instrument shines purple as a large ball of energy knocks over a group of apes but there remains too many for them to be able to rescue the princess.

From the opposite end of the corridor, Commander Teltris, Robert and Simon are working well together in fighting their own way through the attack. Robert catches a glimpse of Juliana being picked up by one of the apes. Simon provides his colleague with cover enabling Robert to get a clear shot of the ape. He fires his glowing arrow, striking the creature but this causes the princess to be dropped to the floor and she becomes unconscious. The remaining apes assess the situation and decide that the resistance is too strong for them to successfully complete their task of kidnapping the princess. The apes leave her on the ground and attempt to escape through the same route they had used to enter the palace and push past Robert and Simon. The other humans dash down the stairs with reinforcements and give pursuit, whilst those remaining in the corridor hurry to aid the princess.

Juliana slowly opens her eyes. Upon seeing Robert she hugs him for dear life. The young royal has been traumatized by the attack. The king steps back, whilst Commander Teltris apologizes to Simon for the way that he has been treating the humans these past few weeks. The king looks to the doors of the queen's chambers, remembering the tragedy of her dying. He is not yet mentally prepared to see her corpse.

As the commander and the two humans remain here to help his daughter recover, he quietly walks away to return the scepter back to the throne room, where he wishes to grieve alone.

The humans and royal guards chase after the retreating apes whom are trying to reach the cellars below the palace. Some of the creatures manage to escape into the darkness of the hidden passageways and the humans decide to call off the pursuit.

Claire fathoms that the apes must have gained access to an unknown entrance of the passageways from the surface. She then realizes that the apes would have needed an accomplice to have unlocked the gates.

The humanoid guards speculate that at least twelve apes have managed to escape. Derek instructs them that once the palace is secure, to continue with their search of the passageways in order to establish how the apes had managed to get into the palace. Hideki warns his colleagues that Yoshi is bleeding and needs medical attention.

Rachel quickly tares the sleeve from Yoshi's robe and tightens it across the wound to stop the bleeding.

She warns everyone, "We must get this dressed". The humans' then run back to their chambers' to get some bandages.

Inside the throne room King Ridley closes the doors behind him. Since the guards of the palace are in pursuit of the apes he assumes that he is alone. He gazes at the grand throne, amazed by its splendor and walks up to it, reflecting on what has just happened. He is distraught that he did not have the opportunity to say goodbye to his wife and could not hold her within his arms for one last time. He then realizes that due to his failure in assessing the threat, his daughter had almost been kidnapped. The king then drops the scepter on the floor, it has fallen from his grasp as the realization of the events begin to sink in. His head lowers and his legs begin to buckle.

Emotionally drained and physically beaten from the entanglement of battle, the king slumps to the floor, crying in sorrow. A woman's voice suddenly speaks from inside the room, "Poor King". The royal is startled and asks, "Who, who's there?" The woman speaks again, "Now you realize that you are all alone". The leader of Sephire stands up to face the person talking to him but cannot recognize the woman's voice or be able to see anyone else within the shadows of the hall.

A slender figure then steps out before him wearing a black cloak with her face concealed behind a hood.

Before the king can ask her who she is, the figure raises her arm and fires a laser shot, directly hitting the king in the chest. He falls backwards from the impact and lands on the floor of the throne room.

The humanoid leader begins to feel numb and is unable to pull himself up. The decreasing beats of his dying heart are heard inside his head. He looks up helplessly to the ceiling as his attacker approaches and removes her hood, the king instantly recognizes his attacker's face and is shocked with terror of who it is.

"You!" He says and attempts to scream out a name to give her identity away but his breathing stops and the last image he sees before dying is the woman concealing her face behind the black hood.

Chapter Ten

Derek asks his companions if they know the whereabouts of the King. Simon presumes he has gone to the throne room. Robert suggests, "Come on we had better look for him". Rachel chooses to remain with some of the handmaidens to look after the distraught princess.

As Robert and his colleagues approach the big wooden doors to the entrance of the throne room, Simon notices there are no guards on duty and wonders where could they be. When Derek places his hands onto the handle the doors are opened from the other side by Gwelyn. The yellow cloak of her uniform is visibly shaking. She appears to be in shock and begins to scream uncontrollably. Concerned, the humans' dash past her and enter the throne room where they soon discover the king laying motionless on the floor. With other members of the royal guard now arriving, Commander Teltris rushes to the fallen leader to feel for a pulse. The commander notices that King Ridley holds a laser within his grasp. Looking at the laser wound, Commander Teltris instantly knows that his leader has a slim chance of surviving the extent of his injury.

Everyone within the room looks desperately at the commander, hoping he is able to feel for some sign of life but he regretfully announces that the majesty is dead. Those within the room gasp in shock and Gwelyn begins to scream loudly once again.

Several weeks have now passed by. The feeling of sorrow is felt deeply amongst the people of Valadreil.

The grieving of loosing both of her parents has been too much for Juliana to cope with. Only the support from Rachel and her human friends, provides the young royal to find the strength to continue. The princess strongly denies the rumours that have been whispered of her father committing suicide due to the shock of loosing his wife. Juliana speaks to her guest alone in her chamber, "Father would not have wished

121

to leave me abandoned like this even if he was terribly upset with mother dying". Juliana still sobs at the thought of the events which happened on that dreadful day. Rachel tells her she must remain strong for her people and tries to remind her of the duties that she must soon accept. The princess is well aware of what her friend is implying and replies, "But Rachel, I am not strong enough to do this on my own, I cannot become leader of Sephire and give hope to the humanoids when I have none myself".

Rachael looks her straight in the eye and truthfully tells her, "Even in the most gravest of situations, there is always hope". Juliana wipes away her tears, feeling mentally stronger and thanks Rachel for her continuing support. There is a knock at the door and the guard outside speaks, "My lady, it is time". The two women in the room know what he means for they are to attend the burial of the dead majesties.

Once outside they are accompanied by Rachel's human companions and proceed towards the courtyard where they find five thousand humanoids, assembled of guards', handmaidens' and other loyal servants to the royal family. They stand encircled around two horses that are each linked to special carriages containing the coffins of the deceased King Ridley and Queen Avril.

Upon seeing the princess, dressed in her black robes, everyone lowers to one knee in mark of respect.

Juliana notices the carriages bear the flags of the horse and crescent shape to Sephire's sun. She allows everyone to rise and then pulls down the veil to conceal her face. Rachel stands alongside Juliana and gently grasps her hand to allow her to know that she is not alone. Juliana does not let go of her hand and they stand directly behind the carriages as the riders on the horses slowly lead the solemn march through the capital. Each person of the parade stands in pairs behind the princess and Rachel, before joining the march of respect for the fallen.

The carriages move very slowly through the streets of Valadreil. Each of the townsfolk stands silently outside their homes, bowing their heads as the precession marches past. Princess Juliana looks at the common people, most she senses are still in shock, others are crying. Juliana realizes she has now been able to come to terms with loosing her parents but she does not know if she will ever be able to provide these people with hope and believe. The march takes an hour before the carriages reach the way out of the town. The royal guard forces bow their heads, as it is seen to be the end of the journey for the king and queen who once governed the humanoids. The gates open and the precession leads outside the town towards a specially constructed tomb, which has been built.

Simon recalls that whilst reading through the ancient manuscripts, there had been several references of tombs being the symbolic place for kings and queens to be buried. The procession halts and twelve royal guards carry the coffins into the tomb. The princess accompanies them, as she helps to bury her parents.

Those who have not entered wait patiently outside the tomb for the ceremony to commence. After a short while Juliana reappears with her guards and the horses are slowly ridden away to the stables of the town.

The mourners are then led to a grassy knoll, where they see a young boy standing on top of a large rock and a harpist sitting in a chair behind the rock. They wait for everyone to gather around the top of the small grassed hill to become silent. The harpist begins to play and the young humanoid starts to sing, his voice is heavenly in tune with the crystal clear sound of the harp. The words sung are from texts of ancient times as a celebration to the life of the dead majesties.

The spectators on the hill are moved with the harmonious sound. Claire considers the scene to remind her of a choirboy singing a Christmas carol. The majority cannot help but shed a tear as everyone begins to join hands for unity and strength.

The singing continues for several minutes, with the harpist dictating the speed that the boy must sing, whilst changing the pitches of the harp. The musician then begins to play at a high note, which the boy reaches with his voice and holds onto it for as long as his breath will allow.

Then both the harpist and the boy stop at precisely the same moment and the song of respect is complete.

Slowly the mourners depart back to the safety of Valadreil, the princess knows that a month from this very day will signify the moment when she will have to take the pledge to become Queen of Sephire and ruler of the humanoids. She prays to herself that she will somehow manage to find the strength from within and not let her people down.

Chapter Eleven

In the northern rocklands of terror, the daunting site of Roshtu's fortress paints a bleak picture across the landscape. The weather is continuously wild with rain falling heavily. Any humanoid that strays past the northern borders are never seen again. Sharp jagged rocks surround these lands for miles where concealed trenches full of apes await in ambush. The dark knight's fortress is located across a wooden drawbridge and is well protected against an attack. With its gates and walls both tall and strong it would require the entire humanoid forces to be able to break through.

Thousands of apes prepare for battle with the humanoids as they are busy assembling large wooden weapons that will fire heavy rocks that would cover a great distance. The ground is muddy but the weather does not deter the apes as they have had to deal with far worse on other planets that Roshtu controls through the portal.

The fortress contains a maze of dark candlelit corridors that are guarded by apes. Inside the battle room Riesk and Gormosh greet the few members of the ape strike team that had been sent to capture the humanoid's princess. The circular room is large with curved walls, in its center, a holographic image of Sephire displays strategic battle plans of the tribe army and royal guard forces. Riesk addresses the apes and asks them why had their mission failed? The leading ape of the strike team replies, "The humans still remain at Valadreil, it is due to the witch's failure to remove them that had caused our attack to not succeed".

Riesk relays to them that Finch had provided a warning of the humanoids intercepting a message, which had been sent from the witch. Gormosh remembers that he wishes to speak to the tracker and requests an ape servant to collect the feline from his chambers. Thanks to the tracker, the tribe army has been able to commence with their battle preparations much sooner than anticipated and have saved valuable time.

Riesk asks the strike team why had they taken so long to return to the Northern Rocklands of Terror? An ape replies, "We were surprised not to have been chased from the palace by the humanoid forces, so we decided to remain hidden to make our observations. We then saw the humanoids construct a tomb and witnessed the burial of their king and queen".

The two large ape brothers look to one in shock and check to confirm that they have just heard correctly, "You mean they are leaderless?" Gormosh asks the strike team. The apes respond that he is correct.

Riesk quietly forgives the witch and reminds himself it was foolish to ever doubt her powers. He tells his brother, "Everything is happening how Roshtu said it would. The princess not being captured is insignificant, our main objective was to create panic and turmoil within the very heart of Valadreil. Now that has been accomplished Peirlee will soon strike her attack on the troublesome humans, allowing Roshtu to finally return".

The doors are then opened and Finch is escorted into the room. The creature appears to have been well looked after. With his fur shiny he stands nibbling on a piece of meat that is clenched between his paws.

Gormosh notifies Finch with news of a task that he requires him to do. Finch asks without any hesitation what will be the reward?

Riesk tells him that he will become the richest tracker throughout the entire galaxy. Finch is astonished and drops his stick of meat to the floor. Gormosh then tells him, "Finch you will return to Valadreil and look for any signs that the humanoid forces will mount an attack". Riesk commands the ape strike team to also accompany the tracker and dismisses them from the room.

With the two ape brothers now alone Gormosh comments, "If everything goes according to plan, by the time the humanoid forces commence their attack on us, Roshtu would have been able to open his portal, allowing re-enforcement's of our army to come through". Riesk smiles at the prospect and they both gaze through the glass window panes that overlooks the muddy courtyard, where through the rain, thunder and lightening they can see the portal that will signify the end of the humanoids.

Meanwhile in Valadreil, Juliana sits in a chair, her eyes focus on everything within the room, it has been a month to the day since her parents were laid to rest. Juliana is no longer a princess and the seat she sits on is no ordinary chair as it is the grand royal throne. This is the moment that Juliana has become the Queen of Sephire and leader of the humanoids.

In front of her are crowds of humanoid dignitaries, royal servants, handmaidens and her human friends.

Queen Juliana feels strange being inside the same room as where her father had perished. One of the servants then passes Juliana the royal scepter. She grasps hold of it and stands in front of the audience.

Everybody within the room begins to applaud the newly appointed queen.

Once the gathered spectators become silent, Queen Juliana speaks defiantly to her people, "We will not concede to the threat that lingers in the north of our planet. I will continue my father's attempt to restore freedom for our people, where we can live once more in peace". The audience applauds again and the queen departs under the protection of her guards. Whilst approaching her small group of human friends whom are gathered at the back of the room, Juliana looks across to Rachel, who acknowledges to her that the speech was fine.

The queen passes through the open doors with her face showing concern of the next announcement that she must address to the townsfolk of Valadreil. Once the last of her speeches for defiance has concluded, Juliana knows that it will be time to prepare for the evening festivities for the banquet to honour her appointment as the humanoid's leader.

Later that day, within the housing quarters of the royal handmaidens, Robert waits patiently outside Gwelyn's chamber. He carries some flowers and has made himself presentable. For the first time that he can recall he has decided to leave his weapon of special powers behind in safekeeping. The Welshman knocks on the door, hoping he is not too early to collect Gwelyn to accompany him as his guest to the banquet.

He receives no response and knocks once again. Concerned, he places his ear to the door to hear if there is anyone inside the room. As he applies some pressure to the door it opens and allows him to stumble accidentally inside. Robert looks around but cannot see that anyone else is within the room. He wonders where could the handmaiden possibly be, but decides to make good use of the time that he has available.

The human attempts to check that his appearance remains acceptable but is unable to find a mirror. The Welshman then inspects his breath and confirms the flowers he holds remain fresh. The room is much smaller than he had anticipated considering that Gwelyn is one of the senior handmaidens. He then looks at the bed, which suggests that it has not been slept in.

The curtains have not been drawn, allowing some of the evening light to shine into the room. Robert then notices there is a display stand with a silk cloth covering the top. Curiosity gets the better of the human and he attempts to lift up the cloth to find what is hidden underneath.

The doors suddenly open and Gwelyn appears with one of the other handmaidens. She looks suspiciously at Robert. Had her co-worker not accompanied her inside the room, Gwelyn would have wanted to know why he had entered her room. The Welshman smiles innocently and asks if she is ready to go to the banquet.

Gwelyn accepts the flowers that he offers her and dismisses the other handmaiden. She then informs Robert that she is ready and they leave the room with Gwelyn locking the doors behind her.

The ceremonial dinner is in full swing where fresh fruit and meat is available to pick, whilst music of violins and harps play within the throne room that creates a harmonious atmosphere. Everybody is smartly dressed in their formal clothes where the attendees consist of the humans and loyal members to the royal leader.

The humanoids have not forgotten the severity of their situation with the threat of the tribe army apes.

The royal guard forces are patrolling the town and the palace in case of an attack. Should the apes decide to strike, the queen will soon be warned. She walks inside the room dressed in her stately clothes whilst being accompanied with Rachel as they greet the guests.

The guards outside the throne room open the doors to allow more visitors to enter. Derek asks Simon if he has seen Robert. The English legionnaire has no idea where their companion is but expects that he will soon be joining them. The dark haired man has been relieved that ever since the skirmish with the apes he has managed to be back on speaking terms with his friend. He now accepts that Robert enjoys being with Gwelyn, so long as it does not hinder with their progress for the search of valuable information as to the whereabouts of the two lost books.

Meanwhile in the throne room, Bobby attempts to charm his way with some of the pretty humanoid women whom are present in the banquet. The influence of sampling the homegrown wine causes the young sandy haired teenager to feel too relaxed. Claire pulls her teenage brother aside to prevent him from causing any further embarrassment. She is unsure if he is too young to be able to handle drinking alcohol. Bobby assures her, "Relax sis, they have no age limit for drinking booze on this planet". He then hiccups and proceeds to stumble across to the other side of the room to obtain further alcohol. Claire looks concerned to Naomi, who can only smile at the boy's attempt to walk in a straight line.

Simon then notices that Robert has now arrived and points him out to Derek but the American comments, "What does Robert think he is doing parading with one of the handmaiden. Does he not know she can't come back to Earth with us?" Not wanting to unsettle things once again with Robert, Simon shrugs his shoulders and they continue to mingle with the other guests.

Bobby finally manages to make his way through the crowd of people and arrives at the table containing wine. So far he has consumed purple, green and turquoise coloured drinks. Feeling jolly and adventurous he decides to pick up a yellow colored wine. Bobby then gazes into the mirror placed on the wall. He looks at the reflection of himself and watches a group of humanoids walking past. The teenager then recognizes one of his human colleagues and realizes that it is Robert who appears to be accompanied by someone. Bobby stares hard at the mirror trying to see through his blurred vision of whom the person is so that he can spread the gossip back to his friends.

Suddenly the image in the mirror shows him the face of a scary old hag with green wrinkled skin.

Shocked by what he has seen Bobby spins around and dashes towards Robert but in his attempts to save him he accidentally bumps into some of the other guests. Just before he prepares to attack the threat to his friend, Bobby is then surprised to see that the person accompanying Robert is actually the attractive handmaiden called Gwelyn.

Once the commotion has subsided and having been provided with a disgruntled look from Commander Teltris, the teenager stops in his tracks and wonders what could have fooled his eyes. He then remembers the wine he had previously consumed. Bobby decides to place his glass of wine back onto the table and instead picks up a glass of spring water, where he then rejoins Claire and Naomi.

Upon seeing the non-alcoholic drink, his sister praises him for using some common sense. Bobby smiles back at her but silently ponders that when people had drunk too much they were supposed to see pink elephants not scary witches.

Chapter Twelve

When the start of a new day arrives, the humans awaken with hope that they might be able to discover the location of the two remaining lost books. Only then can they attempt to find a way of combining the power from each of the books in order to find a way of returning to Earth.

As they assemble in front of the queen's chambers, Simon believes the task ahead will not be easy but his companions try to remain positive. Bobby wonders where Robert is. Hideki comments, "I have not seen him since the banquet last night". Derek suggests that maybe he spent the night in Gwelyn's chambers. Robert's younger cousin is slightly concerned as she is certain that he knew about this mornings meeting. Rachel suggests they should go without him and look for her Welsh relative as soon as the discussions with Queen Juliana have concluded.

Commander Teltris then informs the waiting humans that the humanoid leader is ready to see them and allows them to enter the room, where they are then left alone. Each member of the group vouches to the new leader of Sephire that they will continue to help the humanoids to resist any further attacks to Valadreil.

The queen looks seriously at them and announces determinedly, "We have been on the defensive for too long. The apes attack to Valadreil will not go unpunished. I hold them responsible for triggering the death of my parents and I'm afraid that the hatred within my heart will not subside until they are brought to justice. Our forces outnumber the tribe army apes and we shall therefore plan our attack to claim their fortress in the north".

The humans look uneasy and Rachel urges the queen not to be too hasty with her decision or to speak about her plans to anyone outside of this room until the spy within Valadreil has been caught. Otherwise the humanoid attack strategy will be in vain as the tribe army will be alerted of their plans and they would loose the element of surprise.

The determined queen pauses to reflect of what Rachel has said and grudgingly accepts her heed for patience. She then allows her guards to enter the chambers and grants the humans to have access to the archives once again.

Elsewhere inside the palace walls, Robert wakes up from a deep sleep. He is still fully dressed in last nights banquet clothes but has not got the faintest idea whose room he is in. Robert attempts to stand but without being able to control his weary legs he stumbles to the drawn curtains. Yawning loudly the young man pushes back the curtains to reveal bright light into the room, which does nothing to help ease his pounding headache.

The Welshman recollects the banquet from the previous evening but does not recall drinking too much alcohol. He finally realizes this is Gwelyn's room although he has a distant memory of being here before.

The handmaiden suddenly enters the room, which startles the human. Upon seeing Robert she comments, "Sephire's wine must be too strong for you". She then eases him back down onto the bed.

Robert thanks Gwelyn for looking after him but then recollects he was supposed to be with his companions for a meeting with the queen. Gwelyn tells him to rest until he feels better. Robert attempts to stand up but he does not have the energy and is rapidly becoming concerned with his health.

The handmaiden picks up a bottle of perfume from a table and sprays some of it into his direction. She then sits next to the Welshman on the bed and looks at him. He can smell the sweet perfume and immediately feels drowsy. Robert's head feels as if it is spinning and his eyes become heavy.

Just as the human falls unconscious, Gwelyn stands over him and looks down menacingly at Robert who is now fast asleep. She then attempts to pick up an object concealed from underneath the bed, when she suddenly hears a knock to the door. Gwelyn walks over and wonders who has disturbed her. She partially opens the entrance only to be greeted by the other humans. She carefully slips past the open doorway, where Rachel asks her if she has seen Robert.

The handmaiden closes the door behind her and replies, "Yes I saw him earlier this morning he had made an early start with his search through the archives and brought this book up to me". At this moment Gwelyn produces a book that she had previously concealed inside her cloak and passes it to Simon. The thin Englishman whom wears a golden legionnaires outfit immediately notices that the book's spine has writing that is written in gold leaf lettering and begins to flick through the pages. Gwelyn continues to inform the humans, "Your friend told me that he was going to explore The Tomb of Zemlin, which is situated close to the eastern border".

Simon discovers a page that he has been desperately searching for these past five months and declares, "I think Robert may have found the location of the missing Blue Book of Wisdom!" And with that he dashes along the corridor, leaving his colleagues excited by the possibility that their search might be over.

They quickly thank Gwelyn for the information and hurry along the corridor to catch up with Simon whom can be seen moving towards the stables.

As she watches the humans' leave, Gwelyn smiles, for she is pleased with her deception. She then turns around to enter her chambers in a bid to kill the troublesome human that she has drugged when suddenly a handmaiden approaches along the corridor and calls out to Gwelyn that her services are required by the queen.

A frown of annoyance appears on the pretty handmaiden's face but she reluctantly obeys her order and considers to herself that Robert can wait for later. The potion she had sprayed will keep him sleeping for a few hours. His friends will abandon him once they find the lost book and be tempted through the gateway that will appear. Soon she can leave this place with her objectives complete and return to her dwelling in the west as her true identity of Peirlee the witch.

The humans manage to persuade the stable boys to let them borrow some horses and they depart Valadreil on horseback with great haste, leaving the vast town of Sephire's capital far behind in the distance. The trail of dust is seen through the air from the horses' hoofs as they ride on the pathway that leads to the east of the planet. Derek warns the others that it will take them a couple of hours to get there since he had previously seen the tomb whilst on patrol with the royal guards.

Simon remains impatient and feels that it is imperative they catch up with Robert as quickly as possible.

He would never forgive himself should anything happen to his friend. Claire has a nagging suspicion that something is wrong, her powerful weapon of intuition is trying to warn her of something. She wonders what could it possibly be? Is it to do with Robert, or perhaps the humanoids? She concludes that her thoughts may become clearer once they reach The Tomb of Zemlin.

The team of humans, continue to ride eastwards. After an hour of traveling has passed by Naomi uses her enhanced vision to notice a stream, which is further ahead. She notifies her companions and they decide to deviate from their current route where their horses trot towards the creek.

Once they have stopped Bobby jumps down from the uncomfortable saddle that he had shared with his older sister and complains that he will never be able to walk properly again.

As the horses begin to drink from the water, Rachel speaks to the others that she is surprised Robert had decided to leave them behind. Simon agrees with her but hopes their friend has not come to any harm.

Derek comments that without Robert's leadership will impact their chances of success and will add strength to Roshtu's power.

Claire suddenly clutches her head in pain and falls to the ground. Concerned, her friends rush to help her and Rachel offers Bobby's sister some water from the flask. She takes a sip from the cool spring water that slowly eases her pulsating pulse and the throbbing in her head subsides. Naomi asks, "What is wrong?"

Panting, she replies, "I sensed a great evil threat, but I was unable to see clearly what it was. I fear something terrible is about to happen". Her breathing becomes stable once again and she appears to have recovered. Simon is still worried about Claire's health but having heard this warning he suggests they should continue with their journey to catch up with Robert before it is too late. Derek tells them it should only be six miles until they reach the tomb but most of their journey will be uphill, which will slow their progress. The band of humans' saddle onto the horses and ride as fast as their creatures will allow.

* * *

Elsewhere on Sephire, Robert's eyes briefly open. His head feels numb and the human wonders how long has he been in a deep sleep dreaming as it feels that an eternity has elapsed. He forces his sleepy eyes to open but is unable to focus on anything from inside the room as everything has become a blur to his vision. Still sweating from the encounters he had experienced in his dreams, the images slowly come back to him. "What is wrong with me!" Robert asks out loud but the Welshman has no way of knowing what to do in order to make his problems go away.

He feels so hot, as if burning up from the inside of his body. Robert decides to allow some air to cool his skin and fumbles to unbutton his shirt. With his energy levels evaporated he struggles to sit up from the bed but his head begins to roll from side to side. In an attempt to stop the spinning he closes his eyes otherwise he fears he will be sick. Suddenly the image of the last nightmare flashes before him. To his horror

Robert finds himself inside a dark tunnel, being chased by a frightening old woman who carries a small-glassed ball. Scary monsters begin to come out of the circular object. They have sharp teeth and want to taste his blood. The troubled man sees himself frantically attempting to run away from them but as he glances over his shoulder he can see the enemy is closing in on him. Robert suddenly trips over an obstacle and falls to rocky surface where he receives cuts to his arms and legs.

Attempting to get back to his feet he pushes himself up but something within the floor grabs hold of his ankles that prevents him from moving. Robert is trapped and looks up to witness his demise where he sees the scary woman look down at him, whilst still holding onto her crystal ball.

Robert then awakens with a startle, "What, where am I?" he asks. Recovering his breathing, the human wipes the sweat away from his forehead and decides to try and stand up but when his feet touch the floor, his legs give way and his eyes suggest that the room has spun upside down. Falling to the ground, Robert knocks into a cabinet, which causes a small piece of furniture to tumble down. The sound of the impact forces Robert to open his eyes, where before him an object that had previously been concealed, unrolls from a cloth.

He attempts to focus his eyes onto the item, but his vision is still bleary all that the human can hear is the sound of an object moving towards him. When the noise suddenly stops Robert's vision begins to clear and to his terror he recognizes it is the crystal ball belonging to the scary woman who had been pursuing him in his nightmare!

Robert realizes that he must get away from this place and find a way of warning the others but in his attempts to stand up he collapses back to the floor through exhaustion and falls unconscious.

* * *

Meanwhile, the humans' approach to the top of the hill has been with slow progress. At the summit they find The

Tomb of Zemlin, where large rocks surround a stone carving of the first king to Sephire. Rachel wonders why Robert's horse is not here. Naomi suggests that perhaps his horse has bolted.

Derek attempts to call out to their companion but receives no reply. "Maybe I can find some tracks around the area". Hideki says and begins to look closely at the grass along the slope to see if it has recently been trodden on. The others reach the rocks and become aware of some steps that lead into darkness underneath the tomb. Simon turns around to Claire and asks her if she senses any threat. The slender brunette woman responds, "I cannot sense any sign of danger here".

Fastening the reigns of their horses around some of the rocks, Simon looks to his companions, unsure of what to do. Rachel recommends that Naomi should keep watch for any signs of patrolling apes that may be in the area. Derek volunteers to look after the horses whilst Yoshi searches for any of Robert's tracks at the top of the hill this leaves Simon, Claire, Rachel and Bobby to explore the passageway beneath the tomb.

Chapter Thirteen

Claire walks alongside Simon down the steep steps that lead to the underground passage. Her headband shines a way through the darkness. Rachel and Bobby follow closely behind them, suddenly the teenager catches sight of a face looking back at him, he yells out and grabs hold of Rachel for protection. The teenager's outburst causes his three other companions to jump. Claire and Simon turn around to Bobby but he whispers to them that he had seen a face within the darkness. His older sister shines her light into the direction of where Bobby points. They soon realize he had seen a humanoid figurine. Claire's light shines further along, showing several other sculptures of humanoids whom would have been of some importance.

The tunnel smells of dry grass and soil but as they continue to creep forwards the air becomes foul.

A frightened Bobby looks frantically around him but is alarmed when he sees several creatures slithering within the ceiling! Looking up he realizes there is no ceiling just the land of earth above them, which is full of worms.

Wishing to get away from this place, Bobby recommends to his colleagues that he is returning to the surface in case anything should have happened and quickly departs for safety. Claire rolls her eyes and mutters under her breath, "Chicken".

* * *

Within the humanoid palace, Robert opens his weary eyes. He remains on the floor and feels terribly weak. The human catches sight of the crystal ball again and knows whom the object belongs to but does not wish to wait for her return. "I must get out of here!" He shrieks and somehow manages to rest against a cupboard where he uses it for support to haul himself back to his feet.

Robert attempts to walk but despite his legs feeling unstable he succeeds in stumbling towards the door.

Taking a few gulps of air Robert hopes that as soon as he is through the other side of this door he can call a humanoid guard for assistance but he senses that his eyelids' are becoming heavy once again and that his legs are beginning to give way. The concerned Welshman knows that there is precious time remaining to escape the witch's trap. Robert turns the handle of the door but is mortified to discover it is locked and falls to the floor in anxiety. Unable to get away from his confinement he feels abandoned to await the reality of his haunted dreams.

Directing his gaze at the last rays of sunlight from the closed window, Robert wonders if there could be signs of a possible escape from that end of the room. He crawls across the floor where he eventually reaches the window that overlooks the town of Valadreil. A sudden burst of hope pulses through his veins when he becomes aware that the catch on the window has not been locked. Sliding the panel to the side he manages to clamber outside and onto the ledge where strong gusts nearly send him backwards, which causes his unbuttoned shirt to flap uncontrollably within the wind.

Robert grabs hold of a railing to prevent himself from tumbling over the edge of the tall building. Unable to see a way down and still trying to focus properly, he decides to climb up in order to reach the roof. Calling on all of his energy, Robert begins to pull himself up a pole but soon comes to a grinding halt and pleads, "Simon, why aren't you here, why can't you help me?" Tears begin to trickle down his face as he realizes that his human companions cannot save him.

* * *

At The Tomb of Zemlin, Claire leads Simon and Rachel to the end of the passageway, where they find a container. Rachel questions, "Where is the book?" Simon believes it must be here and frantically pushes the container open. He soon discovers The Blue Book of Wisdom and sighs in relief, but in doing so, allows some dust to be swept away from the book's cover.

Cautiously they look to one another but just as Simon is about to attempt to open the book, Claire grabs hold of his hand to stop him. He asks what is wrong? Claire then points to a carving of images that are behind Simon and suggests that they should first attempt to understand these before pulling back the cover.

Simon turns around and studies the drawings, he voices his interpretation, "These imply that the book once possessed great powers. Powers that were beyond the humanoids control. In an attempt to bury it from sight, a group of humanoids were selected to carry out the task in this location. However in the search for seeking power of wisdom each of the humanoids turned against one another and eventually killed themselves". Simon then concludes, "Just before the last humanoid died he, or she must have sketched this carving, warning anyone else who should discover the book to the dangers of its contents".

Rachel asks what should they do now? The group cannot resist the temptation any longer and they decide to find out what is inside. Simon cautiously turns to the first page. An inner light, shines from the book and the humans notice that the words, which have been written in the ancient text are scribbled in gold leaf lettering. Claire recognizes some of the letters and phrases from each of the three lines. "I think this words reads, past, the one on the last line is, hereafter". Rachel wonders what the words mean.

Simon replies that he does not know but then delicately lifts the paper over only to find that the first page has a large black square, which covers the middle of the paper. Nothing happens and the legionnaire is about to turn overleaf when suddenly images and colours' slowly begin to take shape, which eventually shows eleven elderly humanoids.

Unable to take their eyes away, the humans watch in amazement. Claire believes that these humanoids must be members of the original governing council. Simon suggests "Perhaps this is an image of something, which had happened a long time ago". Rachel agrees with him and recollects that on the previous page the word 'past' had been written on one of the lines.

From the opposite end of the tunnel, Bobby looks down the darkness and is curious with what the others may have found but chooses to remain where he is. The adolescent then sees a bright light from the end of the passage and hears Simon's raised voice. Afraid to be missing out on something the teenager attempts to place his fears to the back of his mind and starts to crawl nervously down the tunnel when suddenly a loud booming sound is heard from above their heads. Rachel manages to divert her attention away from the book and points out, "It's Naomi's warning signal!" She turns around to head back to the surface only to bump into Bobby. Together they quickly make their way towards the steps whilst Claire and Simon remain transfixed on the images from the book.

"Where are they?" Naomi yells at Derek, hoping that he can see their companions from the tunnel. At the top of the hill Yoshi quickly approaches and gasps by what he sees in front of him. Derek points out, "Look it's a gateway, similar to the one that appeared when we found The Book of Spells!"

Naomi drops her weapon to the ground and tells her boyfriend that she is leaving this place and begs for him to follow before the African woman then runs towards the entrance of the gateway. The image stops flickering and Derek realizes what his girlfriend has seen. He cries out in disbelief, "Home!" Yoshi asks him to elaborate but Derek is already running to catch up with Naomi and he shouts back to the Samurai "This gateway leads us back to Earth".

Yoshi is bewildered and stares at the image of an amusement park. The Japanese man cannot help but follow when he suddenly remembers Hideki. Yoshi manages to run towards the edge of the hill and calls out to his fellow countryman,

"Hideki, hurry we've found a gateway that leads back to Earth". Yoshi notices that his friend still has quite a climb to catch up but turns around only to witness Naomi going through the gateway shortly before Derek who then throws himself through.

As Yoshi approaches the entrance to the gateway, he begins to smell sea-air and hears various musical tunes coming from within the amusement park. The Japanese warrior suddenly thinks about the humanoids' fate, should they leave and decides that he cannot let them down. He attempts to stop himself but a powerful force of energy grips hold of him and starts to pull him ever closer towards the opening.

Unable to prevent his legs from moving Yoshi looks back helplessly and catches sight of Hideki reaching the top of the hill. Hideki witnesses his friend departing from this planet where he fades within the gateway. The Japanese ninja calls out to Yoshi but he has already gone. The image of the gateway suddenly begins to flicker, which suggests that it is loosing power and is about to be closed. In an attempt to join his friend, Hideki sprints towards the gateway.

Rachel and Bobby make it up the steps of the underground passageway and watch in amazement.

The female wizard explains to him that she cannot abandon the queen and that she has decided to stay until their task has been completed. The teenager looks at Rachel as if she is mad and argues that this might be their one chance to be able to return home. Bobby then explains that he must get his sister.

Hastily retreating back down the steps Bobby shouts emphatically for his sister to hurry up but after receiving no response he decides to go and get her.

Upon reaching the end of the passageway the excited youth is frustrated that both Claire and Simon have chosen to ignore him but he then has to shield his eyes from a bright light that protrudes from the book that his weak companion holds open.

With time running out Bobby grabs hold of his sister and leads her to the exit of the passage, Claire objects to this and voices her disapproval, "What do you think you are doing?" But her brother quickly replies that a gateway, which is linked to the amusement park at San Francisco has appeared.

The New Yorker is shocked and then shouts out to Simon for him to follow but the Englishman continues to remain mesmerized by the pictures from within The Book of Wisdom. Once they reach the end of the tunnel, Rachel grasps hold of Claire and Bobby's hands to pull them quickly up the steps.

Along the end of the passageway, the pictures before Simon's eyes become increasingly powerful with each passing second, providing him with valuable insight to events that have happened in the past, events that are currently taking place and events soon to take place. The energy bursting out from the book, forces a strong gush of wind to blow into Simon's face, forcing the helmet to fall from his head and his hair to be swept back. Forcing his eyes to remain open, he stares at the image of a scary elderly woman.

Simon suspects this must be the witch. The picture then changes to a terrifying sight where masses of apes belonging to the tribe army are assembling huge wooden weapons in a dark and rainy environment, through thick mud and sharp rocks.

A lightening bolt flashes before his eyes, forcing him to momentarily blink. Simon then recognizes the face belonging to Roshtu, whom seems to be much older and wrinkled than the previous time he had encountered the dark knight at the Argian Waterfall. Simon then notices Roshtu standing in front of a portal within the rocklands of the north.

Suddenly the image of Robert appears. He is lying motionless on a bed. Simon can see that his friend does not look well as his skin is yellow and he appears to be sweating. The figure standing over Robert causes Simon's blood to run cold and he gasps in shock at the sight of the witch grasping onto her staff, ready to bring it crashing down onto Roberts exposed chest to kill him. Before the image can be played through, Simon forces himself to look away and slams the book shut. Breaking free from its power he falls to the ground panting. Without stopping to regain his breath, he hastily dashes back along the corridor and grasps onto the book.

On the surface, Hideki is just ahead of the other humans. He continues to run as fast as his legs will allow.

As he nears the gateway the images become heavily distorted. With only a meter away from the opening, a door suddenly covers the entrance. Hideki lunges to grasp hold of the handle but as his fingers touch it the door and the gateway disappear, leaving Hideki to fall with a thud onto the grass.

Rachel, Claire and Bobby catch up with Hideki, where they help the upset warrior to his feet. Simon then appears but he realizes that some of his friends are missing and asks where are they? Rachel is left to inform him of what has happened.

The group is despondent knowing that their chances of defeating both Roshtu and his witch have diminished due to their lack of numbers and that they have perhaps missed their one opportunity of returning home. Their thoughts turn to their three friends whom they might never see again and they begin to wonder if Derek, Yoshi and Naomi have made it safely back to Earth. As Simon allows his mind to drift he then exclaims that he realizes whom the spy at Valadreil is. Claire asks, "Who is it?" He answers, "I cannot believe that I have been so blind. There is one person that has access to valuable information and can walk past guards unnoticed without being questioned. We have been deceived all along and have fallen for the witches trap".

Rachel is still unsure whom Peirlee is disguised as but with the legionnaire making his way towards the horses, everyone suddenly notices that Bobby has already mounted into his saddle. His sister asks, "Bobby, where are you going?" The determined teenager replies, "I know who it is, the witch is disguised as Gwelyn. I saw her through the reflection of the mirror during the banquet but was too blind to realize".

He then places his powerful club next to the saddle and rides quickly down the slope in order to save Robert. Claire screams out for her brother to stop immediately but he fails to listen.

Hoping to prevent Bobby from attempting to confront the witch on his own, the remaining humans' quickly gather their weapons along with those of their departed companions and saddle back onto their horses to catch up with him.

Chapter Fourteen

Robert clings desperately onto the metal railing that he uses in his attempt to climb to the rooftop.

Pausing to catch his breath the Welshman shuts his eyes and still attempts to block out the frightening images from his vivid nightmares. Robert begins to feel groggy once more and his grip on the pole begins to loosen. Realizing that should he fall he will plummet to his death, he opens his eyes and looks at his cold white knuckles. Despite the sick Welshman's best efforts to resist the spell that surrounds him, with each passing second his body become weaker and weaker.

Unable to move any further, Robert shivers from the cold wind and the falling temperature of the night. He gazes at a pattern of stone chipping within the palace wall but through the vision of his watery eyes Robert can see an image of Simon's face. The human stares at it believing it is his friend that looks at him.

"Simon, I'm sorry, you tried to tell me, tried to warn me, but I didn't listen, I have been deceived by the witches spell and now I've fallen so far beyond her powers that I can't break free. Save me Simon from what I may become, I can feel my spirit slipping away from me. Guide me back to safety, out from the darkness, for the witches shadow continues to haunt me". Suddenly a voice shouts down to him that snaps him out from his trance. Robert looks upwards and realizes that the sound had come from the rooftop of the palace.

Dazed, the human looks up and barely identifies the figure of a royal guard. The humanoid guard manages to get some help and throws a rope down for Robert to hang onto. Several more humanoid guards pull back on the rope and eventually manage to drag the freezing human over the ledge and onto the surface of the roof. Robert lands hard to the ground and falls unconscious.

The humanoid guards carry Robert to the queen for her to decide on what they should do with him. As they enter the royal throne room, Queen Juliana looks shocked and distraught by the state that Robert is in. Realizing that he is barely alive she quickly instructs her handmaidens' to get some blankets. Queen Juliana attempts to ask Robert what has caused him to be in such a state but she receives an incomprehensible response.

With Juliana concerned of Robert's health, one of her servants appears with several blankets, the queen recognizes her handmaiden and asks, "Could you attend to him? I fear he is showing the same symptoms that my mother did before she became ill". The handmaiden turns around but in that moment Robert opens his eyes and looks on in horror, as he now knows whom the witch is disguised as. In his attempt to move away the guards immediately have him restrained. He tries to speak out to everyone but he is still under the influence of Peirlee's spell and cannot speak properly. Annoyed that he is not being taken seriously he decides to yell instead.

Gwelyn smiles at him knowing full well that his resistance will not be enough to save him. The queen looks on in concern as the guards carry Robert out from the throne room and take him away towards Gwelyn's chambers.

Once the handmaiden dismisses the guards, the doors to her chambers close and Robert finds himself back where he started as it appears that his fate has been decided. Lying on the bed he is powerless to do anything. The Welshman looks up to the ceiling where flickers of candlelight indicates that a shadow approaches. Gwelyn's face appears before him, she remains in the beautiful form of the handmaiden but reverts to her natural voice of the witch, "You have got in the way of my plans for the last time!" Robert shuts his eyes and grimaces as he recognizes the voice from his nightmares, when he opens them he sees the witch has taken her true identity and that she grasps hold of her staff. Peirlee raises her weapon high above her head ready to bring it crashing down onto his exposed chest to kill him. Robert suddenly asks her, "Why?" She halts and sees no harm in telling the human, since he is about to die and tells him, "Why you, is that what you are asking?"

The human nods his head as she continues, "Fool, you did not see, but then you do not know". She says in her cackled voice. Robert uses all of his remaining energy to ask her to explain what she means. The witch elaborates, "I saw it and so too did Roshtu, he feels threatened by what you may become". Peirlee smiles knowing that she has not provided Robert with all of the answers to her riddle and decides it is now time to carry out the execution. As she raises her staff aloft, Robert closes his eyes and awaits the inevitable moment of doom when suddenly the doors of the chamber shatters to smithereens.

Surprised by what is happening Peirlee looks across the room at the small figure that has charged through. The distraction causes the witch's spell over Robert to be broken and the human awakens but then becomes aware of Bobby rushing to attack the enemy.

The battling blonde teenager swings his powerful club to block the first couple of shots of energized light that Peirlee fires in his direction from her staff. Bobby realizes to his peril that he is unable to progress any further with his attack and wishes he had not been so rash with his decision to confront the witch by himself. He then looks to Robert for assistance but sees the Welshman trying to shake away the weariness of Peirlee's spell.

Fortunately aid arrives from the royal guards who have heard the commotion from the hallway. Upon seeing the sorceress they quickly ignite their shields and begin firing laser shots from their spears, but the witch's staff is too powerful to allow her to be hit by their shots. Suddenly one of the guards is knocked down from a mighty bolt of power that Peirlee has fired, causing everyone in the room to look at the fallen humanoid.

Seizing her opportunity, Peirlee uses her staff to knock Bobby over the head that sends the unsuspecting human to fall unconscious to the floor. She then fires a bolt of energy towards the window and thus shattering the glass as a means for her escape. Peirlee then picks Bobby who is motionless, up from the floor and makes for the broken window. Upon seeing this Robert manages to get to his feet, finally restored to his former self but then becomes aware that he is completely defenseless.

Simon and the other humans then burst into the room. The legionnaire lunges across the room and uses his shield to protect both the group and Robert. He reaches his friend just in time as the witch sends a bolt of energy that would have been fatal had Simon's shield not deflected it.

Placing the crystal ball inside her black cloak, Peirlee warns the humans that this battle is far from over and falls out of the palace window, whilst holding onto Bobby along with her staff. Robert sprints to the opening within the wall and is quickly joined by his companions. They are horrified that the witch would kill Bobby but they watch Peirlee sitting on her staff through the clouds whilst grabbing hold of the motionless teenager, where she flies them away from Valadreil and into the night. Robert screams out Bobby's name in distress and outrage, knowing that he is at fault for their friend's sacrifice, as they helplessly watch the captured human disappear into the western sky.

Robert is later consoled by his companions but still blames himself for Bobby having been taken prisoner by the witch. The Welshman realizes that not everyone has returned and is told by his cousin that upon the discovery of The Blue Book of Wisdom a gateway appeared, which had sent Yoshi, Derek and Naomi back to the amusement part on Earth. Robert is surprised this has happened and is upset that part of their team has been diminished. Without their friends powers it seems impossible that they can confront both the witch and the dark knight but through all of his disappointment Robert is somewhat relieved to hear that they have managed to retrieve one of the lost books leaving just one more to find.

Queen Juliana accompanies the remaining humans within the palace watchtower. She cannot believe that she has been so blind to the witch's deception. The humanoid leader is very relieved that Robert has managed to survive the ordeal and asks if he remembers anything whist he was under Peirlee's spell.

Robert barely recalls anything that has happened over the past month.

Claire then gives The Blue Book of Wisdom over to the queen for safe keeping with The Green Book of Spells. Queen Juliana promises to keep the books hidden until the humans require them again and that she will aid their attempt in rescuing Bobby. Claire tells her that the battle with the witch is for them to deal with alone. Bobby's sister remains distraught for fear that her younger brother could be subjected to pain and torture.

Robert quietly speaks to Queen Juliana, recommending that she should now prepare her forces to march north and attack the apes. Since the threat of a spy no longer remains on Valadreil her battle strategies will not be given away. The queen nods her head in approval of Robert's suggestion.

As the morning sun begins to rise, from the top of the watchtower each of the humans' turn to the western horizon, determined in rescuing their captured companion but know that in order to save Bobby they will have to face a difficult confrontation against the witch.

Robert's companions walk down the winding staircase to begin their preparation for the long journey ahead, leaving Queen Juliana and Robert alone to gaze across the horizon. They turn and then look at one another both unsure of what to say. They have both recently had to overcome terrible circumstances.

Robert has admired the way in which Juliana has become the humanoids' leader but in some way he feels responsible for the death of her parents and apologizes for his failure. The queen replies to him, "Your eyes are full of honesty, and sorrow. Do not blame yourself there was nothing you could have done, the witch is very powerful". Juliana can sense the pain that Robert keeps locked up inside and she takes hold of his hand. They both make eye contact and Juliana tells him that he is the one person who has battled against the witch's spell and managed to survive.

They continue to stare into each others eyes, drawing ever closer to one another when the sound of someone approaching from the staircase can be heard. Queen Juliana and Robert immediately step away from each other and then Commander Teltris appears. He glances at Robert and looks to the queen before bowing his head and declares, "Your highness, the dignitaries you have requested to see are ready for you". The queen replies, "Very well Commander, please lead the way".

With the commander's back turned, Juliana provides Robert with a fleeting glance of affection before she walks down the tower.

Soon after Juliana has departed, Robert regains his composure from what had almost taken place. He promises himself that he will do anything within his powers to rescue Bobby and bring salvation to the humanoids. Robert then clenches his fist and taps the wall of the watchtower with his knuckle to indicate his determination to succeed and then walks down the spiral staircase to join his companions.

Book Three
The Battle of Sephire
(The Black Book of Barmothenue)

A female humanoid dressed in the white robed uniform of the governing council, walks hastily away from the council temple in floods of tears. The upset woman runs along a corridor but stumbles into a chair and falls to her knees sobbing tears of pain and frustration. Her handmaiden has seen what has happened and quickly dashes over to help her mistress. Concerned she asks, "Peirlee, are you okay?"

The middle-aged humanoid looks up and recognizes the long flowing blonde hair of her loyal handmaiden.

Peirlee calms herself before replying, "Carmen, I have been relieved from my duties". Carmen is surprised that Governor Terris would be so bold but realizes he would not have done so without good reason.

The handmaiden whilst helping her mistress to sit onto the chair asks, "My lady what has happened?"

Peirlee does not register the question as she contemplates the decision she has just made. Her eyes reflect anger and she warns Carmen, "I will show those fools not to take my opinions seriously. I am going to find the dark knight and show everyone that I am not afraid of him".

Carmen is shocked to hear this and reasons for her not to disobey Governor Terris. Peirlee stands up from the chair and replies to her handmaiden, "I have been wrongfully denied of my powers to lead.

Without power, I have no reason to live". Peirlee then hurries along the corridor and walks towards the stables.

Carmen is in a dilemma of knowing what to do. A part of her knows that she should go to the governing council temple and warn the other governors but her heart tells her something else. Carmen turns around and chases after her mistress hoping to save Peirlee before it is too late.

Having reached the stables, Carmen sees no sign of her mistress and frantically asks the humanoids nearby, "Have any of you seen Peirlee? Do you know where she has gone too?" Most of the stable boys shake their heads but one of them comments, "I saw her leave on a horse just a short while ago, she left heading that way". The young boy points towards the distant tall gates to the exit of Valadreil.

Carmen immediately jumps onto an already saddled horse. The handmaiden ignores the stable boys' objections in taking a horse, which belongs to Governor Terris and rides the stallion along the cobbled streets of Valadreil whilst passing startled humanoids on her way. She leaves the vast town behind her and charges towards the forest where she chooses to ride in between the trees in hope that it will provide her with a shortcut to the north.

Without stopping to rest, Carmen eventually reaches the borders of the forest and soon comes across a dusty pathway. Looking down at the surface, Carmen discovers the marking of a horse's hoof that appears to have been placed recently. The handmaiden assumes her mistress must only be a short distance away and urges her horse to continue along the path when suddenly a loud boom is heard from nearby and the ground begins to shake violently.

Carmen's horse is spooked by the noise and the creature stands upright on its hind legs, which causes the rider to fall from her saddle. The startled handmaiden lands hard onto the floor alongside a sword, which has come out from its sheath. The horse bolts back along the path leaving Carmen abandoned where she holds onto the sword and picks herself up from the grass. With the ground still vibrating the humanoid makes her way towards the sound of the explosion.

The young curious woman wonders what has happened but then Carmen sees a circle of fire. Before she can look into the circle she notices two figures standing within a clearing in between the trees. Carmen recognizes that one of the figures is her mistress but relief to find her soon turns to horror when she realizes that the other tall person is the terrifying dark knight.

Without being able to think clearly, Carmen runs towards them and screams, "Peirlee get away from him!"

Her warning echoes throughout the forest but her mistress placidly looks around at her. Stopping only meters away, Carmen drops her sword by the sheer presence of evil surrounding Roshtu and takes a step backwards.

With the dark knight choosing not to attack her Carmen asks Peirlee, "What are you doing? Have you lost your mind?" The older humanoid walks up to Carmen and responds quietly, "The time of the humanoids will soon be over. Our race will fall to the power of the dark knight's ape army that is preparing to enter Sephire through a portal built by the ancient priests of Barmothenue". Carmen stares back in bewilderment, silently praying that this is not happening. A chill runs down her spine when she glimpses the terrifying image from inside the gateway and sees a planet of fire. Her expression shows fear of what the humanoids will soon be up against.

Carmen comes to her senses and warns Peirlee, "We must act now in order to save our people".

Peirlee fails to listen and gives one final command to her handmaiden. "Return to Valadreil and pass on what I have said to the governing council. They must prepare for the surrender of our planet". Carmen shakes her head refusing to accept the order and demands to know what Peirlee intends to do. The middle-aged humanoid responds, "I have formed an alliance with Roshtu, he has granted our people their existence in exchange for my loyalty, I do this only to save our race". Carmen stares back in disbelief.

The dark knight walks towards the gateway and tells Peirlee that it is time to go. Carmen screams out, "I will not let it end this way!" The determined handmaiden picks up her sword from the ground before charging towards the evil knight in an attempt to kill him. However, before she can raise her weapon to strike the enemy, Peirlee releases a surge of energy from a staff, which she had previously concealed underneath her robes.

The blast directly hits Carmen and she falls to the ground. Lying on the grass and powerless to do anything she stares up in shock of what her mistress has just done. Carmen's breathing begins to fade and the humanoid defector kneels close beside where she whispers, "I could not have you kill the dark knight you would spoil my plans". Peirlee winks at her dying handmaiden before walking away to join her new ally.

Carmen witnesses the disloyal humanoid rejoining the evil knight where they both fade into his dark and terrifying domain. The circle of light suddenly diminishes, leaving Carmen alone within the trees. She notices her flesh is changing colour and shines glittering green. Believing that her afterlife is rapidly approaching, Carmen closes her eyes and awaits her fate.

Chapter One

The frail figure of Peirlee walks down the dark spiral staircase of the tower to her dwelling and moves past candles that have been left to flicker. An echoing sound comes from the impact of her staff as it touches the concrete slabs. The tribe army apes previously stationed here for protection have long since departed and returned to the northern rocklands of terror to prepare against the humanoids final assault. Peirlee knows that her opportunity of leadership will be gone should the humanoids be victorious. She will do anything to prevent the humanoids from reclaiming their planet without her help.

Reaching the last step of the staircase, Peirlee pushes a wooden door that opens with a creaking sound.

Walking along a dark narrow tunnel that has a dry stale smell, the old sorceress slowly approaches the human that she holds captive. The young teenager is held within a force field restrained by crackling bolts of blue energy. Bobby can only watch helplessly as the witch strides towards him.

The young human teenager quickly attempts to close his eyes in hope that the witch will assume him to be sleeping and will leave him alone but Peirlee reaches down to a cloth, which is placed inside a bucket of cold water and smothers the damp cloth over the boy's face. Bobby gasps from the cold sensation and opens his eyes. The witch cackles, "You're no good to me dead". She then places the damp garment back to the floor and raises a flask containing water up to Bobby's mouth. At first he refuses to drink from the flask but common sense prevails and the teenager accepts a few drops of water.

Bobby is frightened of the witch's appearance and power but realizes that should she want him dead she would have done so by now. Bobby pushes his head backwards trying to get away from her and yells, "Leave me alone!" Peirlee looks back at him and remarks, "So you've finally decided to start talking, good".

The young human attempts to question the witch to determine a motive to her madness and asks, "Why have you betrayed your people?" Peirlee narrows her eyes and responds bitterly, "Who have you been speaking to?" Bobby fails to answer and attempts to outstare her but soon forces himself to look away from the terrifying eyes.

Peirlee warns the human, "You should have taken the opportunity to return to your home planet when you had the chance. Now you will suffer the same fate as the humanoids". Bobby silently wonders if the witch is right. Maybe he should have gone through the gateway that appeared at the Tomb of Zemlin but had he done so then Robert would have been killed.

Peirlee has had enough of being polite and tells him, "I will leave you be, if you provide me with information". Bobby is intrigued and asks, "Information, what sort of information?" Peirlee takes a step backwards in irritation and mutters under her breath, "Questions, questions, don't you ever stop asking questions? I almost wish I had taken one of the other humans instead of having to cope with your obsessive complaints". In a quiet but threatening voice Peirlee demands to know the location of the two magic books that his companions have retrieved.

Bobby replies truthfully, "I don't know where they are, they're just boring old books covered in a lot of dust". Bobby soon becomes scared and shakes with fear by the sight of Peirlee's furious expression.

The witch bellows, "Those books have more importance than you think. I must have them". Bobby immediately tells her, "Robert is the one who is looking after them". He then realizes that he has been too forthcoming. Peirlee knows the teenager had been trying to keep this news secret from her and is satisfied that she has extracted all useful information from the teenager. Bobby attempts to scare the witch by threatening her, "My companions will soon come to rescue me".

Peirlee grabs hold of her staff and looks back at him, replying in a chilling voice, "I am counting on it". She then begins to walk away. With the fading echoing sound of Peirlee's staff touching the floor Bobby is left alone once more to fear his surroundings and of what the witch has in store for his friends.

In the humanoids' capital, word has spread throughout the town of the important meeting called by Queen Juliana to determine a course of action against the threat that has invaded their planet. Within the darkness of evening, many humanoids gather along the streets of Valadreil and anxiously await news of the final outcome. Despite the humanoids feeling relief in having the alliance of the remaining humans, they do not yet know how the prophecy to the Saviours of Sephire will be realized.

Inside the royal palace, Queen Juliana sits on the throne once occupied by her father. She is within the company of her dignitaries whose opinion has often been called upon, along with Commander Teltris and seven of his captains. The flickers of candlelight within the grand hall reflect solemn expressions on each of their faces. The meeting has lasted for some time and so far they have not reached an agreeable conclusion.

Queen Juliana informs the audience of what Simon had seen through the retrieved Book of Wisdom.

Alerting them of Roshtu's portal, which increases the threat that should it become activated it would allow further apes to enter Sephire and place any chance for freedom to be beyond reach. Some of the captains are skeptical of Simon's story and of the power to the long lost book.

One of the dignitaries suggests the humanoids should leave to attack the Northern Rocklands of Terror straight away, "Every hour we delay only provides our enemy with further time to prepare for battle".

Another dignitary immediately voices his objections to the suggestion, "What of our preparations? Once our royal

160

guards have left Valadreil, who will protect those that cannot travel with us into battle and must remain behind such as the women and children?"

Commander Teltris looks up. His battle-scarred face clearly shows his frustration with the constant bickering of this debate. He begins to speak and instantly silences the room by his presence and with his powerful yet calming voice, "We have members of our royal guard who are currently working on instructions provided by our former king". The commander pauses to glance at the queen, hoping she is not upset to hear of him talk about her dead father. The chief officer continues speaking, "When King Ridley was freed from the witch's spell he issued me with two instructions. One was to strengthen the defenses to Valadreil in case of an attack. The other command was to send a detachment of guards to go into the forest and commence building a village within the safety of the trees, should the need arise if the capital could not be defended".

Quiet whispers begin to mutter within the hall as Commander Teltris announces, "I have received word before this meeting that the construction of the encampment is almost complete. With extra help we will be able to protect the women and children".

Queen Juliana senses that time is not on their side and gives her approval of the commanders suggestion whilst silently thanking her father for his intuitive decision. The royal leader addresses her audience, "Very well, once our people are ready, everyone will leave Valadreil. As soon as the encampment has been completed we ride north for battle".

The queen allows those around her to digest the realization of her decision before asking the dignitaries to inform the townsfolk to evacuate Valadreil but stresses that the travelling humanoids need only bring essential items with them. Commander Teltris speculates they should be ready to begin the journey within three days, which will give them enough time to gather supplies of food, water, armour, carriages and horses.

Queen Juliana concludes the meeting has now finished and allows everyone to be dismissed. The gathered audience obediently bows to their leader before walking out through the open doors of the throne room.

As the high-ranking humanoids begin to carry out their specific duties, Commander Teltris asks Queen Juliana, "What of the humans? How will they figure with our plans for battle?" The queen delays her response knowing the commander will struggle to accept her decision and she informs him, "I have allowed the humans to leave for the western lands of Sephire where they will attempt to rescue their companion held captive by Peirlee". The commander politely reminds Juliana they must have the humans' help in battle if they are to break through the ape blockade.

Juliana reasons for him to appreciate what the humans must be going through in not knowing if their friend remains alive. Commander Teltris nods his head in acceptance and replies, "The humans' have already proved their loyalty. I only hope the witch will not be too formidable for them". The commander then briefly moves away to discuss some orders with one of his captains.

Queen Juliana stands alone in the corridor and takes a moment to reflect of the many thoughts that are currently going through her mind. The burden of power now rests heavily on her shoulders and she sighs from the weight of her responsibility and the uncertainty of what will happen in the future. Juliana looks beyond the commander and notices the Saviours of Sephire are approaching from the corridor. Seeing the Welshman who leads them, provides her with hope of safety.

From the opposite end of the corridor, Simon walks at the back of the group and attempts to force a sleeping rug to fit inside his tightly secured holdall. Hideki notices that Simon is not walking in a straight line and grabs hold of his arm to steady him. Just in front of them Rachel tries to speak with

Claire but notices she is lost in her thoughts. When the wizard touches Claire's arm to get her attention she accidentally startles her. The tall slender brunette woman apologizes, "I'm sorry I was busy thinking about Bobby and how much I miss him". Seeing how she feels upset by the thought of not knowing if her brother is still alive, Rachel decides to place an arm in sympathy around her shoulder.

Rachel's older cousin reassures Claire, "Bobby is still alive the witch does not want him. She is using him as bait to get to me. Your brother is very tough and I am sure he is giving the sorceress a rough time".

Claire manages to raise a smile, as she knows that Bobby will not be a quiet prisoner. She thanks Robert for his words of encouragement. Simon looks to Robert and is pleased to see that his close friend has recovered from the witch's dreadful spell and continues to lead them through this terrible time.

Robert turns around and notices that from further along the corridor Juliana is looking at him. After what had happened earlier when they had almost shared a kiss the Welshman remembers the tender moment and begins to blush. He leads his companions towards the royal leader whilst barely managing to keep his composure and they each bow their heads to the humanoid majesty.

Queen Juliana smiles briefly and asks them to raise their heads. Her smile soon fades away and she announces to her friends in a soft yet saddened tone, "The fate of my people shall be decided in battle. By our estimations we outnumber the tribe army apes and with Roshtu gone, we must use this opportunity to destroy the portal in the north of our planet. Valadreil will empty and those who cannot fight will be led to safety where we have built an encampment within the trees of the forest".

The five humans are pleased that the queen is not afraid to take on her father's quest to go on the offensive and battle the enemy.

Commander Teltris now joins the small group and acknowledges the humans before informing the queen, "Your message has been passed onto the townsfolk to prepare to leave Valadreil". Juliana silently hopes that the humanoids will continue to stand by her decisions.

Robert is concerned that his team cannot be in two places at the same time, firstly to rescue Bobby and secondly to help the humanoids in battle. He asks, "How long do we have to rejoin your forces before you leave for the Northern Rocklands of Terror?" Commander Teltris replies, "The longest our forces can wait would be in nine days time".

The Saviours of Sephire realize that time is already running out and hastily pick up both their weapons and holdalls before bidding farewell to the queen. Robert declares to Queen Juliana, "You can rely on us to return and fight alongside you in battle, I give you my word". Robert's face reflects the determination he has to keep the solemn oath. Juliana wishes that she can confide her feelings for him but decides that now is not the time. Instead she tells her friends, "We shall position several scouts along the borders of the woodlands who upon your arrival, will provide you safe passage to our camp".

Commander Teltris offers to escort the humans to the western pathway. As they walk away, Robert has a last fleeting look at Juliana, before catching up with his companions where they walk out onto the courtyard.

Juliana watches the humans leave until they are out of sight. Already she feels saddened without them being here but chooses to remain hopeful to see them once again. Her waiting handmaidens then accompany her towards the palace chambers to carry out their own preparations for the journey ahead.

Chapter Two

With the morning sun beginning to break through the clouds, Hideki proceeds to take off the dark cloak of his uniform. Rachel is surprised to see this, as the Japanese warrior is rarely seen without it on and asks Hideki if he is okay. Hideki gestures to the weather and replies, "Even at this hour of the day, there should be a coolness within the air but today there is not, it will be very warm today, I wish not to sweat". Robert is not happy to hear this as he knows the warm weather will only slow their progress.

The humans walk closely behind Commander Teltris, through the streets of Valadreil. Simon notices the humanoid townsfolk are giving them suspicious glances almost as if they have realized the humans' intent to leave. Whispers and muttering can be heard and Claire senses the anxiety building within the people around them. Many humanoids have begun to follow the humans to find out what is happening.

Upon reaching the tall gates of Valadreil the Saviours of Sephire look to one another, hoping they encounter no resistance from the guards and that the people of Valadreil will understand the reasons for their departure. Commander Teltris orders his guards to allow the humans to pass through the open gates. The guards raise no objections but appear dumbfounded to see them leaving. One of the humanoids asks Robert where are they going, but the guard receives no reply.

Stepping out from Valadreil the commander points to where the western pathway can be found and then wishes Robert and his four companions good luck on their mission.

Commander Teltris watches the humans reach the pathway that leads to the western plains. He is joined by a crowd of humanoids' wishing to know why they are leaving. One of the captains' asks his commander, "Should we not follow the humans?" His superior replies, "We cannot follow them, their route into battle may take a different course from

165

ours but they will be there in battle nonetheless. We have much to accomplish before we can leave the town, I suggest you all return to your duties".

The humanoids are relieved to hear that the Saviours of Sephire are not abandoning them and go back to complete their preparations to leave Valadreil.

Within the tall grass fields outside the humanoid capital, the head of a concealed tribe army ape lowers back down behind cover. Alongside the ape are other members of the small strike team assigned to observe the humanoids' movements to ascertain when they will be ready to march for battle. The second in command crouches next to the strike-team leader and asks, "What is it? What have you seen?" The ape leader quickly replies, "There's movement, the humans are leaving, but not for the north". He then pauses to think if they should follow but the irritating sound of someone eating noisily distracts him. The ape does not need to turn around to establish who it is and whispers. "Finch, don't you ever stop eating?"

The feline creature enlisted by the dark knight, momentarily stops nibbling on the bone that he clutches and retorts, "Don't you ever stop smelling?" The ape leader grimaces through annoyance and he attempts to control his temper. He would like to grab the insubordinate creature and teach him to learn some respect but knows their cover would be blown. Instead he tells his second in command, "We can't wait here forever and must assume that the humanoids are preparing for war". He then turns around and informs the rest of the strike-team that they are going to return to the north. The other apes are pleased to hear that they will be returning to their preferred climate of driving rain and ferocious wind but before any of them can move the commanding ape suddenly grabs hold of Finch's arm.

The tracker is caught unawares and drops his bone onto the grass. The ape whispers in his ear, "You will not be joining us, follow the humans". At which point Finch is given a paw full of coins. The feline's eyes widen in delight and he accepts his mission. As the small group of concealed apes crawls cautiously back through the tall grass, Finch moves in the opposite direction towards the path that the humans have taken.

With the red glow of the sunset being cast over the valleys to the eastern lands of sephire. Dark shadows begin to form. Shadows from trees and from the hills. Suddenly a new shadow appears. Slowly the image begins to materialize, it is not a shadow but a rider dressed in dark robes who sits upon a black menacing horse.

The rider brings the horse to a halt and looks across the surrounding landscape, searching for signs of prey. Immediately the creatures within the fields begin to flee for places to hide. The hood of the rider turns to where in the great distance, lightening can be seen but being so far away the sound of thunder cannot be heard. The dark figure then rides its horse towards the distant storm.

Meanwhile in the western lands, Hideki and Rachel are returning to their companions with pieces of wood to be used for a campfire. The humans are resting against some rocks on the side of a slope, which overlooks a large open field. Robert helps his cousin and Hideki to start the fire by rubbing some sticks together whilst Simon is in the midst of whispering to Claire of the images he had seen through the Blue Book of Wisdom. "The sight of the Northern Rocklands of Terror made my blood run cold. There must have been an army of apes too many to even count but they appeared to be preparing against an attack.

There was something else the book was trying to tell me but I do not know what it was".

Claire concentrates and closes her eyes to gain some understanding from the headband that provides her with the power of intuition. After a brief moment she begins to tremble by the growing realization and speaks out, "Roshtu". Upon hearing the name, Robert drops a piece of wood from his grasp and his other companions become unsettled. Claire opens her eyes. She appears calm, as she has now developed the strength to handle the pressures of her special powers and informs Simon, "You saw the dark knights return". The group begins to feel despondent, as they had hoped Roshtu would not be able to find a way of coming back to Sephire. The humans silently recollect the battles they have already encountered against the dark knight and how on each occasion they have barely managed to survive.

Unawares to Robert and his companions, a figure crouches nearby and listens to what they are saying in hope of gathering valuable information. Finch notices the shiny piece of jewelry that one of the humans wears on their head and he mutters quietly, "Sparkly, shiny, it must be expensive. I have to get it".

However in Finch's eagerness to get a closer look at his bounty, he does not notice a stone, which is close to the edge of a rock. The paw from the feline accidentally brushes the stone where it falls down and lands on the ground. The noise immediately stops Claire speaking in mid sentence. Her colleagues are wary against an attack and instantly grasp onto their weapons.

After a few minutes has elapsed there appears to be no indication of anyone approaching and the humans eventually decide that the threat no longer remains.

Having placed their weapons down they settle once again and Robert attempts to reassure his friends.

"Everything Simon has seen is only the possibility of what might happen in the future. Nothing is for certain, the end has not yet been written. We still have a chance of success".

Once Robert stops talking, Hideki manages to get the campfire started, which makes Rachel jump. The humans then decide to rest their weary heads down onto their sleeping rugs. Closing their eyes they each reflect of what Robert has spoken and try to dream of a happy ending. Whereas Finch continues to hide from a safe distance and remains to be unnoticed.

Chapter Three

Queen Juliana is alone in her chambers and has just finished dressing into her military garments. She looks towards the partially drawn curtains and sees through the windows that it remains dark outside.

Juliana realizes she need not be awake at this hour but the troubles on her mind prevent her from sleeping. She is aware that the coming of the new day will mark the time her people will leave the capital of Sephire and begin their journey into the forest.

Juliana cannot help but wonder if the humans remain safe, for the witch is a formidable opponent and will not allow Bobby to be rescued easily. Juliana feels guilty to have not been able to send some of her guards to help the humans with their quest. Although deep down inside, Juliana has an incline that the powerful Welshman who leads the humans' will return to fight by her side in battle.

Before sitting back onto the comfortable bed, Juliana stands in front of a mirror and looks at her reflection in the glass. The queen notices her facial appearance seems tired. Trying to recollect the last time she has slept peacefully, Juliana remembers it was when her parents were still alive. Staring blankly at the mirror Juliana considers the importance of her responsibilities to lead the humanoids and decides to get some rest.

As she sits down the thoughts swirling around her mind force her to ponder the inevitable battle that will decide who will rule this planet Sephire. Juliana is certain that even in victory her people will suffer many casualties. No matter how many times she attempts to think for a safer alternative, Juliana reaches the same conclusion of the importance in destroying Roshtu's portal to prevent him from strengthening his ape army.

Suddenly Queen Juliana is alerted to a knock at the chamber door. She opens her eyes and wearily sits up from the bed. Immediately noticing that daylight shines into the room, Juliana realizes she must have dropped off to sleep. The door opens and in steps one of the queen's handmaidens.

Juliana instantly recognizes it is her loyal servant called Ishma, they bid good morning to one another and Ishma brings in the queen's morning meal. The loyal servant informs her majesty, "My lady, the people are almost ready to leave the capital". The queen acknowledges her handmaiden, "Thank you Ishma, please could you let Commander Teltris know that I shall soon be ready". The handmaiden bows her head and departs from the chambers whilst closing the door behind her.

A short while later, Queen Juliana makes her way outside the palace and onto the courtyard where she meets with Commander Teltris who is joined by a large number of riders. The queen is assisted to mount onto her horse, which bears the flag of Sephire. The humanoid leader looks around at the solemn faces before her, whilst observing the banners, shields and the spears that the royal guard forces carry. Juliana wants her people to ride out of Valadreil with a steady heart and she attempts to lift their morale. The roal leader asks everyone to become silent and addresses those around her.

"People of Sephire, we leave this great town that we call our home. We leave not through defeat but with a desire to keep it ours and to restore freedom to all of the humanoids throughout Sephire. One day our people will return and unite as one to live without fear or danger, in a time of peace".

The queen completes her lifting speech and Commander Teltris gives the order for the commencement of the evacuation to Valadreil. A loud booming sound of horns are blown, which can be heard throughout the streets of the capital and immediately the guards open the large wooden gates to allow the humanoids to leave.

Queen Juliana leads the march, steadying her horse as she observes the crowds of people who watch her ride past before they join the traveling convoy. Juliana is relieved the people remain to stand by her decisions. She then looks across to the commander who rides alongside her and notices a look of determination on his face, almost as if he senses that the time for battle is not far away.

Leaving the vast capital trailing in the background, Juliana denies herself the opportunity to have one last look back at the tall glistening towers. She refuses to believe this will be the last time that she will see Valadreil. The commander and several of his captains' ride in front of the queen to be certain the pathway ahead leading towards the woodlands is clear from any danger. Whilst at the back of the convoy the transportation of weapons and food supplies are heavily protected by royal guard riders.

Within the dark and rainy environment of the Northern Rocklands of Terror, heavy catapults and other weapons of destruction are being strategically positioned. Legions of apes' pull on thick cords of rope to drag the heavy artillery across the muddy and rocky terrain. A commanding ape that stands at the top of a mountain grasps onto a torched flame, which flickers in the wild winds. From the view of the mountainside he witnesses thirty to forty legions of the army completing the final preparations for battle. Suddenly the ape notices another torch that has become lit from a lookout post, which is positioned close to the northern borders, indicating of something approaching. The muscular creature instantly turns around and strikes an enormous drum. The loud sound provides the tribe army apes with the signal of a possible attack and the apes stand poised for war.

Inside the fortress of the Northern Rocklands of Terror, the threatening ape brothers in charge of the army are busy examining the holographic images to their tactical plan of attack against the humanoids.

Gormosh and Riesk are both aware that without the portal being activated they have only the advantage of knowing the northern lands.

Suddenly an ape servant enters the control room, Riesk demands an explanation from the servant and is clearly annoyed to be interrupted. The small ape replies, "The lookouts have sited an unknown cloaked rider that is heading this way". Gormosh and Riesk silently look to one another and then hear the warning sound coming from outside. With his duty completed the ape servant steps away from the control room and closes the doors behind him, leaving Gormosh and his brother wondering of the identity to the person approaching.

Chapter Four

Robert is seen to be waiting for his companions to catch up with him. They have been travelling across large sweeping fields these past few days as the search to find Peirlee's dwelling continues. The tall brown haired man hopes that their captured companion has found the strength to survive. The Welshman notices that his colleagues are not far behind as they walk wearily down a slope. Suddenly a raven distracts Robert's gaze as it hovers overhead before gliding effortlessly away. He remains to stare at the raven, seeing the creature use its tail and wings as it soars over a tall hill. Robert then gasps when he sees the route, which the raven has taken and his heart begins to pound by the sight at the top of the hill of the witch's abode. Even from this distance it looks a terrifying place. The Welshman places an arrow to his bow and urges his friends to hurry.

The raven that Robert had seen, flies past the watchtower of the witch's dwelling and lands gracefully on the balcony that overlooks the fields below. A hunched figure walks towards the bird and places down some dead mice for the raven to take as its reward. The creature carefully picks up the food with its claws and flies away to feed its young. Peirlee the witch had seen from her crystal ball, the image of the humans' through the raven's eyes. She gives a cackle and takes hold of her magic staff before leaving the watchtower and walks down the spiral staircase.

Hideki and Robert both offer their assistance to the two female members of their team to reach the top of the steep hill. Before Robert turns around he remembers that Simon will also require a helping hand.

Once they are all at the peak of the hill they crouch behind some trees for protection. Simon whispers, "I am surprised not to see an army of apes past those gates". Robert asks Hideki if his trained ninja senses suggest this to be a trap. Claire overhears and quietly interrupts, "Of course it's a trap but for some reason I'm not sensing any threat here".

Rachel asks her cousin, "Now what should we do?" He replies, "We can't wait here forever, I suggest we enter the courtyard and try to find a way into the tower but should remain close to one another". With one last look in awe of the tall tower that stands before them, the humans raise their weapons and move cautiously out from behind their cover.

An eerie silence greets their arrival. Relief not to find any apes slowly turns to anguish when they each consider if anyone else is here. Simon speculates, "This place appears to be deserted". Claire is concerned that they will not be able to find her younger brother in time. She attempts to use her powers of intuition to sense a feeling of Bobby but something is blocking out her concentration.

Simon deactivates his energy shield and comments, "It would appear the witch and the apes must have left for the north". Hideki is bewildered, "Then it has all been in vain, we have traveled this distance and accomplished nothing". Feeling despondent the humans' lower their weapons and look around the courtyard in search of finding a way inside the building. Rachel's gaze turns upward where she had thought she had seen something floating down from the sky. Her eyes suddenly widen in horror when she sees an object hurtling towards them.

"Get back!" She cries out to her companions. Before Simon can reactivate his force field to protect them, Robert falls over, as a large object crashes to the surface with a loud bang, which just misses hitting him.

The Welshman whilst still lying on the floor, notices that attached to a flag thrown down from above is a large heavy chest that would have killed him had it made contact.

As he is helped back to his feet, Robert looks angrily from where he assumes the object had been thrown and catches sight of someone retreating into the watchtower and hears the person cackling. The humans realize they had been purposely led to feel a false sense of security. Robert seethes, "Peirlee!"

Without attempting to find out if the nearest door is locked, Robert releases an arrow from his bow, which knocks the entrance off from its hinges. Simon begs Robert not to go charging off in a rage. The Welshman turns around, his eyes sparkle with fury and he replies, "The witch has much to answer for".

He then proceeds to lead the group through the doorway and into darkness.

Once inside, the flamed arrow from which Robert has drawn to his bow along with the shining light from Claire's headband allows the humans to find themselves inside a large corridor. The darkness beyond does not indicate what else is around them. Robert advises his friends to stay close and they move cautiously forwards with their weapons ready for use as they expect an imminent attack from the witch.

After a short while the humans' realize they are moving along an endless corridor. Hideki suggests they should turn back and attempt to find a route that may lead elsewhere. However before any of them can move Rachel notices a fog is quickly developing around them. Simon asks nervously, "Is that a fire from somewhere?" Robert assumes it is another trick used by Peirlee to separate them.

Walking blindly, the Saviours of Sephire stumble into one another and against various items of furniture.

With the air beginning to smell foul they each place a hand over their noses. Robert is able to see Simon and Hideki standing alongside him but he cannot see where the two women have gone too. Coughing from the fumes of the mist he attempts to call out to them but is alarmed not to receive a response.

Suddenly the Welshman catches sight of the light shining from Claire's headband and is barely able to see the outline of her body through the thick mist but within an instant both women scream out in terror as a floor panel slides back from underneath their feet. Robert hurries across to help them but is too late.

He desperately calls out their names but is unable to see where they have gone. Simon then stumbles against a door and discovers that it is unlocked. Hideki pulls Robert to the doorway and the Welshman reluctantly leaves the fog filled corridor, hoping this route will reunite them with Claire and Rachel.

Tumbling down what appears to be an endless slide, Claire fears the inevitable impact and can hear Rachel's screams from close behind her. The darkness plays tricks with her mind, she does not know if her eyes are open or closed and the two women continue to plummet deeper underground.

Claire becomes aware that the decent is beginning to level out which slows their speed and both women find themselves sliding safely into a room that is filled with hay. With their pulses racing, the human women look to one another relieved to still be alive. As the wizard attempts to recover from their ordeal her friend suddenly senses the presence of her younger brother. Whatever it was, which had previously been blocking out her powers of intuition has now diminished. Claire yells enthusiastically, "Bobby is alive!"

Claire decides search for a way out from their confinement. She finds a door but becomes distraught to discover that it is locked from the other side. Fortunately Rachel's magic hat has remained on her head and she uses its power to allow her to walk through the solid door.

The brunette woman has to blink her eyes when she sees Rachel vanishing from sight but then the sound of a click from the other side of the door is heard and it is pulled open by her friend who now re-appears.

Claire hugs her colleague and the two women dash up a flight of stairs. Claire leads the way as she runs towards the trail leading them to her captured brother.

Elsewhere Robert informs the events of what he had seen to Simon and Hideki who are disturbed to hear of what has happened to their two companions. Robert notices some stairs that lead down and suggests they walk that way in hope of finding Claire and Rachel. Before any of them can move, they each hear the chilling sound of a loud cackle echoing from the bottom of the staircase. Assuming it is the witch, the three humans' are in pursuit where they go on to discover another doorway.

Without knowing what may be waiting for them on the other side of the door, Robert advises Simon to activate his energy shield in case they should find themselves under attack. Once Hideki pulls back the door, Simon grips onto his shield and cautiously leads his friends through the open door. The humans' find themselves inside a dark and narrow tunnel. Simon immediately hears the distant sound of running water. He glances back anxiously to Robert for instructions but his friend motions him to continue. Robert wonders if Claire and Rachel might be here and decides to call out both their names. His voice bounces against the walls of the tunnel and the sound echoes further ahead within the darkness. The three humans are suddenly surprised to hear distant calls for help coming from a distinctive male voice. Simon gasps, "It is Bobby!" and they hurry to rescue their friend.

The depth of the water now reaches as high as their ankles and they can still hear Bobby's pleas for help.

Robert tries to reassure him, "Don't worry Bobby we're on our way to save you". However unknown to the commanding human and his colleagues, a rope surges towards them from underwater. Simon instantly trips over the rope and plunges headfirst into the murky water along with his companions.

Stunned and surprised they struggle to retrieve their weapons. Suddenly the group finds themselves under attack from Peirlee as she haunches on a walkway above and shoots crackling fire bolts in their direction.

Barely managing to avoid being hit, Robert realizes that Peirlee has the upper hand and yells out for his team to quickly find shelter behind some of the pillars. The humans' attempt to return fire but the witch does not remain in the same location long enough for them to make any contact. Robert desperately wishes to rescue Bobby but knows that without any kind of distraction he would become an easy target.

With the stone from the pillars being demolished from Peirlee's continuous attack, Simon begins to feel the power from his energy shield fading away and he quickly alerts his companions. In an attempt for the energy shield to regain enough power to protect them, Robert fires a barrage of shots. However the witch is now only meters away from them and uses her staff to easily deflect the arrows.

Peirlee then releases a huge blast of energy directly towards Simon. The impact is so powerful that it totally diminishes all energy from the legionnaire's shield and it falls from his grasp. The humans have no other place where they can hide and Peirlee tells the humans, "Admit it, you have been defeated".

Hideki, Robert and Simon look to one another wondering if this is the end when all of a sudden the door from the end of the corridor opens. Claire and Rachel both enter the tunnel to come to their rescue.

Before the witch is able to react, Bobby's sister releases a laser shot that causes the witch's magic staff to fall from her hands. Peirlee cries out in horror as she realizes that she has no defense against an attack and dashes into the murky shadows. Peirlee quickly flicks a concealed switch within the wall, allowing a deluge of water to plummet into the tunnel.

Claire immediately senses her brother is in danger of drowning and gives up the incline to waste precious time in attacking the witch and hurries to rescue Bobby. The moment of indecision allows Peirlee to retrieve her powerful weapon where she successfully parries an arrow that had been fired from Robert's bow. The witch decides to leave the humans to suffocate by water and uses her staff to allow her to fly through the open doorway where she then locks it behind her.

With the water level continuing to rise, Claire, Simon and Rachel are relieved to reach Bobby who appears to be in good health. The teenager cries tears of joy to see his friends' again but relief soon turns to concern when they realize they do not have a key to unlock his chains. Simon uses his spear to fire four carefully placed shots allowing Bobby to be freed. Claire hugs her younger brother and the group quickly wades through the water that now reaches as high as Bobby's waist.

Upon reaching Robert and Hideki at the locked door, Rachel uses her magic hat to allow her to pass through the solid object of the door and opens it from the other side. With water spilling out into the corridor, the humans do not pause for breath and immediately run up the staircase of the watchtower to give pursuit of the witch.

Chapter Five

Peirlee walks past the last steps to the staircase and opens the door of the watchtower. Her breathing is heavy from the encounter with the humans and the betraying humanoid knows that she has been fortunate to have come away unscathed.

Upon entering the watchtower, the sorceress immediately notices her crystal ball is shinning. Curious to find out what it is trying to tell her she walks across to the round object and glimpses into the clear object.

The image she sees causes her eyes to widen in surprise. Peirlee recognizes the dark cloaked figure of Roshtu as he rides upon his horse. Thousands of apes stand to attention by the sight of their master as the dark knight's horse canters toward the drawbridge of Roshtu's fortress.

Peirlee cackles to herself, "So Roshtu has finally returned, soon it will be over and my time will come!"

The old sorceress then gasps in horror when she sees the image from within the globe changing to show the group of humans pursuing her from the staircase. The withering hag says in annoyance. "Aaah, those scoundrels won't give up. Never mind there will be another time to be rid of them once and for all. For now, I am needed elsewhere". The witch then gathers her crystal ball and takes hold of her magic staff before walking towards the balcony.

Robert and Hideki are the first to reach the top of the winding staircase and both of them charge into the room whilst closely followed by their companions. Upon entering the watchtower they witness the witch flying away on top of her staff where she fades into the distant horizon. Robert attempts to aim an arrow at their enemy but realizes it will not reach his intended target. The humans' lower their weapons and are each disappointed to have not won the battle against the witch as they realize the sorceress will be plotting further terror against them and the humanoids.

Robert turns around to look at Bobby and sees Claire hugging onto her younger brother but the teenager is more interested to receive the food that she had been carrying for him. Robert walks up to the teenager and thanks him for his earlier attempt to save him from when the witch had been disguised as Gwelyn.

Bobby accepts the gratitude but apologizes to everyone, "I know I was wrong to have thought I could defeat the witch on my own".

Bobby looks around the circular room of the watchtower and notices a sundial that captures the light, where along the perimeter of the wall are shelves that are stacked with books. Uninterested in learning of the books contents, Bobby continues to be inquisitive and jumps up and down enthusiastically when he finds his special powered club. He quickly dashes to retrieve the weapon and then carefully inspects it to be certain that it has not been tampered with.

The other humans decide to search for valuable information that Peirlee may have left behind. Rachel walks across to a desk where the young blonde haired woman reviews some paperwork. Upon closer inspection she observes several text references to the Black Book of Barmothenue and gathers her companions. The humans' are able to establish that the ancient humanoid priests who once lived in the castle of barmothenue had written the magic book.

Simon wonders why the witch would be interested in the book. Bobby interrupts Simon and comments, "That evil sorceress had interrogated me to find out what had happened to the other two books we had found". Robert becomes alarmed that Bobby has told the truth to Peirlee and placed Juliana into danger.

He asks, "What did you tell her?" Bobby replies sheepishly, "I said nothing". Simon is doubtful with the teenagers response and comments, "If the witch discovers the last of the lost books before we do, she will prevent us from ever being able to return to Earth".

Unknown to the humans' a shadow appears from the doorway that is slightly ajar. The feline tracker called Finch listens intently to the humans' discussion. The tracker squints through a gap to see where the group has gathered. Finch observes that one of the females wears a sparkling piece of jewelry upon her head. The fury creature's eyes widen in delight by the prospect of stealing such jewelry. He is debating whether to creep into the room and take it from the unsuspected woman.

During this moment Simon translates to his friends, "Apparently the castle of barmothenue was once the capital of Sephire and is located within the northern lands. This is where the ancient humanoids worshiped. The humanoids would come from many miles, bringing with them valuable items to give to the priests in order to appease their gods".

Bobby asks the legionnaire, "Do you mean treasure?" Simon confirms that the youngster is correct and continues, "At the time when the dark knight and his armies invaded the planet, the faithful humanoids prayed for peace but when the calls for mercy to the gods were unanswered the priests committed suicide. However before they carried out their own executions they had buried the treasure. The location of the hidden treasure can only be discovered inside the contents of the Black Book of Barmothenue".

Finch hears this part of the conversation and decides to continue following the humans', hoping they will blindly lead him to the treasure where he will steal it for himself. The tracker quietly tiptoes down the staircase to wait in hiding outside.

Hideki and Claire both try to understand the readings from the sundial, Simon sees them struggle and lends his assistance. He informs everyone, "Today is the second day of the sixth month". Robert is aghast, "What, are you sure you have taken the readings correctly?" Simon nods his head quite certain he is accurate. Robert realizes they are running out of time and must leave immediately if they are to reach Queen Juliana in time before her forces leave for battle. Robert urges his companions down the winding staircase where they commence the next phase of their journey to rendezvous with the waiting humanoids in the forest.

Elsewhere on Sephire, thousands of humanoids that have fled Valadreil continue to arrive deep into the woodland forest where huts and walkways have been built high within the treetops. Queen Juliana walks through the path of fallen leaves. She witnesses the women and children queuing in front of tall ladders that lead upwards. They wait patiently to be given directions of which hut they are to use as their place of shelter. Juliana can see women making their climb, some with young babies fastened to their backs.

Whereas men on platforms pull heavy items of belongings including supplies of food and weaponry that are tied together by ropes.

Suddenly one of the queen's loyal handmaidens approaches through the congestion of people. Ishma notifies her leader, "My lady, the commander and his captains are ready to begin the battle discussions and are waiting for you". Juliana asks Ishma to accompany her to the meeting. The handmaiden leads Queen Juliana through the crowd and they walk towards the area where the tents for those who will be riding into battle have been built. Upon the sight of their leader each humanoid bows their head in respect and honour. The queen politely acknowledges them and continues to walk towards the tents.

The two humanoid women are allowed to walk past guards who keep watch and they enter the tent. Once inside the chattering and gossiping immediately becomes a deathly silence and everyone stands to attention. Queen Juliana recognizes her dignitaries, Commander Teltris and ten of his captains who are responsible for individual sections of the royal guard. Juliana is certain there are those who are present that do not believe her to be strong enough to lead the humanoids into battle. She places the negative thoughts to the back of her mind and allows everyone to be seated.

As soon as everyone is settled, Commander Teltris asks for the queen's approval to begin the meeting.

Queen Juliana nods her head and a large drawing is placed onto a stand for everyone to see. Captain Jessop has been given the task of giving the presentation and proceeds to walk confidently towards the stand. The young captain sees this as an opportunity of raising his profile and hopes he will be rewarded with promotion.

He begins, by enthusiastically explaining to the watching audience that the drawing on display is a map detailing how far they have to travel before reaching the northern borders. The captain then over exuberantly strikes his pointer against the drawing to indicate their current position but in doing so a considerable amount of dust escapes from the canvas and causes Captain Jessop to cough uncontrollably.

Commander Teltris sees the captain attempting to recover his breath and the high ranking humanoid decides to take over the presentation. With his powerful and commanding voice he informs everyone, "The estimated time it will take for our forces to reach the northern border would be in four weeks but only if the weather remains favorable". Queen Juliana is not happy to hear this and voices her concerns, "We cannot wait that long as it provides the tribe army apes too much time to be prepared for battle".

Captain Jessop, having recovered from his coughing fit warns his majesty that rain is on the way as he has noticed along their travels, the behavior change within the animals. One of the elderly dignitaries advises the queen, "We must bring forward the day to leave for battle". Juliana shakes her head and replies, "I will not leave until I am certain that all of our people have arrived safely into the forest. Besides I gave my word to the humans' that we would wait for them. Without the Saviours of Sephire we will not break through the ape blockade". The dignitary understands her reasoning and sits back down on his seat.

Captain Jessop allows everyone to see drawings of the intended route towards the northern borders. The information suggests they are to travel across hills and ravines. Queen Juliana asks to see the route, which leads them to the fortress. Captain Jessop hesitates, as he was not expecting this question. He looks across to Commander Teltris for help. The commander informs his leader, "We have no information of the passage beyond the northern border. Ever since Roshtu's arrival those who have entered the northern lands have never been seen again".

The queen and her dignitaries are astonished to hear this as it means they can only strategize their attack once they reach the battlefield. This not only gives away the element of a surprise attack but will place the royal guard forces at risk.

Captain Jessop attempts to seize his opportunity and volunteers to take a small detachment of his section to the north where they can take sketches of the unknown lands. The other captains whisper their doubts of the mission and the commander withholds his approval, believing it is too risky. However the senior dignitaries suggest to the queen that it would be wise to accept the captain's request. Juliana takes a moment to consider. She knows the information would prove useful despite the dangers involved and regretfully allows the bold humanoid to prepare for his mission. The captain walks exuberantly away from the tent whilst being closely followed by the commander and the rest of his men.

With only the dignitaries and Ishma left within the tent, Juliana stands up and asks if the suggestion to hold a forest banquet for all of the humanoids would be suitable. The five dignitaries consider her proposal to be a good idea as it will lift the morale of the people and will leave a lasting impression on those who are going into battle of what it is they are fighting for. Juliana asks Ishma to gather the other handmaidens and begin announcing tomorrows evening banquet to everyone.

Stepping outside from the tent, Queen Juliana watches more of the travelling humanoids enter the camp with the knowledge that she will soon be riding away with her forces and leaving behind the women, children and those that are too old to fight. Juliana gives a silent prayer to the gods and asks them to look after her people.

Her troubled thoughts remind her of how lonely she feels without Robert being here. Juliana is concerned that her scouts who have been placed near the edge of the woodlands have yet to see the humans return.

With the sun beginning to set Juliana realizes that the Saviours of Sephire have two more days remaining before she and her forces commence their journey north.

Chapter Six

The humans' continue their route eastwards through the fields of Sephire, hoping to regain lost time in order to reach the humanoids. The group has not stopped to rest for several hours. Tired and weary they each find it difficult to block out the mental pressures of fatigue. Robert cannot help but let his concentration wander, his thoughts reflect on those who are no longer here with them. He wonders if Naomi, Derek and Yoshi had returned safely back to Earth when they had gone through the gateway.

The Welshman considers if their way of life has been turned upside down as a consequence of what had happened to them and ponders if they had returned to the same time period as the one they had left.

Robert's thoughts dwell of his friends and family back home, he does not know if they are aware of where he is. The sad feeling of missing his parents' remains, yet despite his longing to return home, he has a strange sensation that as each day passes here on Sephire he sees images that suggests to him that he is already home. Before Robert can pursue his thoughts any further he suddenly hears Bobby yelling. The sound snaps Robert's attention back to reality.

Looking towards the young teenager, Robert looks to where the teenage boy points and notices that the early morning sunlight sparkles against the water of a stream. The humans' forget their tiredness and dash across the grass with a zest of renewed energy having realized they can finally drink, clean and rest their worn out feet.

Without hesitation they each sit on the grass, hurry to unfasten their boots and proceed to dip their toes into the ice cold water of the stream. Feeling instant relief, they rest their backs onto the grass and gaze up to the shiny green sun of Sephire where they smell the freshness of the morning. Suddenly Bobby jumps up and screams out that something was trying to nibble his big toe. The others laugh when they notice that it was only a harmless fish. This is the first time in quite a while that any of them has been able to raise a smile.

Hideki suggests they should make good use of the weather and continue their journey eastwards but Robert advises everyone to rest for a little while longer as they will not be stopping again until nightfall.

The warmness of the sun dries away the last drops of morning dew from the grass. Simon decides to replenish each of their flasks with water from the clean stream. Claire helps Simon and they begin talking about happier times. After washing the dirt away from his face, Simon gazes into Claire's eyes, staring at the softness of her face. He is mesmerized by the kind American woman and wishes that they were sharing this moment under different circumstances. Suddenly the skinny Englishman fears that his gaze might become obvious and decides to direct his sight away from her in case he is causing her to feel uncomfortable. Claire senses that Simon wishes to tell her how he feels for her but she knows they must concentrate on their duty to the humanoids.

The rest of the group looks at the map of Sephire from Rachel's magic book and gather around her to determine how much further they have to travel. Bobby decides to leave them to do the thinking and walks away but soon catches sight of his sister scratching Simon's itchy back. The young teenager is horrified to see that his sister's actions could be misinterpreted as being romantic and that she might feel an attraction for a man who Bobby considers to be nothing more than a wet blanket. Desperate to ruin Simon's chances, Bobby calls out to his sister, "Claire, I think I have a splinter in my toe". He is relieved to see her hurrying to help him.

A disgruntled Simon mutters under his breath and attempts to dry his feet before sliding them into his legionnaire sandals. After picking up the gold and shiny helmet, he notices Robert sitting on a rock, evidently in deep concentration. The quiet

Welshman is busy thinking of what Simon had previously told them about Roshtu coming back to this planet and how the dark knight would be able to activate his portal, thus allowing thousands more of his tribe army apes to enter into the battle, that would render all chance of victory to be completely hopeless. Robert honestly cannot think of a winning solution in defeating Roshtu although he does not dare to share this thought with his companions.

Closing his eyes through tiredness the Welshman fears to visualize how they will meet their deaths but hopes it will be honourable. The vision Robert sees is not the scene of battle but is instead an image of a beautiful woman dressed in a white satin dress with flowers in her hair. He recognizes the woman is Queen Juliana, he cannot help but hope to be with her once again. Robert knows they owe a great debt to the Queen of Sephire, as she has showed her trust towards them. He admires the fact that despite her parents dying she has remained strong and brought hope back to her people. The Welshman decides he will fulfill his sworn promise to Juliana. Standing up from the rock he advises his companions that it is time to continue their journey.

With the sound of birds chirping the humans' trudge away from the stream, knowing they have a long way ahead of them.

After the next six hours has elapsed, the humans still find themselves walking through endless fields, hoping they will be able to see some sign of trees in the distance. The pace from each of their strides gradually decreases. Robert feels the straps of his holdall are beginning to cut into his shoulders. The sun in the western sky still beats down upon their backs, which adds to their tiredness. Being so thirsty they have drunk most of the water that had been gathered from the stream. Bobby complains that unless they find a place to stop soon, he will not have any feet left to be able to walk into battle. The group momentarily pauses to allow Rachel to understand their current position from the map before continuing onwards.

With the sun setting their eyes begin to feel heavy and they barely have the energy left to pick their feet up when all of a sudden Hideki notices some trees upon the horizon. At first he cannot believe it is real but when he blinks again and sees the trees are still there he cheers enthusiastically. This startles his friends but as soon as they notice what he has found they are just as relieved as he is.

Desperately hoping they have not arrived too late, Robert tries to search for signs of the humanoid scouts who are supposed to be waiting for them. An uneasy feeling grows within the pit of his stomach when there remains to be nobody here to greet them. The six humans' look to one another hoping someone can suggest something when suddenly Robert hears inside his head the familiar sound of the soothing voice from Carmen.

"The woodland forest, welcomes the return to the Saviours of Sephire".

Robert gleefully informs his colleagues, "The guiding angel is here I'm still able to listen to her". Rachel prompts Robert to ask Carmen, which way will lead them to the encampment. The guiding angel instructs Robert and his companions to remain where they are and to look behind them towards the fields.

Turning around slowly, Robert opens his mouth in amazement as he sees below the twilight sky six glittering white horses that ride towards them. The creatures gallop gracefully and obediently stop in front of the humans to allow them to mount.

Once Bobby manages to sit onto his saddle all six horses ride the humans into the forest and weave in between the trees at fast speeds. The breezing air brushes against the humans' faces. Simon is worried that he will fall off and holds tightly onto the reigns. He ducks his head to avoid hitting a branch and looks back to see how close the branch was but suddenly sights a group of riders that are gaining on them.

Simon panics and calls out to alert his companions but then becomes horrified to discover that his horse is beginning to slow down. The legionnaire pleads for his creature to continue riding when he suddenly notices that his friends have also stopped just ahead of him.

Robert looks back along the trail and tells his colleagues not to be concerned as he recognizes by the emblem on the white cloaks that the riders approaching are the humanoid scouts. The pursuing horses are brought to a halt and the humanoid riders bow their heads to welcome the Saviours of Sephire.

Robert asks urgently, "Have the queen and her royal guard forces left for battle?" One of the scouts replies, "Come we will show you save passage to the camp, Queen Juliana is anxious to hear of your arrival".

The scouts lead the humans deeper into the forest where after a short space of time they reach a slope.

Below them is a clearing where Robert and his friends witness thousands of humanoids dancing to piped music, laughing and telling stories as small camp fires flicker around them. Bobby suddenly begins to hear voices talking just above his head and looks up to see people looking down at him from platforms and bridges that have been built high within the treetops. The humanoid scouts bid farewell to the humans and return to the forest borders where they will keep watch in case of an attack.

As Robert and his companions' attempt to take in their surroundings, the horses cautiously guide them down the slope and away from the lively crowd where stable boys help the humans' to dismount. With the music still playing in the distance the team of humans turn around and notice Queen Juliana approaching.

Robert feels a rush of emotions to see Juliana once again but does not know how to show his feelings for her. The humanoid majesty greets them and tells them, "It is wonderful to see you all again, I was beginning to fear the worst had happened". Simon regrettably informs Juliana that despite rescuing Bobby they had failed their secondary objective because the witch had managed to elude them. Robert defiantly announces, "The sorceress will be punished for her betrayal to the humanoids".

Hearing the music and the noise of people being merry, Rachel asks the queen what is the reason for the celebrations? Juliana responds, "The festivities are to allow friends, families and loved ones to share these precious hours together, for many this could be the last time they see each other. I want everyone to be reminded what it is that we are fighting for, but come let me show you to where you can recuperate. I am sure you are exhausted from your long journey".

The humans follow behind Queen Juliana who leads them to some tents where the sound is quiet and peaceful. Before Claire opens the entrance to the tent, Juliana informs them they are welcome to join in the celebrations once they have rested. The humans accept her invite and allow the royal leader to return to her people. Bobby wonders what is inside the tent and pushes past his older sister. Claire chases after him but before she can raise her disapproval of his rudeness she and her companions stare in bewilderment at the sight of steaming bowls of water to be used for washing, fruit juice for drinking along with forest berries to eat and beds of straw to lay upon.

As soon as the humans' have bathed eaten and rested they decide to join in with the celebrations outside.

Rachel sees her cousin is still sleeping and suggests for her companions not to disturb him. The group quietly leaves the tent and allows Robert to rest. Within the darkness the Welshman's body twitches as he is in a deep sleep. He pictures in his dream the beautiful image of Queen Juliana. He can see her standing in a field surrounded by summer flowers, she turns around to him and offers him her hand to hold whilst smiling. Robert feels his heart pounding and he runs towards her. He then notices a dark shadow from above that blocks out the sunlight upon Juliana's face. He becomes concerned to see her smile disappear. Quickening his pace to reach her, Robert then sees the shadow on the ground in front of him is forming into Roshtu who now blocks his path to the queen. Robert looks down and sees a sword by his foot. Picking the weapon up he charges towards the dark knight. Suddenly, Robert's eyes open and he finds himself back in reality, awake and alone in the tent. He begins to hear the sound of the distant piped music and of people cheering, which enables him to slowly remember where he is.

Chapter Seven

Robert decides to find out where his friends have gone to and walks outside the tent. With his eyes and ears becoming accustomed to the darkness of his surroundings he can see the distant flickers of small campfires. Around this area of the forest, gathered humanoids are feasting on what little food is available, celebrating their existence and marking their determination to survive.

As Robert notices several humanoids sitting within the treetops whom are playing musical instruments, a line of dancers pat Robert on the back and welcome him to the party. Robert smiles back at them and continues to walk forwards. He recognizes Simon sitting down and decides to walk over towards him when he then sees his close friend is cuddling Claire. Robert is pleased that Simon has overcome his shyness and has allowed the young brown haired woman to know how he truly feels for her. Robert knows only too well how difficult it can be to have an infatuation for someone especially when you are not certain if the other person feels the same. The Welshman walks away from his English friend but fails to notice Bobby whom stands in the shadow of a tree and walks straight past him. The facial expression of the young teenager does not reflect happiness instead his glare shows anger as he watches disapprovingly at the man who is in the arms of his beloved sister.

A short distance away Claire embraces Simon before heading off to get some refreshments. Simon stares longingly at her, his gaze follows her until she is out of sight when he suddenly feels an object being prodded against his back. Before he can turn around, a voice whispers in his ear. Simon instantly recognizes the tone of Bobby's voice. "If you think I am going to sit back and watch my sister make a fool of herself you're mistaken".

Simon senses that the boy is aggrieved and asks him for an explanation, Bobby remarks, "You're not worthy of my sister's affections. You're taking advantage of her vulnerability". The puny legionnaire attempts to reason with him, "Do you not think it is for your sister to decide whom she can fall in love with?" Bobby replies, "We're here to fight for the humanoids so I am warning you to stay away from my sister, otherwise I'll make your life a misery".

Simon realizes by the threat that the teenager is not prepared to negotiate. Picking up his legionnaire's helmet Simon walks away in annoyance, wishing he could tell Bobby some home truths. In all honesty Simon is more upset with himself for not standing his ground and realizes that he has let Claire down with his cowardliness to have a confrontation.

Claire then returns to the table and carries two goblets of wine. She asks her brother if he has seen where Simon has gone? The teenager replies, "I saw him dancing away with an attractive humanoid woman". Claire clearly shows her disappointment that Simon would be so fickle and stares at Bobby in disbelief. The teenager takes advantage of her lack of concentration and with a smug satisfied grin on his face he accepts one of the goblets of wine.

Further ahead another line of dancing humanoids' dashes along the grass, which is covered with fallen brittle leaves. Robert sees them approaching when suddenly one of the dancers breaks away from the chain and grabs hold of his arm but then stumbles to the floor. With the dancers moving away into the distance, Robert looks down embarrassed and offers a hand of assistance to the young woman that is dressed in rags.

The Welshman is startled to discover that the woman dressed in peasants clothing is none other than Queen Juliana. Before Robert can speak, Juliana motions for him to be silent, she then accepts his hand to help her up and leads him towards a quiet area within the forest.

Juliana whispers to him, "I wanted to move around freely amongst the common folk without drawing too much attention to myself". Robert looks into her eyes, wishing he could relax and talk openly with her.

They sit down alone on the grass within a clearing of trees where they talk about their childhood. Robert listens intently to Juliana as she tells him about her exciting adventures. His emotional barriers of protection slowly begin to lower and he begins to feel at ease. Even though Robert can hear Juliana talking to him, when he gazes into her soft eyes the words do not register inside his head.

The human then blinks and his concentration returns to where it should be. Juliana continues to whisper to him. "I have been warned that the journey north will be a dangerous route to take, with steep hills added by wind and rain. I hope the royal guards will continue to stand by my leadership. I am certain there are those who would prefer Commander Teltris to be the one to lead our people into battle". Robert assures her, "Everyone has strong faith in your leadership, besides I will always support you". Juliana is thankful for his encouragement and holds onto his hand.

Robert feels his body beginning to tingle by the feel of the touch of her gentle and smooth hands. Juliana talks quietly, sharing with Robert about something her late father had once told her. "My father was right, I should have taken the opportunity to have found a husband to help lead our people. I had no idea when I was going to be ready to decide, I always believed that it would happen in the future once the war had ended but love comes in the most strangest of circumstances. I must admit I never expected to fall in love with a human".

Her voice stops and Robert gulps in surprise and his hand falls from her touch. Once he recovers his breath he asks Juliana who is it that she has an attraction for? Juliana draws closer to him and tells him he should know by now who it is and then she promptly kisses him softly on the lips. Before

Robert realizes this is not a figment of his imagination the sound of someone approaching distracts him. They both pull free from each other through fear of being discovered and quickly rise to their feet. Juliana points to some greenery, where Robert lets go of her hand and dives for cover to keep their secret hidden.

Juliana tuns around and realizes that Commander Teltris has found her. Before the commander has the opportunity to ask why is she dressed as a peasant she informs him, "I think it is time for everyone to get some rest". The commander replies, "Your majesty, Captain Jessop is ready to discuss his mission with you and is waiting inside your tent".

Juliana asks the high-ranking humanoid to lead the way. As Commander Teltris steps forward he notices the queen looking back to an area within the trees. Placing one hand onto the handle of his sword he asks if she has seen something? Queen Juliana hesitates to respond but then informs him it is nothing to be concerned about. They both walk toward the tents and see the celebrations are ending. Robert continues to crouch down within the undergrowth, watching Juliana until she is out of sight. Once he realizes the route is clear, he stands up and returns to the camp. With the music now finished and the noise nothing more than of quiet chattering, the humanoids climb up ladders to get to their shelters within the treetops.

Robert makes his way towards the tent when he then bumps into Simon, Hideki and Rachel. They ask him where has he been, Robert replies innocently, "I went to stretch my legs". However his mind is in a daydream as he silently recollects the tender moment he had shared earlier with Queen Juliana.

A short distance away Commander Teltris escorts his leader inside her tent where they are greeted by Captain Jessop and five members of his section whom are all dressed in battle garments. The earlier expression of enthusiasm on the captain's face has now changed to a serious and professional look.

Commander Teltris informs his Queen, "Captain Jessop believes the strike team can reduce the time it will take to reach the northern lands by travelling light. Upon reaching the northern border they will split into two separate teams to detail the route and to establish any developments of how far the enemy has prepared for battle".

Queen Juliana whom is still dressed in her peasants clothing, asks the captain when will his team be ready to leave. Captain Jessop replies, "Straight away your highness." The queen looks at her commander before nodding her head to approve the captain's mission. The strike team leader turns to his colleagues where one by one they each place on dark cloaks to conceal themselves and put on their steel helmets and step outside where their horses await them.

Before mounting onto his horse Captain Jessop is told by Commander Teltris not to take any unnecessary risks and above all to avoid being captured. Once the captain climbs up and settles into his saddle he looks down at Queen Juliana and informs her, "I will not fail you". He then raises his sword into the air to give the order for his strike team to charge. The six riders leave on their mission and the horses gallop into the darkness with the sound of their hoofs fading into the distance.

Queen Juliana stands alongside the commander both of them remain staring into the darkness of where the riders have disappeared to whilst silently wishing that they return safely.

Chapter Eight

In the early hours of the next morning, Robert opens his eyes and is surprised be awake with the feeling that he is needed elsewhere. Sitting up from the bed he notices each of his human companions are still fast asleep. Robert decides to crawl out from underneath the tent so as not to alert the royal guards on watch outside. Creeping into the dense woodland of the forest he sees a shimmering glow and recognizes Carmen walking closer towards him. Robert now understands that she has summoned him here.

With the morning green sunlight beginning to break through the gaps in between the leaves and branches of the trees, the guiding angel's brightness causes Robert to shield his eyes. She whispers for him to follow and after a brief walk they arrive to an area where two white horses await them. Upon seeing Robert, one of the horses' obediently lowers down for him to mount. Robert looks across and notices Carmen has already sat upon her horse. She speaks inside his mind and instructs him to follow her.

Without any reigns or a saddle to sit on, Robert hopes the horse will not ride too fast. He decides to hold gently onto the back of the creature's neck as it canters alongside the other horse.

Whilst riding steadily through the forest, Carmen tells Robert, "The gods continue to watch over you". He replies, "We wasted our one opportunity to defeat Peirlee". Carmen reasons, "The witch may still have a part to play in Roshtu's demise". Curious to find out exactly how Carmen would know of this Robert considers questioning her when he suddenly becomes aware that the two horses have stopped.

Seeing Carmen dismount, Robert also climbs down from his horse when the guiding angel then begins to answer Robert's question before he has even asked it. "You are probably wondering how I can sense what might happen in the future. I have a connection with Peirlee that dates back long ago. I was there at the time when Peirlee decided to betray the humanoids, which signified the moment when the gods chose to make me immortal and I became the guiding angel of the forest".

"You must try to understand that the witch's presence surrounds all three of the magical books. Peirlee is looking to retrieve all them in order to combine their power and become so powerful to overcome the dark knight and become Sephire's true leader". Robert looks back at her aghast, as he comprehends the need to find the location of the last hidden book before the disloyal humanoid does. Robert asks Carmen if she can help them to learn of the whereabouts of the Black Book of Barmothenue. The guiding angel replies, "The hidden book is within the walls of Roshtu's fortress located inside the Northern Rocklands of Terror. Only the dark knight knows the precise location of the book, this is why Peirlee continues her allegiance with him". Robert reminds the guiding angel that Roshtu had fled from Sephire through his own gateway. Carmen looks sadly at the human and informs him, "I am afraid the dark knight has already returned. Right now he is using all of his resources in trying to find a way of activating his own portal to allow thousands of his tribe army apes to enter into Sephire".

The majestic humanoid pauses to allow Robert to digest the bad news. Robert looks around to clear his head as he is still in shock. Within bright daylight Robert notices from below this high vantage point he can see the most beautiful crystal clear watered lake reflecting the image of the hillside trees. The scenery causes him to forget his concerns of Roshtu's return. Gazing down at the lake, Robert sees through his mind's eye, the beautiful image of Queen Juliana.

Robert quickly decides that now is not the time to be dwelling on his own problems of knowing what to do to understand his affection for the humanoid queen and attempts to force the issue away. Carmen whispers to him, "Why do you choose to disregard your feelings for Queen Juliana?" Robert is embarrassed to have let his feelings for Juliana be known but eventually decides to confide with the spiritual humanoid. "I am confused why I keep allowing myself to feel the way that I do about Juliana, I mean the queen".

Carmen looks back at him warmly and asks, "Why prevent it? You have a connection with the humanoids, which dates back to your past". Confused by what the guiding angel is telling him, Robert listens to her explaining, "When the time of destruction first began with the arrival of Roshtu the humanoids requested for one of their own people to go through the portal to Earth and ask the humans for help". Robert interrupts her, "I've heard about this, the humanoid failed to return to Sephire and had cast shame onto the humans as it had seemed they would not help". The guiding angel quickly corrects him, "No, the volunteer who asked to go on the mission was a kind, brave person. He failed to return because he could not find a way of activating the portal, which had been damaged on Earth. So he spent the remainder of his life as a human, living as one and eventually dying as one. However when he died he left behind a strong family bloodline that would continue for generations. Now on this day, at this time I stand alongside a member of that same bloodline".

Robert looks at her with his mouth open in shock but for some reason he knows that everything of what she has told him helps him to understand the reason why he feels at home here on Sephire and why he so desperately wishes to help the humanoids to restore their freedom. Carmen explains to him, "Deep down inside you know you belong here, that you are fighting not just for the humanoids, but for your people. This is why you have a strong connection to Queen Juliana. Your destiny is to be by her side. Roshtu sensed this through his dark magic. He fears your potential. This is why the witch targeted you. They both fear you will unite the humanoids and become King of Sephire".

Robert's legs begin to quiver at the prospect of becoming king and being married to Juliana. He asks how can he let

Queen Juliana know of this revelation. Carmen replies, "You cannot tell any of this to the majesty for everything must happen the way it is meant to be. Although your journey into battle must take a different route from the queen and her forces".

Robert looks up at Carmen in horror and pleads, "But I can't leave Juliana to be in battle without me. I've promised to protect her". Carmen informs him, "Focus your attention to preventing Roshtu from activating his portal. That is your priority, otherwise not one of you will survive". Robert cannot help but think of Juliana's safety and asks, "Will she be killed in battle if I am not with her?" Carmen responds, "The future is too uncertain to determine who will live and who will die, all you can do is fight for your people and do what is right".

Carmen then sits up onto her horse and looks back at Robert before saying gently, "I will instruct the animals of the forest to keep watch and protect those who are to remain. May you triumph to defeat the enemy that awaits you in battle". Her magnificent horse leaps back onto its hind legs and Carmen allows the white stallion to ride her into the distance.

With Carmen now gone and still attempting to comprehend all of which he has learnt, Robert gets back onto his horse. The creature proceeds to ride the human back to the outskirts of the humanoid encampment. Robert eases down to solid ground and gently pats the horse on the back, the creature rides away into the forest and the Welshman turns around to make his way back to the tent.

Without wishing to explain his adventure to the guards and his companions, Robert decides to crawl underneath the tent as he had done so previously. Once inside he finds his colleagues are still fast asleep and is thankful Hideki's snoring has proved useful in helping his coming and going.

Sitting back down onto the bed, Robert closes his eyes but his mind is too active to be able to fall asleep.

He continues to think of what Carmen has told him and how his life now suddenly seems to make perfect sense.

Chapter Nine

Two royal guards burst into the humans' tent and inform the awoken group with news from Queen Juliana that her forces are to ride for battle later today. The humans are then left alone in order to begin packing their belongings. With the countdown to war ticking ever closer to the end, Robert and his companions can feel the tension building inside of them. The Welshman looks across to his friends to see if they are okay and notices Simon offering a hand of comfort to Claire but she refuses to accept his support and looks away from him.

With his items already prepared, Robert steps outside the tent and asks one of the guards if they know where Queen Juliana can be found? The sentry informs him that his majesty is having discussions with her dignitaries. Robert thanks the guard and returns to his companions. Bobby asks him where had he gone to? But the tall brown haired man quickly asks for his friends' attention and requests for Simon and Hideki to accompany him to see the queen whilst suggesting to the remainder of the group to gather some supplies before they embark on their journey.

Walking towards the center of the encampment, Robert cannot help but notice that Hideki has been very quiet and decides to ask the Japanese warrior what is wrong. The ninja replies, "I dislike the waiting of battle it can play tricks with your mind". Simon groans at the prospect of having to travel once again and remembers the frightening images he had seen from within The Blue Book of Wisdom.

They soon arrive at the queen's tent and are allowed to enter by the guards who keep watch from outside.

Once inside Robert catches sight of a large map, which has been placed onto a table for everyone to see.

With the available space found to be lacking, Robert is unable to see Juliana but he can hear her addressing the audience. He assumes there must be at least fifty humanoids in the tent consisting of dignitaries and other high ranking officers.

Standing in between the heavily armoured humanoids, the Welshman can only catch a glimpse of the queen dressed in her ceremonial robes as she directs her speech to the seated dignitaries. With the sound of people shifting in the audience to make space for the humans, Queen Juliana pauses and looks at the gathered crowd. She instantly recognizes Robert and smiles briefly before diverting her gaze to the rest of the tent's occupants and informs everyone, "Due to the lack of knowledge of the route beyond the northern borders, Captain Jessop has left with a small strike team. They will attempt to sneak past any ape blockade and enter The Northern Rocklands of Terror where they will take note of valuable information to help us with our battle preparations".

"Once we reach the northern borders we will rendezvous with the Captain and then our forces will separate into two sections. Commander Teltris has volunteered to lead the main bulk of our attack and meet the tribe army apes head on. I will lead the remainder of our forces from the east".

As the queen pauses, the sound of quiet muttering begins to spread from the back of the audience as some of the humanoids question the intelligence in minimizing the size of the attack. Robert looks around at the humanoids, wishing they would give their leader the benefit of the doubt. Queen Juliana attempts to explain her reasoning, "If we can draw out the apes, this could open up a gap in their defenses that will allow us to ride directly to the castle of barmothenue and destroy the portal".

Each of the dignitaries silently considers her proposal of attack. Commander Teltris stands next to the queen to offer his support of her suggestion but his facial expression is one of a man who already knows that he will be outnumbered in battle.

Suddenly someone coughs from amongst the audience to get the queen's attention. Everyone looks around to see who it is and Robert steps forward. "Your highness may I suggest that your section of the attack should send reinforcements to Commander Teltris". Juliana is shocked that Robert would choose to upstage her and bitterly reminds him of their priority to destroy the portal to prevent further apes from entering into Sephire.

Robert replies calmly, "I agree your majesty but I request my team of humans' should be the ones to destroy the portal. I know there may only be six of us but we will use the humanoid attack as a diversion to infiltrate the fortress". Those who are standing close to Robert suddenly become silent and the soldiers within the tent begin to nod their heads in approval of the human's proposal. With the dignitaries whispering to one another in making their decision, Queen Juliana wants to tell Robert that she fears it is too dangerous. Commander Teltris whispers in her ear that the outspoken human should be taken seriously.

Simon and Hideki look to each other in shock. Both are wondering what their colleague hopes to accomplish in sacrificing their lives on some foolhardy mission. In an attempt to convince everyone Robert speaks out, "If we truly are the Saviours of Sephire, now is the time for us to prove it and end this war once and for all". The humanoid guards begin to applaud the Welshman's short speech. Simon can sense that the soldiers belief has been lifted. The sound within the tent becomes silent once again as Robert waits for Juliana's decision.

The queen reluctantly nods her head in approval of the suggestion, as do the dignitaries. She then informs Robert that his request has been accepted and announces to the audience, "Our forces must begin the journey north immediately, there is precious time to waste". She then concludes the meeting has now finished.

The tent begins to clear quickly with humanoid guards making their way outside. Simon and Hideki remain close to Robert and attempt to ask him for an explanation but the Welshman is busy trying to make his way through the oncoming crowd to be able to talk with Queen Juliana. He can see her in conversation with the elderly dignitaries but before he can move further forwards, Commander Teltris greets him.

Robert immediately stops to look up at the imposing humanoid. The commander looks down and shakes his hand telling him, "You made a very brave decision and have raised the morale of my soldiers". The human looks up in awe at the warrior and replies, "It felt the right thing to do at the time, although I do not know how we are going to get to the fortress". The commander pats him on the back and explains they can discuss that later. He notices Robert is not paying any attention to him and is staring at the queen.

The commander assures the watchful human, "Don't worry about the queen being annoyed with you, she will soon understand. Although I would give her some time to talk with the dignitaries". The Commander ushers the three humans out from the tent and advises them to begin packing. The humans bow their heads to the commander and turn around to return to their companions.

All around them, humanoids are frantically packing and saying their good-byes to loved ones who must remain in the forest. Simon remains uncertain about Robert's actions and asks, "Should you not have waited to talk your proposal through with the others before making the decision to volunteer all of us on your mission?" Robert informs them both that he had no choice and quietly shares with them the news of what Carmen had confirmed to him this morning about Roshtu's return and the threat of his portal being activated. Simon and Hideki both nod their heads in appreciation that time is running out.

Later that day within the late afternoon sunshine, the royal guard forces accompany the queen who is now dressed in her military garments. She bids farewell to those who look down at her from platforms and shelters built high within the treetops, hidden away in case of a tribe army attack. Juliana holds back her tears as she reflects that these humanoids may be all that will be left of their race. She is assisted by her handmaidens up onto her horse and is passed the royal scepter once held by her father.

The call of a horn is heard to mark the start of the journey that will end in a month's time upon reaching the Northern Rocklands of Terror. The queen waves goodbye to the tearful handmaidens before joining the solemn procession of that leads away from the camp.

A female humanoid looks down at the convoy from a platform built within the tall trees. She stands next to her young six-year-old boy and watches the last of the queen's handmaidens being helped up the ladder to the platform. An elderly male is assisted in pulling the ladder up. The inquisitive child asks its mother, "How will we get down?" The mother replies to the young boy, "From now on everyone must remain within the trees for their safety". All around sobbing can be heard from those who have been left behind.

The boy asks, "Won't the queen and the guards be coming back?" The mother pretends not to have heard the question and silently reflects to herself of the certainty that she will not be seeing any of those who have left, ever again.

Chapter Ten

Within the north of Sephire, streaks of lightening form across the dark red night sky. Along the rain-drenched terrain of mud and rocks, tribe army apes continue to prepare for battle. Within the walls of the fortress, Gormosh and Riesk whom are the two ape brothers that control the ape army have been summoned to meet their leader. Both walk into the room fearing the person they are about to see.

Upon entering the room the large doors are quickly slammed shut behind them. With only the flashes of lightening shining through windows from the wild storm that rages outside the brothers look around to try and see their master. Before Riesk can ask Gormosh as to what they should do he jumps out of his skin when a loud calming voice speaks to them from the windows that overlook the muddy courtyard.

"Tell me how far are you with your preparations for battle". Recognizing their master's voice, the apes hesitate to respond. Gormosh can see the outline of a hood above the top of the seat, which suggests that Roshtu has his back turned on them. Seeing the apes' hesitation against the reflection in the glass of the window their master asks again, "What do you have to tell me?" Riesk decides to answer but does not dare to look back at the face in the window's reflection. "My lord our army is almost ready for the humanoids attack, the witch has assured us she has been making progress in finding a spell to activate your portal".

Riesk stops talking when he hears a slow screeching sound that suggests the chair is swiveling around to face them. Both apes step back by the sight of Roshtu, whose appearance remains terrifying. His glowing red eyes and pale white skeletal face makes the ape brothers to feel afraid and they notice that Roshtu has aged significantly as a consequence of going through the gateway.

The dark knight asks them both, "How long will it take for Peirlee to activate the portal?" Gormosh replies nervously, "She estimates one month my lord". Roshtu immediately picks up an object from his desk and throws it in anger across the room. The object hits the wall and shatters into pieces. Roshtu yells, "I do not want to hear estimations and assumptions. I want to know exactly when the witch will be able to activate the portal and it had better not be as long as a month because the humanoids will be here to attack us before then. Tell the witch to find a solution sooner. I don't care if you have to starve her. Now get out there and watch over her. Tell Peirlee she must get the portal open!"

The two apes hastily retreat from the room and would prefer to be in the storm instead of being subjected to any further of Roshtu's rages.

* * *

With light beginning to fade and the wind blowing in strong gusts, the humanoids have halted their journey much sooner than they would have liked. Robert has by now informed their task to the remainder of his group and is relieved they have not argued against his decision. Although he has pledged his promise in restoring freedom to the humanoids, he is equally determined to help his loyal friends find their way back to Earth.

As the royal guard forces attempt to pitch their tents of shelter through the difficulties of the wind, Commander Teltris talks with Robert. The high-ranking humanoid informs him that once they reach the beacon in five days time Robert's team will have to commence their separate route into the Northern Rocklands of Terror. Both men look somber when suddenly Queen Juliana approaches and they both immediately bow before her. She allows them to rise and asks her commander, "When will we be able to move onwards?" Her loyal servant looks upward and replies, "Judging from the clouds within the sky the wind is coming from the north. I doubt it will not ease up until morning".

Juliana is disappointed to hear this as they have already fallen behind schedule. She asks if he can inform the soldiers to be ready to continue within a moment's notice and asks for a handful of men to keep watch of the weather conditions throughout the night to report if there should be any improvements. The commander bows his head and departs to obey his orders.

The queen looks beyond Robert and notices Bobby is struggling to fix the humans' tent. Robert turns around, upon seeing this he asks Hideki to assist the teenager. Attempting to keep her hair from blocking sight of Robert, Queen Juliana gives him a smile. Robert is relieved she has not remained cross with him for speaking out in the discussions back in the woodlands. Juliana tells him, "Despite my understanding for the reasons of your mission, I am concerned that our attack will not draw out the apes guarding the portal". She quietly fears for Robert and his team's safety.

The Welshman is touched with her concerns and assures her, "I believe the task of destroying the dark knight and the portal is my duty and purpose for being brought to Sephire". Juliana nods her head in acceptance but voices her wishes that they did not have to be separated once again so soon after having been reunited. Robert tells her, "You will find the strength from within and rally your people to fight when the time comes. One day we will be together in a time of peace".

Without thinking, the pair hold hands and gaze at one another but then remember where they are and decide to return to their duties. Walking back to his colleagues Rachel walks up to him and whispers, "Why is your face red?" Robert attempts to disguise his infatuation for Juliana and replies, "Oh it must be the gusty wind". Rachel is less than convinced and argues, "But it is not a cold wind that blows. Is something going on between you and Juliana?" Robert's face glows a brighter shade of red and he walks away replying, "Rachel, I have no idea what you are suggesting". He leaves his cousin to smile cheekily upon her theory.

At the sign of first light the humans talk quietly amongst themselves inside their tent. Whilst outside the wind continues to blow fiercely. Simon has managed to be on speaking terms with Claire, much to Bobby's annoyance. Hideki asks Robert if he knows the details of the northern route they are to take. The Welshman informs his companions, "Commander Teltris believes we should encounter little resistance should we choose to take the remote path, which leads us across the high rocky mountains".

Bobby wonders why the apes will not be there. Robert responds, "The path will be unforgiving with winds that none of us have ever encountered before added by thunder, lightening and torrential rain, the apes probably assume nobody would be foolish to travel by that route". Claire asks jokingly for Robert to remind her why are they going in that direction.

Speaking seriously to his friends, Robert relays all of what the commander had told him, "We will begin our separate journey from the humanoids as soon as we reach the beacons, apparently we must leave by crossing a lake. Once we reach the other side we travel across the mountains to reach the north. We must not take longer than three weeks as it is imperative we get there before the humanoids begin their attack".

Suddenly the humans are startled by the sound of the humanoid calling horn. The bellowing sound is to instruct everyone to pack away their tents and commence the trek northwards. After catching his breath from the surprise, Simon points out to Robert, "The queen must be anxious for us to move on if she wishes for us to travel in these conditions". Robert remarks to his childhood friend, "I think the weather will only get worse from here onwards".

With the commander urging everyone to hurry, the royal guard forces are soon ready to continue towards the next region of the forest and a step closer to the northern border.

Chapter Eleven

The bearded humanoid guard called Azeem of the sixth unit to the royal guard forces, currently under the command of Captain Jessop, manages to find a foothold where he is able to catch his breath whilst attempting to climb the rocky mountain within the Northern Rocklands of Terror.

With his notebook full of sketches still tucked inside his cloak, Azeem checks he still has the drawing utensils within his possession. The humanoid is no stranger at having to try and remain inconspicuous.

Many times in the past before battle, King Ridley would ask him to detail the opponents strategic positioning, each time his feedback had proved invaluable. However this time he finds himself within a part of Sephire where he has never been before, where the rain pours down heavily. Azeem hopes that what he intends to sketch upon reaching the top of this mountain will not be ruined by the rain.

Suddenly a small stone hurtles past his face. Squinting his eyes from the falling rain he looks upward and sees Captain Jessop just ahead of him signaling that having slipped he is okay. Azeem grimaces, wishing the captain was not so eager and would choose more caution. Azeem whispers to their other colleague just behind that there is no alarm and they are going to continue to climb. Azeem hopes the remainder of the strike team that are keeping control of their horses at the base of this mountain have not been discovered.

With the captain tiring, Azeem soon catches up with him when he suddenly sees a ledge, which is not far away. He points it out to his superior but the captain does not wish to deviate from his current course and continues to ascend to get a better view of the battleground leaving Azeem to scramble across towards the ledge.

Once he reaches solid ground the humanoid notices the path cut along the side of the mountain is very narrow.

Assuming that his other companion will follow after Captain Jessop, Azeem clenches the drawing utensil between his teeth and precariously crawls along the ledge with his cloak flapping against the strong winds.

A short distance higher from Azeem, Captain Jessop nears the summit of the mountain with the incline that he has not much further to go. With one arm outstretched the captain finally manages to place his hand onto a solid object to help elevate him upwards to the top of the mountain. However the facial expression on Captain Jessop's face of anticipation and excitement soon turns to horror when he realizes that he has grabbed hold of a tribe army ape's paw. Immobilized through fear the captain meets the dreadful gaze of the fully armoured ape who brings it's wooden weapon crashing down onto the defenseless humanoid.

Hearing the distant thunderous sound of marching, Azeem rounds the corner of the mountain still struggling to keep his balance along the narrow and uneven ledge. As soon as he reaches the other side his eyes widen in terror and his drawing utensil falls out from his clenched teeth. The startled humanoid sees an enormous army that coves the entire rocky landscape. Below the thunderous sky he witnesses large wooden weapons of destruction. Azeem knows defeat when he sees it and does not think the queen can successfully break through this blockade to reach the distant fortress, which he can now see upon the horizon.

Suddenly Azeem hears the fatal sound of screaming from nearby and hurries back along the ledge but is distraught to witness the captain plummeting to his death. Hoping to reach his other colleague, Azeem crawls back across the mountain but he has to cover his ears upon hearing a deafening sound of warning drums from the top of this mountain. The scared humanoid realizes they have been discovered and must retreat now if they are to escape with their lives intact.

Before Azeem can call out for his companion to descend, he stares up in dread as he sees a terrifying black horse look down from the top of the mountain. The creature sees his other companion trying to hide within the darkness of the mountain when suddenly the horse blows out a fiery flame from its nostrils.

Azeem cries out in distress as he watches the helpless humanoid being unable to withhold his grip and suffer the same fate as the captain.

Azeem begins to climb down frantically. Slipping several times, he refuses to die like this but fear and panic have replaced his concentration. Nearing the bottom, Azeem calls out below to the remaining members of the strike team and warns them they have been discovered. His colleagues look up at him in dismay as he falls to the ground with a thud. Whilst they help him to his feet he pushes them away and urges them to ride hard and fast away from this place. Before he can finish his sentence a sound can be heard of a horse approaching. Azeem turns around and sees the outline of the creature flying towards them. He jumps up onto his horse and grabs onto the reigns immediately causing his horse to gallop.

Azeem gets away just in time as a flame is fired towards them, which catches one unfortunate rider, leaving only three remaining to try and escape.

Zig-zagging in between the hillside trees Azeem hopes to loose the dangerous pursuing flying horse. The three retreating humanoids search desperately for the track they had used to get here but soon find themselves in front of two separate pathways. Knowing they have no time to hesitate, Azeem instructs the other two riders to take the pathway on the left as he then rides his horse along the muddy track to the right. As he holds tightly onto the reigns he speaks a quick prayer that one of them will successfully be able to find an escape but he soon finds himself under attack from the pursuing flying horse. Realizing he needs to use the trees as cover, Azeem changes route and leads his horse down a slope.

The pursuing dark horse looses sight of the humanoid and chases after the other two fleeing riders instead. Azeem looks back and sees the creature fly away into the distance, before he can raise a smile he finds himself now being threatened by a group of tribe army apes. The hostile creatures barely miss his head after having thrown their dangerous curved wooden weapons.

Still urging his tiring horse to continue, Azeem turns back to see the apes are in pursuit. The humanoid looks straight ahead and notices that a pile of stacked logs blocks his route forwards. Deciding to charge towards it the determined soldier encourages his horse to jump. The obedient creature does not ease up and barely manages to clear the top of the logs but through tiredness its hind legs clip the top log. Azeem feels the impact and holds his breath anxiously but his horse is able to stabilize its landing and the soldier manages to remain on his saddle. He gratefully pats the creature's neck as it continues to ride onwards.

Azeem looks back once again and is pleased to see that the pile of logs have come crashing down and now blocks the path behind him. He doubts his other two companions have been as fortunate in their escape and urges his horse to hurry so he can try to warn the queen that the apes are prepared for war.

Chapter Twelve

Making their journey through the forests of Sephire the six people from planet Earth along with the humanoid forces trudge along a muddy track. Recognizing where she is, the queen informs Robert and his friends to look towards the distant trees. Rachel and Claire divert their gaze beyond to where far away they can see a tall pointed beam with two long poles across the top. At either end of the poles are bright red crystallized lights. The entire humanoid force stops briefly to marvel the amazing sight.

Commander Teltris announces to the humans, "This landmark represents the northern beacon". Moving towards the beacon Queen Juliana explains, "The original descendents of Sephire had constructed the beacon it was believed they had built it for the purpose of appeasing the gods. Now it serves its purpose by marking the territory belonging to all that is left of our scattered villages". The queen feels remorse for not having helped the villagers within this region. She decides to move to the front of the traveling convoy and is accompanied by her commander.

Once they reach the gigantic beacon, some ill-faced humanoid villagers greet the royal guard forces.

Wearing torn garments and bodies that appear to be starved, the villagers bow to the commander believing him to be King Ridley. The soldier is more concerned to establish if the villagers have seen some of his men ride through here recently. One of the elderly villagers replies weakly, "A group of riders past through four days ago but not one of them has been seen since".

Commander Teltris does not feel at ease with this news. He had hoped to have caught up with Captain Jessop by now and turns around to the queen, who shares his concerns. The elderly villager informs the high ranking humanoid, "The apes have all retreated from this region and fled to the north".

Commander Teltris remarks to his queen, "The apes have gathered all of their army". Queen Juliana looks at the poor villagers and instructs her colleague to issue these people with some food.

The commander whispers in her ear that there is not enough food to go round for his men but Queen Juliana tells him to take it out from her rations instead. The powerful soldier remarks that it will not be necessary and leaves to give the ten villagers some nourishment. Meanwhile Juliana looks down from her horse and advises the villagers to head south for safety. The ill faced humanoids thank her for her mercy and accept the commander's small offering of food.

Queen Juliana informs everyone they will camp here for the evening before moving on in the early hours of the morning. The commander hopes that by then they might hear word from Captain Jessop's strike team. The majesty is not so optimistic and asks some of her royal guards to search the area in case there are any ape spies lurking around.

With the rest of the humanoid forces setting up their camp for the night, Robert and his companions realize they must soon break away from the humanoids and leave for their own journey. After drinking some water from his flask, Simon tells Robert he is relieved the weather conditions have eased up.

Robert fails to respond but Hideki warns them, "It is the calmness before the storm".

With the pale green crescent shaped sun of Sephire beginning to set in the west, the humans are led away from the camp. Claire sees the faces of the royal guard forces looking at her and her companions leaving, feeling that they are being abandoned to face their doom in battle. Robert is unable to understand what his emotions are doing to him and cannot think of the words that he wishes to say to Juliana. He only hopes it will not be the last time he will be able to look upon her.

The small group reaches the lake just as an evening mist begins to develop across the water. Simon pulls the cloak across his golden legionnaires uniform as the temperature begins to drop. Commander Teltris and Queen Juliana somberly escort the humans to where two tied wooden rafts have been left on dry mud to use as a means of crossing to the other side of the lake.

The commander wishes the Saviours of Sephire good fortune in battle, as he knows they will have an important part to play if the humanoids are to be victorious. He then steps back to allow the queen a moment to be alone with them. The humans hug goodbye to Juliana, she tells her friends not to fear of what awaits them.

One by one the humans separate into two groups of three, Bobby makes certain that Simon does not accompany him and his sister by offering Hideki to put his items into the small raft. Simon rolls his eyes in disgust and helps Rachel to unfasten the knot of the rope that holds the other raft.

Robert is left alone with Juliana to bid his own farewell. Looking into her eyes the Welshman notices a single tear of sadness fall down her soft cheek. Without holding back any further in having to think of what to say Robert whispers to Juliana, "All my life, I have been waiting for the moment to meet the perfect woman to share the rest of my days with. Despite the circumstances that have led us to one another if we survive the battle that awaits us, I promise I will not leave your side". Juliana smiles back at him and tells Robert she loves him, whilst silently wishing that she could do all that she can to never be apart from him.

Upon hearing Simon reminding him that they have to go, Robert drops his shoulders in disappointment.

He clenches Juliana's hands before heading to the raft and passes his items to Rachel who is already seated. Feeling remorse for not saying farewell the way he would have liked, Robert steps away and pats a dismayed Simon on the shoulder telling his friend he will only be a moment.

The Welshman then dashes back to the queen and embraces her. They cuddle each other, now unafraid of whom may be watching. With Simon staring in disbelief the commander tells him to get into the raft as he prepares to cast them away. Robert and Juliana kiss romantically, he then tells her, "No matter what happens I will find a way of destroying Roshtu's portal".

Robert then steps away and vouches, "One day we shall meet again and be together, somehow, someway I will reach you". He takes his eyes briefly away from Juliana to be helped into the raft and be patted on the back by the commander before he casts their raft onto the lake.

Robert continues to meet Juliana's gaze. Their eyes remain in contact with one another until the other person is swallowed up within the twilight mist.

The high ranking soldier leads a tearful Juliana away from the lake to regain her composure, whilst Rachel consoles Robert who hangs his head in sorrow. His cousin attempts to offer him with words of encouragement.

Simon quietly warns them, "I have a nasty suspicion that I am paddling in circles and we might find ourselves back where we started". Robert raises a smile and helps his friend to reunite them with their other companions.

Chapter Thirteen

Upon reaching the other side of the lake, Robert and his team carefully disembarks from the two rafts and secure them with ropes that have been tied against a nearby tree. Bobby teases Simon by asking him what took him so long to paddle across. Simon quietly counts to ten to withhold a bitter response. Before any of them can move away Hideki suddenly spins around with his sword raised. The others are surprised and prepare themselves against an attack but see nothing suspicious within the undergrowth of trees and bushes. After a moment, Robert whispers to Hideki and asks him what had he seen? The trained ninja remains very still whilst watching for signs of any movement and remarks quietly that he had seen something following them.

After a few tense minutes have elapsed Bobby comments, "I can't see anything following us, let's go".

Robert quietly suggests they should continue their journey but to be watchful for anything suspicious.

As they travel along their intended route, Rachel marks off in her book the number of days and nights that have elapsed since they had left the lake. The humans now find themselves a week later out of the forest and up within the hillside. Deciding to rest for the evening the Saviours of Sephire attempt to assemble their flimsy shelter. Rachel speaks a phrase from her special powered book to generate some heat from her pointed hat. After placing the hat upward on the ground the humans gather around to warm their hands.

Bobby asks his sister what has she done with his food. Claire informs him, "I had to cut back your food supply into rations, otherwise you will run out". The temperamental teenager folds his arms and sulks.

Simon attempts to lighten the atmosphere and comments that it is a relief to have finally left the forest.

Robert asks his cousin how many days do they have remaining before they need to reach the Rocklands of Terror? Rachel confirms, "We have seven days remaining". The leading darkly dressed man is certain that the next seven days will prove difficult for them to cross the mountains.

Hideki speculates, "If we discover the lost Black Book of Barmothenue, would a gateway appear that would lead us back home?" Rachel sees no reason why that should not happen but then declares her decision of not returning to Earth until the humanoids have restored their freedom.

Some of her friends are surprised to hear this and she explains her reasoning, "What kind of life would we lead if we were to return to Earth? Forever looking over our shoulders through fear that Roshtu may decide to attack our planet next". Her colleagues nod in agreement. Claire comments that unless they destroy Roshtu and the witch they may never have a home to go back to.

Suddenly the heat from Rachel's purple magic hat begins to cool down and Robert suggests they should attempt to get some sleep before moving onwards at first light.

Later that night, below the sparkling red-crescent shaped moon of Sephire, a shadow approaches the huddled group of sleeping humans. Creeping ever closer towards them the feline creature called Finch can no longer resist the temptation to steal the shiny piece of jewelry worn upon the head to one of the humans.

Seeing the headband capture the moonlight, Finch promises himself that he must have the item but he still wishes to remain unnoticed. Taking time to carefully plan his route, Finch eventually decides to make his move but then pauses very still when he hears a sound that is heard from one of the other humans.

Realizing it is the sound of someone sleeping, the creature continues to edge closer and notices that he will have to clamber across the young human to reach his intended target.

Only meters away from his unsuspected victim, Finch reaches out knowing the device he wears around his neck will make him almost invisible to the humans when suddenly a foul smell from Bobby causes Finch to quickly place his front paws over his nose. This quick movement activates Claire's headband and alerts her to the danger. The startled female wakes up instantly and looks all around. The bright light from her headband shines directly into Finch's eyes. Blinded, the creature screams out in surprise and hastily backtracks but in doing so stumbles into Bobby and lands on his back with his paws outstretched in the air.

Upon hearing the commotion but unable to see anything the humans quickly rise to their feet. Hideki's trained senses cause him to notice the movement of something against the grass. The Japanese warrior reaches out and grabs hold of something. He then clutches onto a necklace, which had previously been worn by a creature that suddenly becomes visible. The angry pointed eared furry creature attempts to snatch its necklace back but Robert warns him, "I have an arrow pointed directly at your head".

Finch realizes he is trapped and attempts to disguise his true identity by telling the humans, "You are trespassing on my land". Claire immediately sees through his deception. Using her special power of intuition she warns her companions. "This creature is a spy sent by Roshtu to follow us!"

The others are stunned and quickly look around suspecting an imminent ape attack. Finch realizes that he cannot plead his innocence any longer and tries to assure the humans, "There are no apes following".

Unsure if they should believe him, Robert chooses to lower his weapon but is still prepared to kill the creature and orders the feline to explain himself. Finch confirms, "Yes I am a tracker, sent by the dark knight but I do not work for Roshtu by choice as he has my family held prisoner on one of his planets".

Simon demands to know why the creature was trying to kill Claire? The creature stutters and pleads, "I only wanted my prize". He gestures to her headband. Bobby thinks they should get rid of this animal before he causes them trouble. Finch falls to his knees and begs for his life to be spared. Robert questions, "Why should we be merciful?" Finch looks up at Robert and informs him, "Because I can lead you directly into Roshtu's fortress without any of his apes knowing".

Having raised his eyebrows with interest, Robert suspects this is a trap and orders him to continue. Finch replies, "I can come and go as I please. The apes turn a blind eye to my activities". Robert is not so certain that the apes will ignore six humans who will be escorting the creature. Finch begins to sense the human's decision is swaying. "You're looking to disable the portal aren't you? I know where the control room is located inside the fortress. I can take you to it".

Looking around to his colleagues, Robert then asks the creature what does he want in exchange for his guidance, except for his life to be spared. The creature replies, "I know you are searching for a lost book, which contains the location of buried treasure. All I ask is to have a share of the treasure".

Simon mutters his astonishment to Robert, "This creature must have been following us for over a month to be able to know of this information!" His broad shouldered friend realizes the creature could save them valuable time and shocks his colleagues by accepting the feline's terms but orders Hideki to fasten a tight fitting rope to the creature. Finch objects to this at first but after realizing that he already has a good deal he then reconsiders.

Whilst the rope is being tied around him, Finch makes a mental note that the dark cloaked human has placed into a pocket the necklace, which activates his ability to become camouflaged.

Simon voices his concerns to Robert, who also agrees with him but points out to the legionnaire, "We do not know how much this creature is aware of the humanoid attack. This means that we can't turn it loose as we have no idea if it's loyalty is with the dark knight. Therefore I think our only option is to let it help us". Simon tells him he still does not like the idea of having to trust the creature. Robert instructs his friends that it is time to move onwards.

Once they have packed away their belongings, Hideki orders the creature to lead the way. The feline informs them all, "Finch is my name". The Japanese warrior holds tightly onto the rope that restrains the creature and says, "Move along, Finch". The others follow closely behind them.

Chapter Fourteen

Having left the northern beacon a few days ago, the humanoid forces have now reached the next stage of their travels. Commander Teltris remains discouraged to have not seen any sign of Captain Jessop's strike team. With the muddy conditions it is impossible for the humanoids to determine if the strike team had made it this far. Queen Juliana informs her leading soldier they cannot delay any longer and must prepare to leave.

Just as the riders are awaiting their signal from the commander to charge further north, one of the humanoids warns of something approaching. Startled, the commander quickly orders his soldiers to withdraw their weapons but to remain silent and to stay away from the middle of the path.

Waiting nervously for whatever it is that comes closer towards them, Queen Juliana grabs firmly onto her scepter ready to attack. They hear the sound from beyond some trees of a creature drawing deep breaths.

Commander Teltris jumps out and notices it is a horse but the stallion is too tired to react. The humanoid warrior calls for assistance when he recognizes the person collapsed in the saddle is one of the captain's men called Azeem. The commander hurries over and helps the soldier out from the saddle and lowers him to the ground. The humanoid is visibly exhausted but does not appear to be wounded.

Upon seeing what has happened, Queen Juliana orders some guards to tend to the horse and fetch water for the humanoid. Azeem opens his eyes and barely has the strength to thank the queen. Seeing him struggling to speak, Queen Juliana dismounts from her horse and kneels down to hear his weak voice.

Commander Teltris gently lifts Azeem's head to stop him from falling unconscious and asks him what has he seen? Azeem looks up at him, still shaking through the shock of his experience and quietly warns them "Wind, rain, fire and our doom!"

The commander looks grimly to his queen, hoping she can make some sense of it all. Juliana asks Azeem, "What of the ape army, are they prepared for war?" The shattered humanoid responds, "They are ready and waiting, with weapons that will kill many of our men". The commander grimaces and asks Azeem, "What happened to Captain Jessop and the others from your strike team?" Azeem closes his eyes, remembering all that had happened and regretfully screams out, "They're dead, all of them". The humanoid then cries tears of sorrow.

Realizing that the brave humanoid has nothing left to give, Queen Juliana asks some of the royal guards to take care of him. She then tells Azeem, "You will play no part in the battle ahead. You have fulfilled your duty". The bearded humanoid reasons for her to change her mind and asks, "Where else do I have to go? I should be with my people to the very end".

Some of the guards carry Azeem away to be allowed to recover but whispers and muttering can be heard amongst the soldiers. Commander Teltris attempts to rally his men, "Royal Guards, listen to me, the enemy may be waiting for us but why should we fear them? Azeem is living proof that they are not all powerful, for he is the first to have escaped from their lands".

The royal guards understand their commander and nod their heads in acceptance of the major task which now looms ahead. Queen Juliana gets back onto her saddle and defiantly states to her people, "We will not hold back any longer. This is our time, our moment to be rid of the enemy once and for all".

The royal guard forces raise their spears in strength and unity. Commander Teltris bellows out the calling horn to issue the order to charge and within an instant thousands of humanoids on horseback ride along the muddy track that heads towards the distant black sky.

* * *

Elsewhere, the humans are guided by the feline tracker called Finch, whom after having been captured must now show them the quickest route to Roshtu's fortress. The creature has led them out from the stormy weather and into a cave.

Everyone is relieved to be sheltered from the wind and rain. So far they have spent the past four days travelling at high altitude across the rocky mountains. The further north they go the more intense the weather becomes.

Rachel comments of the irony that they should find themselves within a cave as it was through previously entering a cave, which had caused them to enter this planet. Her companions each pull down their hoods and try to dry off. Finch asks the humans where do they come from? Simon dislikes the creature and tells him to mind his own business. Finch pretends to be upset and Claire informs him they come from a planet called Earth. The tracker remarks, "Earth, I have heard the dark knight talk of this planet many times".

The humans are concerned to hear this as it confirms that their previous fears of Roshtu's intention to invade Earth, might be true. Simon is skeptical of Finch's story and believes the creature is trying to trick them. Finch looks at Simon and shrugs his shoulders replying, "I have nothing to gain in frightening you all".

Hideki is not interested to hear any more about this debate and asks Finch, "How much further until we reach the fortress?" Finch whilst licking his paws to wash behind his ears responds, "Four days, if the weather holds up". The humans are shocked to hear that the weather could get any worse.

Robert tells everyone they should prepare to resume their journey before daylight is upon them. Finch interrupts, "In these lands, there is no daylight, it is forever dark and raining". The humans' grimace and one by one they each pull up their hoods. Finch, who remains tied at the waist by the rope, which Hideki holds is told to lead them out where the tiring group has to endure the rough weather once again.

Chapter Fifteen

The humanoid forces have now reached the wooden marker points of the northern border. They arrive in the midst of a heavy downpour of rain. Queen Juliana knows her forces have now passed the point of turning back but she does not question the decision of sending her people into battle.

Calming her horse, Juliana approaches Commander Teltris. She has to shout to be overheard from the pounding rain and notices that the tall and powerful humanoid has already gathered the main section of the royal guard forces. She bids farewell to her companion whom has served not only under her leadership but also under her father's. She asks him to remain firm against the ape blockade long enough to allow her section to break towards the fortress and promises the commander that she will send him reinforcements as soon as possible.

The commander remarks, "I am honoured to be going into battle under your leadership". He then tells her, "For the freedom of Sephire". Queen Juliana looks at him with respect and repeats, "For the freedom of Sephire". Queen Juliana now turns her horse around to face her section that she must take into battle and provides her soldiers with the order to commence along the pathway leading away from the forest and towards the steep hillside.

Commander Teltris and the remainder of the humanoid forces watch their leader ride away. The war veteran realizes he now commands the largest number of humanoid guards than he has ever done before. Despite this he is certain that their chances of success will be slim because they will be outnumbered and fighting in enemy territory.

He pushes aside the negative fears and turns to his men. Deciding that actions speak louder than words the leading soldier raises his spear high into the air. His fellow soldiers roar loudly in defiance to defeat the enemy as their blood warms to the battle that soon awaits them. The commander then leads the royal guards onto the muddy track. If Azeem's directions were correct they will shortly cross a large open field before reaching the Rocklands of Terror.

* * *

Still tied to the rope, Finch guides the humans across the mountainous region of the northern lands. The group creeps cautiously and uses the large boulders as cover. The anxious humans glance far below where they can see thousands of gathered tribe army apes that are awaiting the humanoid attack.

Flickers of flamed torches held by the apes indicate the size of the army that Commander Teltris will be fighting against. Simon whispers to Robert, "It appears that the humanoids will be outnumbered". Robert is more concerned by the threat of the catapults.

Robert urges Finch to continue to lead them onwards. Finch is momentarily flustered as he had been trying to secretly find a way of loosening the knot of the rope that he is tied to. The creature beckons them to follow and warns them to remain very close in case any apes are on the lookout.

Hideki looks upward at the dark red sky and is surprised that the rain has now stopped. Suddenly Claire senses from the power of her intuition that something is about to happen and alerts her companions.

Simon automatically triggers the force field of his shield to protect them. Once it is activated the shield's low humming sound is all that the humans can hear and they look to one another wondering what Claire has sensed.

Before she can explain, a loud explosion is heard from the distance. As everyone looks across to see what has happened a bright yellow light from the horizon momentarily blinds their vision. Shielding his eyes from the brightness, Robert notices it is coming from the outline of Roshtu's fortress.

Through this commotion Finch manages to unloosen the rope restraining him and decides to find cover but before he can scarper another loud explosion is heard. The noise causes everyone to cover their ears for protection when all of a sudden the ground begins to vibrate.

Simon looks nervously at the surface around his feet and panics when he notices several cracks beginning to appear on the mountain. The ground surrounding them gives way and they find themselves tumbling down. Powerless to do anything they continue to tumble but eventually land hard onto a pathway, which is further down the mountainside.

Robert and Simon manage to land safely but the others cannot prevent themselves from sliding over the edge. Robert reacts quickly and catches Bobby whilst Simon grabs desperately onto Claire. The others unfortunately continue to fall down the mountain until Hideki and Finch manage to cling onto another ledge whilst Rachel grabs hold of Hideki's ankles. Finch has a distinct advantage over the others and uses his feline claws to good use and successfully climbs up to reach solid ground. Hideki slips away from the ledge but quickly strikes his sword into the stones of the mountainside to prevent him from tumbling but his grip on the sword is weakening.

With Rachel still dangling from his ankles, Hideki holds firmly onto the handle of his weapon but remains to dangle precariously. The Japanese warrior notices that Finch is just above them and Hideki begs the creature for assistance. Finch contemplates if he should help the human, wondering if he would stand to gain anything. The fury creature looks higher up the mountain and notices that the other humans are out of sight, but can still hear their voices from the pathway above.

Satisfied that he cannot be seen, Finch reaches down to Hideki but his paws go past Hideki's hand and instead he reaches inside the Japanese warrior's top pocket. Finch then retrieves his special powered necklace that enables him to become camouflaged within his surroundings. Realizing the creature's motives, Hideki curses the cunning enemy but before he can shout out to the others Finch then knocks the sword loose from the stones. Hideki and Rachel both scream, as they are unable to prevent themselves from sliding down the slope of the mountain, which takes them directly into the path of the ape army.

Once Finch manages to conceal his necklace he uses his claws to climb further upwards and reaches out for the other unsuspecting humans to help him up. Simon and Robert both pull the creature and ask him where have Hideki and Rachel gone? Finch shrugs his shoulders and gestures that they fell. Simon looks anxiously to Robert but Claire senses that their companions are still alive.

Her friends are relieved to hear this and decide to look for a route down the mountain to help them but notice the bright light still shines upon the horizon. Simon asks, "What is that?" Robert realizes to his dismay that it must be the linking device and yells, "The portal! Roshtu must have found a way of activating it". The troubled human knows there are bound to be tribe army apes entering into Sephire that will increase the numbers to the already sizeable ape army. Robert turns to Simon in horror and states, "Juliana will be here soon. The humanoids won't stand a chance!"

Determined not to let the queen down, Robert places an arrow to his bow and points it directly at Finch. The creature shrieks as Robert commands him to quickly lead them on.

Whilst running towards the light, Bobby asks Robert, "What about Rachel and Hideki, should we not try to help them?" Robert replies, "Unless we destroy the portal we will all be dead!" The humans continue to run behind Finch who scurries along the pathway of the mountainside.

Chapter Sixteen

Queen Juliana leads her section out from a gloomy mist where she allows her small band of royal guards' to come to a halt. In front of them is a large muddy hillside where beyond are the Northern Rocklands of Terror. One of the soldiers notifies his leader, "My Lady, we are ready when you are". Juliana swallows and attempts to place aside all feeling of fear and dread, but the noise coming from the distant army of apes and the unnerving environment makes it impossible to ignore the frightful terror that will soon be upon them. With only a limited number of humanoids alongside her, Juliana knows it is essential the ape army is drawn towards the commander's attack.

She silently hopes Robert and his companions have now breached Roshtu's fortress. Juliana takes a moment to look at those who will be riding alongside her into battle. She recognizes the same expression of apprehension on each of their faces. Suddenly her gaze catches sight of something moving along the slope from where they have just come from.

Expecting that the tribe army apes' have set a trap and are attempting to surround them, Juliana quickly warns the royal guards of a surprise attack. Alarmed and caught unawares, the humanoids quickly raise their spears and nervously wait to fire lethal shots into the enemy approaching through the mist.

Queen Juliana is surprised the apes have not yet released their deadly weapons. She is about to issue the instruction to fire when suddenly the shapes approaching come into sight and Juliana is shocked to see hundreds of humanoid villagers arriving.

The royal guards lower their weapons and Juliana rides out to meet the humanoid that leads the villagers.

She notices the villagers do not wear armour and that their leader carries a long sword resembling those used from old times. The other villagers carry primitive sharp pointed weapons such as pitchforks that would easily crush through an ape's shield.

Juliana looks down from her saddle at the bulky humanoid and tells him, "I would suggest you all turn back and head for safety". The bald headed villager replies, "We have spent the last ten years preparing for this day. We once heard rumours King Ridley would attack the apes but he never arrived, tell me where is he?"

The queen begins to think of her deceased father and wonders what he would do if he were still alive. She informs the muscular villager with news of his death and that as his daughter she is now the humanoid leader. The male villager notices the royal scepter that Juliana carries and immediately commands the other villagers to bow before their leader.

With the villagers kneeling in front of the queen they pledge their duty to the queen's attempt to restore freedom to all of Sephire. Queen Juliana is aware they must soon ride over the slope and enter the battle.

Despite their lack of protection the villagers will add weight to their numbers. She gratefully accepts the proposal for their support. However, before she can turn her horse around someone shouts, "It's stopped raining!" Everyone looks upward to the dark red sky in surprise that the constant downpour has finally abated.

Suddenly the ground shakes violently. The royal guard riders have to try their best to remain in their saddles and to control the horses. Queen Juliana believes the commander has begun his attack and without a moments hesitation she decides now is the time that they finally ride into battle.

Raising her weapon high into the air, Queen Juliana turns around to her fellow humanoids and yells at the top of her voice, "For Sephire!" Her people cheer back, "For Sephire". The villagers run behind the riders of the royal guard and travel towards the hillside where they will enter the battle.

Elsewhere in the northern rocklands of terror, Commander Teltris and the large number of royal guards have already begun to combat the ape army. The commander has to put his experience from previous battles into good use. His strategy is to position the strongest guards at the front of the attack to push into the wall of apes. Leaving the other guards to fire laser shots high into the air to fall down onto the masses of apes beyond.

However the fearless soldier and his men are already fighting for their lives as large boulders released from the tribe ape army catapults continue to crush down upon them. The enemy is also taking advantage of the high ground with apes picking off humanoids with their deadly wooden weapons.

Commander Teltris realizes they are slowly beginning to succumb to the onslaught. Loosing men fast they are vastly becoming outnumbered but he refuses to issue the order of retreat. He is willing to make a stand even if it means sacrificing his and the guards' lives. So long as they can keep the apes distracted long enough for the queen to break through and reach the fortress where she can help the humans to destroy the portal. He shouts out for his guards to shoot down the apes from the hillside and urges those around him to remain strong as he leads the charge into the blockade of apes.

Within the darkened corridors of the fortress the two ape brothers, Gormosh and Riesk escort Peirlee through an open doorway and into the command room. Once inside they find Roshtu standing over the holographic display watching intently as he analyses the progress of battle. Gormosh coughs to get his master's attention and states proudly, "Master, hundreds of apes are coming through the activated portal".

Roshtu looks up at them, his smile is as frightening as his glare. The dark knight congratulates Peirlee upon her success. The witch is visibly exhausted, as she has spent all of her energy into finding a spell to release the portal. She looks at Roshtu, hoping that as promised she will be rewarded with power to rule the humanoids that are going to be taken prisoner.

The smile from Roshtu vanishes when he sees from the holographic images, a break in the apes' defenses. He tells Riesk to send reinforcements into that area of the battlefield to prevent the humanoids from advancing. Riesk bows his head and departs from the room to carry out the order.

With his brother gone from the room, Gormosh asks Roshtu, where are they to send the humanoids that they capture. The dark knight's expression becomes menacing as he replies, "Capture, who mentioned anything about capturing the humanoids?" Gormosh appears baffled as he listens to his master's orders, "I want your apes to kill every single humanoid, we will be rid of their existence once and for all!" Peirlee's eyes widen in shock and she cries out, "You promised me you would spare their lives!"

Roshtu can see how the witch is upset and speaks calmly to her, "Peirlee do you think I would consider going back on our agreement?" Roshtu then holds out his hands to her. The old sorceress gratefully accepts his comforting support as she shakes from the thought of loosing her people. Without thinking, Peirlee places her magic staff to one side and reaches out to hold the black-gloved hands. As she draws her hands within touching distance a crackling bolt of blue energy comes out from Roshtu's gloves and binds her hands together.

Realizing she is powerless to do anything without her magic staff, she looks up at the dark knight in anger and screams at him, "You will regret this treachery!" Before she can finish her promise of further threats, Roshtu raises a finger to her head and a crackling bolt of energy sends Peirlee tumbling unconscious to the floor.

Riesk enters the dark room and is stunned to see what has happened to the witch. The dark knight orders his ape servants to take the witch away and lock her in one of the dungeons within the castle. The ape brothers pick Peirlee up from the floor and take with them her magic staff before dragging her out from the command room, leaving Roshtu alone to evaluate the humanoids attack.

Chapter Seventeen

Hearing and witnessing the ferocious scenes of battle, Queen Juliana rides across the rocky surface of the battleground. Leading the charge of her humanoid attack she notices that a large number of apes are attempting to block their route towards the fortress.

The humanoids who ride with the queen deem this will be their final moment when all of a sudden the queen raises her scepter aloft. A bright purple light appears from the top of the object and shines through the darkness. Queen Juliana yells a battle cry and directs the light at the surging apes. A beam of energy is released from the weapon that knocks the enemy aside and momentarily clears their route.

As the villagers catch up with the queen's section she notices some of the apes have been drawn towards a battle near the bottom of the mountainside. Knowing the commander's attack is taking place south from here, Juliana changes course. She soon recognizes the pointed hat belonging to Rachel and the long thin sword being used by Hideki. The majesty quickly orders those around her to help the outnumbered humans to fight off the apes.

Having rescued the two people that come from planet Earth, Juliana is concerned not to see where their companions are and asks Rachel what has become of Robert? The female wizard is still recovering her breath so Hideki responds, "We were making our way across the mountains when a powerful force of energy caused us all to tumble over the side. I do not know what became of our friends I only hope they have managed to loose Roshtu's spy". Hideki is still incensed with Finch for his earlier attempt to kill them. Rachel manages to breathe properly again and informs Juliana, "The portal has been activated".

Juliana gasps as she realizes that Robert must be in danger if he has not yet been able to destroy the linking device.

Some of the humanoid guards quickly alert Juliana of an approaching ape attack. The determined queen grimaces as she senses that time is running out for her people to win this war. She orders twenty guards from her section to ride with her towards the fortress and then instructs the villagers to fight their way south to help the commander with his attack. Juliana asks Hideki and Rachel to remain here with the rest of the royal guards to fend off the oncoming ape attack. Before leaving she assures Rachel, "We will break through the blockade and help your companions". Rachel attempts to thank her but the queen has already begun to ride with her group towards the fortress. The wizard does not have any more time to think of what will happen as she finds herself firing laser shots at the attacking apes Using dark shadows from the boulders, which surround the fortress as cover. The other four humans crouch down behind Finch and watch apprehensively at the frightening apes marching across the suspended wooden drawbridge. Simon has to cover his ears to block the deafening sound coming from the continuous procession. Robert whispers anxiously to Finch, "How are we supposed to get past those apes?" Finch turns around and points a claw towards a large rock, which is just above the murky water of the moat.

Clambering down the rocks, the humans carefully follow behind the feline. Simon voices his concerns of the apes on the drawbridge but he is not heard. They soon find themselves directly underneath the drawbridge and remain unnoticed. Finch jumps up and grabs onto the rope that dangles just above their heads and motions whilst upside down, for them to follow. Simon remarks to Finch, "You must be joking, that rope is not strong enough to support our weight". Bobby tries to convince his sister that Simon is cowardly and decides to do as Finch suggested.

Hanging upside down Bobby sticks his tongue out at Simon, which causes Simon's blood to boil from the teenagers constant ridiculing. Simon also reaches up to the rope but then becomes frightened and lets go. Claire asks him to be brave. Without wishing to show himself up in front of her, Simon tries again and hangs precariously upside down. Robert and Claire also jump up and Finch proceeds to lead them towards the opposite side of the drawbridge.

Simon has to stop several times to retain his grip on the rope. They are only half way across and already his hands and arms have begun to ache. Trying to block out his fears, Simon does not know where to look. He cannot look down at the murky water in case there should be any dangerous creatures but he dared not look upwards through fear of being seen in between the gaps of the wooden drawbridge by the tribe army apes. The legionnaire attempts to focus and relax by concentrating on Bobby and silently reminding himself of how much he would wish to throw the teenager into the moat.

The humans soon reach across to the other side where at the bottom of the castle, Finch shows them the way inside the fortress through a concealed doorway. The feline turns around and giggles when he notices the humans have to crouch down to avoid hitting their heads on the low ceiling of the doorway.

Robert is not amused and orders Finch to show them the way up the winding staircase.

Simon reactivates his energy shield and follows after his companions. Robert's thoughts of Juliana are imprinted in his mind, he knows there is the need for urgency and asks Finch how much further is left to go before they reach the control room. The crafty creature does not look back but responds it is three more flights of stairs from here.

Suddenly Claire senses a powerful force coming from close by and announces, "I can sense the presence of the Black Book of Barmothenue!" Finch stops and his eyes widen upon the prospect of finding the book and learning the location of the buried treasure. The creature suggests, "I can show you to the book".

The Welsh human has no time for his tricks and places an arrow to his bow. Finch shrieks as he is then ordered by Robert to continue to lead him to the control room. The Welshman then turns around and informs his companions to leave and find the last book by themselves. Simon looks back at his friend and asks, "What are you going to do?" Robert replies, "Something that I was born to do".

After leaving his English friend perplexed by his answer he then chases behind Finch who continues To guide him further up the winding staircase whilst muttering his protests in not being able to retrieve the book. Although unknown to Robert, Finch has been able to place around his neck the special powered necklace that enables him to become invisible to the naked eye.

Chapter Eighteen

Meanwhile underground within the dungeons of the fortress, Gormosh and Riesk drag Peirlee whom remains unconscious, into one of the holding cells.

The ape brothers wonder what they are to do with the witch. Gormosh remembers, "Roshtu wanted her out of the way". Riesk comments they are supposed to kill all of the humanoids and argues that the witch is technically speaking a humanoid. The ape brothers would prefer not to disobey their master and want to hurry up so they can participate in the battle outside.

Riesk sees a sharp pointed weapon upon the wall and tells Gormosh to hold the hag whilst he carries out the execution. As Riesk reaches to retrieve the weapon his brother places the witches staff down onto the floor and holds the limp figure underneath the light. Unknown to Gormosh, Peirlee is well aware of what is about to happen. Although she continues to pretend to be senseless, her eyes remain fixed on the magic powered staff that is just out from her reach.

Gormosh waits with bated anticipation to see his brother strike Peirlee, who still has her hands locked in confinement with a mortal blow. As the muscular ape brings the weapon crashing down with a ferocious force, the limp body of Peirlee suddenly reacts to the danger and somersaults across the floor. Riesk is stunned but before he can grab hold of the witch, she kicks the ape in the leg and he falls down to where she had previously laid.

Instead of striking the lethal weapon into thin air, Gormosh is horrified to see that he has struck his brother across the neck and stares aghast at him now lying motionless on the floor. Shocked by what he has done, the steel object falls from his grasp and clangs on the ground. He lowers to his knees to see if Riesk is still alive. He quickly remembers about the witch and looks desperately around the room in an attempt to locate her.

Using the commotion to grab onto her magic staff, the crackling chains binding the sorceress's wrists diminish. Gormosh turns around and the last thing he sees is a bright ball of energy fired from Peirlee before he falls to the floor, dead alongside his brother.

Peirlee walks out from the cell and makes haste away from the dungeons, muttering how she will get her revenge on Roshtu for his betrayal, vouching to do something she should have done a long time ago.

Near the top of the fortress, Robert's footsteps echo as he continues to follow Finch up the staircase.

With his heart pounding both adrenaline and fear, he looks behind, wanting to help the others discover the lost book but he knows of what needs to be done. Robert whispers to the creature in front of him, "How much further?" Finch beckons him round the corner replying, "The end is not far now". The human keeps the arrow fixed to his bow but suddenly looses sight of the fury creature.

Quickening his pace up the stairs, concern rapidly develops, as the feline is nowhere to be seen.

Panicking that his guide has gone missing, Robert decides to call out but before he opens his mouth he notices an open doorway. Assuming that Finch must have entered, Robert walks into the darkened room to follow but is startled when the door slams shut behind him. He immediately observes a red glowing machine within the corner of the large room and a shinning light that comes from beyond the windows.

He does not like this place and attempts to leave but becomes concerned to discover that the door is locked.

Realizing he is trapped, the Welshman turns around to see if he can find another exit but suddenly becomes aware that he is not alone.

Chapter Nineteen

Moving swiftly along the corridor, Claire continues to guide her two other human colleagues closer towards the presence of the Black Book of Barmothenue. Simon has to hurry to catch up and reminds them to be cautious as there might be enemy apes nearby. The brunette woman does not heed his warning because she is preoccupied in understanding where her senses are leading them.

Claire then stops abruptly in front of some closed doors. Her friends wait impatiently as she turns around announcing excitedly, "The hidden book is in this room!" Simon walks over to unlock the entrance but Bobby has already brushed past him and pushes the two doors wide open that pull back with a loud screeching sound. This causes the humans to stand still apprehensively as they wonder whether it is safe to enter the room. Bobby now steps back to allow Simon to lead them all inside where they find a small room that has many shelves containing books. Claire remarks, "Judging by their appearance, these books must date back years ago".

Simon and Bobby both look at Claire but she explains that she has no idea which of the books is the one they are searching for. Simon urges the three of them to start looking randomly at the books that are visible. With precious light available, Claire retrieves one of the dustiest books hoping it is the oldest.

Stepping backwards she attempts to read some of the contents from under the gold light. Claire slowly begins to realize the light from outside does not shine golden. Diverting her gaze upward, Bobby's sister notices the brightness is coming from a book, which is placed on a shelf near the ceiling. Dropping the book from her grasp she looks around the room for a way to climb up and soon discovers a ladder.

Having placed it in front of the bookcase Simon and Bobby watch with interest of what she might have found.

Once Claire has reached the last of the rungs to the ladder she looks at the book and notices the light shining is coming from the gold leaf writing on its spine. From her time in the humanoid archives Claire is able to interpret the written language and reads out, "The Black Book of Barmothenue!"

Feeling relief in finding the last of the hidden books she uses one of her hands to take hold of it. Suddenly she begins to feel strange, knowing that if she were to open the book it would release its power and activate a gateway to take them back home. Simon can see her beginning to wobble from the ladder and asks her what is the matter? Hearing his words, Claire shakes the notion of opening the front cover to the back of her mind and tells her companions, "I am going to make my way down".

As she approaches solid ground, Claire can no longer resist the temptation and stops to open the first page. Simon and Bobby both see what she is about to do and scream out for her to stop. With her finger and thumb touching the book she is barely able to prevent herself from opening it up but stares mesmerized at the pattern on the front cover.

Simon senses her faltering and begs her not to give in to her temptations. He reminds her they have only one chance to use its power and should they do so now then the humanoids would loose their planet to Roshtu. Bobby pleads to his sister, "Robert, Hideki and Rachel will not be able to come back with us if you release the gateway now". In an act of desperation to get away from the book's power, Claire pulls herself away from it but in doing so, falls away from the ladder.

Reacting quickly to save her, Simon risks injury by throwing himself across the room. Bobby is frozen to the spot through fear but is relieved to witness his sister landing safely into Simon's arms. Dazed by what has happened, Claire regains her senses and looks around to thank Simon but is concerned to find him unconscious having struck his head against the floor from the impact. Bobby dashes across to help, and feels terribly guilty at how much he has misjudged Simon.

The legionnaire wearily opens his eyes to see Claire sobbing over him. He asks if he is still alive but before he can clear his vision, she hugs him in relief and gratitude. Bobby then asks his sister, "What happened to the book?" They each try to remember in which direction the book had landed. Bobby is the first to see it and exclaims "It's over there, near the doorway!" However, before any of them can move, much to their dismay Finch suddenly appears and picks up the book before dashing out from the room.

Cursing the feline for his treachery the humans run after Finch but crash into the door when it suddenly slams shut in front of them. Hearing a bolt being locked from the other side of the door, Bobby shouts out in annoyance, "Why you filthy little creature!" As the three of them fall silent they can hear Finch giggling and taunting them from the other side, "Admit it humans, I have defeated you. Finally I can be wealthy".

Simon is more concerned to find out what has happened to Robert. The creature replies, "I sent him to his death", and the creature laughs once more.

Bobby is outraged and raises his club high above his head whilst warning his friends to step away from the door before he repeatedly crashes his weapon against the solid object. Finch realizes what they are doing and tells them, "The door is too thick for you to break through, it is as thick as your heads!" The creature has a smug satisfied grin on his face. However the next impact from Bobby's club causes the cunning creature's smile to disappear when he hears the sound of wood splitting and realizes that the door is about to give way. Finch decides to make haste along the corridor to escape with the book.

The door then comes off from its hinges and the three humans chase after Finch. The fleeing creature cannot see anything along this corridor that will allow him to become camouflaged and elude the humans.

Finch looks back anxiously and sees Simon bearing down on him. Finch realizes he will not make it to the winding staircase and decides to alter his course by entering one of the rooms to find another means for his escape.

Chapter Twenty

Queen Juliana and her riders charge across the platform of the drawbridge, causing some of the apes to plunge into the murky water of the moat. The humanoids manage to fight their way across to reach an entrance to the fortress. Juliana leaves her two remaining guards to fight off the approaching group of apes and hurries along the corridor in search of the control room.

* * *

With the instinctive feeling that he is not alone within the dark and scary room, Robert looks frantically around to see where the other person may be hiding. Whilst holding onto his bow and arrow in anticipation of using it, he notices a large table close by with a holographic image displaying the battle currently taking place outside. Tip toeing towards the table, Robert takes in from the display that the humanoids have not yet been able to break through the ape blockade.

Feeling despondent in not being a step closer to accomplishing his promise to Juliana he takes a look at the machine in the corner of the room. Still keeping his guard up, Robert notices the machine has pipes fixed to it, which run along the wall and leads outside. From where he is standing Robert follows the direction of the pipes and gasps when he sees that the light shining outside in the courtyard is coming from Roshtu's activated portal.

Realizing he is in the control room and is now only moments away from completing his mission, Robert steps back and prepares to release an arrow into the machine but then suddenly hears the sound of a chair revolving. Turning his head around to where the noise is coming from, Robert watches in horror as he recognizes the other person in the room is Roshtu.

Quickly deciding to complete his objective, Robert releases the arrow from his bow, hoping it will cause damage to the machine. The sound from the arrow whizzes through the air as it nears its target but then Robert is distraught to see the arrow bounce harmlessly against an energy shield protecting the machine.

From the other side of the room the dark knight laughs at Robert's reaction and taunts him by saying, "Do you think it would be that easy to defeat me? No you need to make it to the other side of my desk to be able to disable the shield but in order to do so you must first get past me!"

Robert is afraid to look into the glowing red eyes and the tall imposing figure of his enemy as he sees Roshtu standing up and hears the frightening sound of him drawing his sword. Robert instantly pulls another arrow to his bow and fires it at Roshtu, the speed of the shot catches the dark knight unawares.

Roshtu manages to block the arrow but in doing so, drops his sword. Robert warns the dark knight not to underestimate his strength. Roshtu is incensed that the human would consider himself to be a worthy opponent and the incensed evil knight begins to fire continuous fireballs at the human.

Robert is quick to respond but is barely able to shoot his arrows in time to deflect each of the shots.

Suddenly much to Robert's relief, Roshtu stops shooting at him but then the Welshman notices his enemy smiling and gesturing for him to look at the satchel containing his arrows. Robert is not prepared to fall for this trickery and keeps his eyes fixed on Roshtu. Instead he reaches his free hand backwards to retrieve the next arrow but is soon alarmed when he cannot feel any within his grasp. The human's fears are realized when he glances anxiously over his shoulder only to realize that his supply of feathered arrows has run out. He believes that Roshtu has cast some dark magic but then notices there are some of his used weapons that are scattered on the floor, although he doubts that he will be given the opportunity to retrieve any of them.

Deciding that attack is the best form of defense, Robert charges towards the desk to try and deactivate the energy shield but Roshtu blocks his path. The dark knight physically man handles the human and throws him across the room. Robert lands to the floor but he is not deterred and is adamant that he can get past the dark knight but each time he attempts to reach the desk he is repeatedly met with brute force and tossed aside to land exhaustedly on the floor.

With no energy left to pick himself up Robert is shattered and upset that the enemy standing in his way of success is more than a match for him. The dark knight decides he has had enough toying with the human and prepares to fire a mortal blow. Robert manages to gather the last ounce of energy and stands up to face his opponent. With the glowing ball of energy within his palm, Roshtu smiles at the human's determination and asks, "Why do you bother to resist when those who you fight for will all be dead? The queen has lost and you have no future".

A burning rage develops within Robert and he charges towards his attacker with fury but the dark knight grabs hold of Robert by the throat and crushes him against the nearest wall. Suddenly the door that had previously been locked opens on its own accord. Roshtu detect this and immediately drops Robert from his grasp. The human lands hard onto the floor, desperately trying to breathe again and massages his bruised throat. Roshtu moves toward the door in case there should be any more of the foolish humans but he cannot see anyone. Satisfied that the threat no longer exists, Roshtu turns around to execute Robert.

Still recovering from the assault, Robert has already reached towards the desk and pulls back on the lever, which now deactivates the energy shield surrounding the operating machine of the portal. Before he can try to destroy the machine the injuries he has sustained from the battle causes him to fall to the floor in pain and now the dark knight strides closer to kill him.

Suddenly from the corner of the darkened room the white thin staff belonging to Peirlee, comes into vision and a tremendous bolt of power is fired from the weapon that strikes the dark knight directly in the back.

Roshtu gasps in shock and falls crippled to the floor. He looks up in disbelief at his assassin. Peirlee the witch stands over her dying master and whispers to him, "We could have had everything," and then she fires the fatal blow from her staff that kills the dark knight.

With the witch looking over the dead body of Roshtu, Robert is able to retrieve two arrows from the floor before firing one of them into the machine and causing it to burst into flames. Robert feels a tremendous sense of relief to have not let Juliana down but before he can place the other arrow to his bow he notices the witch has already pointed her dangerous weapon at him.

Robert reasons with Peirlee that the war is now over but she warns him, "It is not over for me". Then in a raised and uncontrollable voice she declares her leadership of Sephire. With her staff still pointed at Robert she tells him, "My kingdom has no place for humans". With his final thoughts of Juliana and his friends, Robert waits for the inevitable execution when suddenly Queen Juliana bursts into the room and startles the witch.

The humanoid queen defiantly announces, "I am not prepared to relinquish my leadership just yet".

Robert cannot believe what is happening and both the human and Queen Juliana prepare themselves for a final standoff against the formidable witch.

As the three occupants within the room remain deadly still but poised to react upon the first person's movement, Robert is pleased to see Juliana but is also concerned that she will come to harm. Quickly he places his final arrow to the bow and fires it at the witch. From across the room Queen Juliana also shoots at Peirlee from her scepter. The purple beam of energy from the queen's weapon reaches Peirlee first but the sorceress is quick to react and uses her staff to successfully parry the blast. However before the witch can attack Juliana, the arrow fired from Robert pierces into Peirlee's shoulder and she stumbles to the ground gasping in shock.

Upon seeing the witch lowering her guard, Juliana fires at her but despite her injury, Peirlee is able to avoid the shots and dashes in pain towards the windows as a means for her escape. Before she can open them, a shot fired from Juliana catches her in the back and the powerful blast sends Peirlee crashing through the glass.

Hearing the anguish cries from the witch, Juliana hurries towards the shattered window and watches Peirlee let go of her staff as she continues to plummet towards the flickering portal.

Juliana is convinced that the witch is defeated. She sighs and tells Robert that it is over but the brave majesty is soon concerned when he fails to respond. Turning around, Juliana screams out in horror when she sees him lying wounded on the floor and dashes to him. Juliana assumes he had been hit by the shot that Peirlee had deflected. She kneels close beside him frantically hoping to save him.

Whilst breathing erratically, Robert gazes helplessly up at Juliana. She appears to be mortified by the severity of his chest wound. The Welshman recollects this is what he had seen in his dreams as he looks down and sees blood on his hands, feeling that his life is slipping away. Juliana attempts to stand up to get assistance but Robert holds onto her hand and tells her painfully, "It is too late for me". Juliana cries at the thought of loosing him and cradles his head in her arms pleading, "Hold on my Love!"

With precious time remaining, Juliana tells Robert, "I want you to know I am no longer afraid to admit that it has been your strength that has help guide me to lead my people". Robert continues to grasp onto her wrists, for the first time in his life he has experienced the sensation of true love and hears

Juliana crying out for him not to close his eyes. He wishes he could force the pain away but he is unable to keep his eyes open any longer. Holding onto his last breath, Robert lets go and says his last words "I love you".

Juliana screams, "This is not how it's supposed to end!" Juliana can feel his pulse fading as his death draws nearer. Crying uncontrollably, Juliana notices a light that sparkles against the cold tiles of the floor.

Wondering what is happening the royal leader looks up at the glittering green light surrounding a woman with long flowing blonde hair who stands before her. Juliana stares up in amazement and asks, "Are you an angel?" The majestic female responds, "I am Carmen", and then the glittering green light fades away leaving Carmen to appear as any other humanoid.

After her transformation, Carmen looks down at Robert dying and speaks to Juliana, "The power of the witch is over, I have been brought back to life by the gods and now I will provide life back to this brave human who has saved Sephire from turmoil".

Juliana watches in bewilderment as Carmen pours a potion onto Robert's chest wound. The queen watches anxiously for a reaction from Robert but nothing is happening. She is about to ask why is it not working when suddenly by some miracle his wound begins to heal and Juliana can feel his pulse and see him breathing once again. Tears that were previously cried through sorrow are replaced with tears of joy and Juliana looks down at Robert still cradled in her arms to see him opening his eyes. Juliana tells him, "I love you". Robert smiles but still feels terribly weak.

Realizing the burning of the machine has increased and that smoke pours out from it, Carmen and Queen Juliana together help Robert up to his feet and make their way out from the burning room.

Chapter Twenty One

Elsewhere inside the castle, Finch attempts to escape by climbing down a vine. Just as the pursuing humans enter the room he balances on top of the balcony still grasping the book that will show him where the buried treasure is kept. Finch crawls down but the creeper begins to creak under the pressure of his weight. The creature's eyes widen in shock when the vine begins to sway and he accidentally drops the book onto the balcony.

Trying to retrieve it before the humans can realize what has happened, Finch uses his weight to swing the vine back towards the balcony but the vine snaps and he screams out helplessly as he plummets. Bobby hurries over to look down from the balcony and much to the teenager's satisfaction, he watches Finch splat directly into the murky water of the moat. Simon and Claire are both relieved to find the Black Book of Barmothenue has not landed open and the brave legionnaire carefully picks the book up.

Bobby notices the portal in the courtyard is flickering and watches thousands of apes hurrying to return to their ape planet through fear of being marooned on Sephire. The teenager turns around to inform his sister but groans when he sees Claire and Simon are kissing. Upon hearing Bobby's complaints they part their lips and look out from the balcony where they also see that the apes are in retreat. Bobby walks up to Simon and shakes his hand whilst apologizing for the way that he has been behaving toward him.

Claire suddenly senses the presence of Robert from nearby. Simon is desperate to help his friend and leads them out from the room where they are surprised to find their companion being helped by Carmen and Queen Juliana.

Before they can ask what had happened, Juliana warns them, "Robert is recovering from his attack with Roshtu and Peirlee. I left some guards outside to protect Hideki and

Rachel". She then allows the humanoid guards who have now arrived, to safely carry Robert outside. Claire notifies the queen that the apes are fleeing through the portal that is beginning to close. Juliana sighs in relief, she finally feels the battle is now over. Suddenly smoke from the control room engulfs the corridor and Carmen urges everyone to get out from the fortress.

Surfacing from the filthy water, Finch hauls himself out from the moat coughing and spluttering. He curses the humans for denying him of his rightful fortune and threatens to get even. However he soon finds himself in the path of the stampeding apes who are desperately trying to return through the flickering portal and has to jump out of the way to avoid being crushed. Finch looses his balance and finds himself falling back into the moat once again.

On the battleground the humanoid forces encounter no further resistance and mass as one large group towards the fortress. Hideki and Rachel who had been fighting in battle are told of the portal closing and they embrace one another upon hearing the success of their friends.

The humanoid forces reach the wooden drawbridge and watch the last ape retreating through the portal when suddenly the image of the alien planet vanishes and the shinning light diminishes causing the humanoids to cheer with delight.

Rachel and Hideki receive a grateful welcome from Bobby, Simon and Claire before they gather around Robert in hope that he will soon recover. Queen Juliana is assisted by some of the humanoids to help lift the injured Welshman to a waiting carriage, where he will be looked after by medics.

With the humans bewildered to see that Carman has come back to living existence once again, Claire shows the Black Book of Barmothenue to the spiritual humanoid but Carmen warns them, "With the presence of Peirlee now gone this book cannot be used to open a gateway on its own".

Unsure of what they are to do, the Saviours of Sephire look to one another in bewilderment. Rachel is devastated and asks the special humanoid what happens now? The majestic female speaks calmly to everyone, "The ending of the enemy, now brings the time for humanoids to unite".

Queen Juliana momentarily leaves Robert's carriage to ask her royal guards if they know where Commander Teltris is? The bleeding leader of the villagers has heard the question and regretfully informs his queen, "I am afraid the commander perished from the attack. He fought for you, your highness and for Sephire". Queen Juliana hangs her head in sorrow and looks at what is left of the humanoids. She notices their torn clothes and cut faces, knowing that her people have paid heavily for this victory.

Juliana announces to everyone, "The commander and those who have died to save our planet will be remembered in honour. We shall build a burial temple here in the north to remind those in years to come of the sacrifice many gave to restore our freedom".

Before she can continue, a loud explosion is heard coming from within the fortress. Juliana warns everyone to step away for their safety but as she speaks a downpour of rain falls from the sky. The burning fires become controlled and are left to smolder. The rain, washes away the dirt and grime from everyone's uniform and the humanoids begin to bury their fallen comrades.

A month from the passing of the evil power that once loomed in the north the rain suddenly stops and much to the humanoids' amazement, plants and grass begins to grow across the harsh landscape. With salvation restored in the north the time has now come for the humanoids to gather their forces and search for those who have sought refuge in the forests before returning to Valadreil.

The villagers have decided to remain in the north, where they will live and complete the temple to honour the dead from the battle of Sephire. Queen Juliana bids farewell to the villagers and tells them she will send help as soon as she can. Juliana then leads her horse to rejoin the front of the slow moving convoy that travels south. They take with them the painful memories, which will carry with them for the rest of their lives.

Robert, the human responsible for bringing hope back to her people, accompanies Juliana. She can no longer hide her love for him. They look fondly at one another, unafraid of what others may be thinking.

Chapter Twenty Two

The humanoids along with the Saviours of Sephire, return along paths that were once unknown through fear of the threat in the north. That threat, no longer remains and the convoy manages to find those who are in hiding. Upon hearing the news, many cannot comprehend that the dark knight the apes and his witch have been defeated.

The humans have fulfilled the prophecy and become the Saviours of Sephire. They travel with the increasing number of humanoids, taking the next four months to arrive at the tall wooden gates of Valadreil and enter the humanoid's capital.

Queen Juliana sits in her saddle and takes in the familiar surroundings. Valadreil is exactly how she remembered it to be, although she is saddened that those killed in battle are not able to see the glistening towers once again.

With the season being autumn, the air is crisp and the sun begins to set much earlier in the day. Robert shares the relief felt from the people all around him. He gets down from his horse and helps Juliana to dismount. She briefly holds onto his hand before letting go and follows her waiting handmaidens into the palace. Robert turns around and is joined by his human companions. He looks at each of their faces and realizes how much they have changed since two years ago when they had first entered Sephire. So much has happened since that eventful day, where they had found themselves lost on the beach.

Robert smiles at them not knowing of what to say. He feels honoured to have known this group of friends.

The Saviours of Sephire huddle together at the top of the stairs to the entrance of the palace, finally realizing their adventure is now over.

Once Carmen has been handed all three of the special powered books she informs the humans, "I will go down to the archives and research on how to combine the power from each of the books to create a gateway". She then departs, leaving the humans feeling disappointed. Tired from the long journey they decide to recuperate and walk towards their chambers.

As they walk inside the palace, Simon suspects it will take Carmen some considerable time to be able find the information. Robert replies, "There has always been doubt if the books would be of any use, we must be hopeful that Carmen is successful". He then asks if they will continue to offer their assistance to the humanoids in whatever way they can. Simon, Claire, Bobby, Rachel and Hideki each agree that they will lend their support to the humanoids.

The free people of Sephire have already begun the process of re-sowing crops and growing trees hoping to rebuild their civilization.

Robert spends the next few weeks working with a farmer, helping him to plant seeds within the long sweeping fields and to tend to his livestock. The Welshman still has the bruises from battle and carefully gathers his tools. He is separated from his human companions who remain in Valadreil to help with the restructuring of the cobbled streets and education of the young.

Dressed in farmer's clothes Robert spends most of the day working alone in the fields. With Juliana being away to help the villagers he has felt lonely. He wishes he could be with her so much but at the same time he does not wish to place her leadership into jeopardy. Even though his companions are expecting him to return to Earth with them, he cannot push away the desire he has to remain here on Sephire and be with Juliana.

Robert looks up at the sky realizing the sun will soon be setting and decides to leave his problems for another day. Picking up his rake and fork he places the farmer's cap onto his head before walking in between rows of corn and into the direction of the farmer's hut that is situated on top of a small hill a mile away.

Mopping his sweaty brow from the physical work he has done toady, Robert then notices smoke coming out from the chimney of the farmer's hut and assumes they are preparing for dinner. As soon as Robert approaches the hut his heart begins to pound upon the sight of four beautiful horses with one bearing the royal emblem of Sephire on its saddle. The farmer's boy is looking after the horses. Robert calls out to the boy, who informs him they have guests waiting inside.

The curious human wonders who could it be and hurries to put his tools away whilst doing his best to make himself presentable. Unable to delay the moment any longer, he opens the barn door and instantly hears the familiar voice of the farmer. The Welshman sees the back of three people in front of him but as the wooden barn door closes the sound causes the elderly farmer to stop talking and he looks up from his chair.

Wondering what is happening, Robert waits nervously hoping not to receive bad news but then a slender dark cloaked figure in the middle of the group turns around and pulls back the hood. Robert smiles at the face of the person in front of him and Queen Juliana smiles back at him. Robert desperately wants to dash up and cuddle her but suspects the two royal guards who are now bowed before him would not be best pleased.

Acknowledging the guards Robert gratefully accepts Juliana's hand and she leads him back outside to watch the beautiful sunset where they can talk alone.

Walking a safe distance away from the hut the two hold hands and gaze fondly into each other's eyes.

Juliana tells him, "Since the ending of the battle, many things have changed but my feelings for you have remained". Robert confesses to her, "I don't like to be apart from you but I understand that as queen you must support all humanoids on Sephire". Juliana reminds him there could still be a chance of Carmen finding a way for him and his friends to return to Earth.

At this moment Robert steps away from Queen Juliana, which surprises her and he looks to where the sun has set, finally understanding the decision he has just made. Turning around, Robert informs Juliana, "I will not be returning to Earth". Juliana is shocked but also relieved to hear this and asks, "What about your friends will you not miss them?" Robert admits, "Yes I will, but I want to stay with you. If I were to go back to Earth, the strong feelings that I have for you would be lost and never rekindled".

Queen Juliana is touched by his honesty and confesses to him, "All my life, I have felt alone, with only my parents to give me their affection, that was until I met you. There is no other person who I would like to spend the rest of my life with". Queen Juliana then takes hold of Robert's hands and asks him to marry her.

Robert is surprised at first, but he fears the consequences to Juliana should he agree. Robert says, "I cannot deny you of your leadership. I could not ask you to step down from power to be able to marry someone who is not noble". Feeling despondent Robert lowers his head but Juliana is quick to gently hold his head up and explains to him, "You and your companions have become legends of our time. My people have already accepted you to become King of Sephire".

With all fears now cast aside, Robert kisses Juliana and says he will be honoured to marry her and then cuddles her. They hold onto the moment for as long as possible before returning towards the farmer's hut to celebrate and to tell the first of many with the good news.

Over the next few days the happy couple rides along the pathway leading towards the capital. Robert notices his human companions are just ahead of them and appear to be embarking on another journey.

The two groups greet one another before Queen Juliana tells Robert, "I must leave to speak with the dignitaries and inform them of our decision". Bidding farewell, the queen rides with her royal guards and enters Valadreil, where she is welcomed back by her people.

Claire asks Robert, "What is going on?" The Welshman cannot withhold his excitement any longer and tells them, "I am going to marry Juliana and become King of Sephire!" His friends sit on their saddles and stare back at him in astonishment. Rachel is the first to congratulate him and gives her cousin a hug, saying emotionally, "I always knew you would make a name for yourself".

Hideki and Bobby both shake Robert's hand to congratulate him. Robert then looks at his childhood friend but Simon is too dumbfounded to comprehend what he has heard. The Welshman senses that his close friend is struggling to come to terms with the news and tries to ease the tension by taking his mind away from the subject. Robert asks Simon, "Where are you all going?" The Englishman replies bluntly, "Since there is no longer the need to have our weapons we are going to return them back into the large chest, which is buried at the monument of stones and retrieve the clothes we wore when we came here".

Robert nods his head in acceptance that his friends are anxious to return home and wonders if Carmen has made any progress. Hideki replies, "Carmen feels she is close to finding the information to activate a gateway". Simon comments, "We must leave now if we are to reach the monument of stones before sunset". He then rides along the pathway, leaving the others to follow. Robert is surprised with his friend's reaction as he had hoped Simon would give him his blessing. Bobby attempts to catch up with the legionnaire to try and talk some sense into him.

Rachel holds Robert's arm and assures him, "Don't worry, Simon is just upset I'm sure he will come to understand, he just needs some time". Robert hopes that his cousin is right and then passes his bow and holdall containing the arrows to Hideki whilst asking him, "Please could you take this with you, I won't be needing it any longer". The Japanese warrior looks after the weapon and the group bids farewell to their companion, hopeful to be returning in a couple of days.

Robert watches them go and feels saddened that their lives will take them along a different path from his own but he then remembers the woman he intends to marry. Robert smiles and guides his horse to move forwards to enter the town of Valadreil, he is unsure of what kind of reaction he will receive from the townsfolk.

Upon his arrival, thousands of humanoids have aligned the streets having heard the rumours of him becoming their future king. Robert is relieved to be welcomed back to Valadreil with cheers and messages of congratulations.

Chapter Twenty Three

After a months work of preparations the wedding day has finally arrived. Robert is waiting inside the royal throne room and stands at the front of a large audience who are waiting in silence. Dressed in the best humanoid clothes available, Robert continues to be patient. Beads of sweat begin to develop on his forehead and he looks to his best man for support. Fortunately Simon had finally accepted Robert's decision to remain on Sephire and stands alongside his friend as he has done throughout their time together. Simon knows Robert is lucky to be marrying a woman as special as Juliana but he still feels depressed that his friend will not be joining them should they ever find a way to return home.

Upon seeing how tense Robert is, Simon teases him by asking him if he remembers what he has to say.

Robert's expression does not express confidence and he glances to the back of the grand hall towards the doors hoping that any second now Juliana will enter and then be led down the aisle by Rachel who has been chosen to be the maid of honour.

As each passing second ticks by, Robert hopes Juliana has not had a change of heart. The people within the grand hall slowly begin to mutter and his concerns continue to mount. Suddenly the doors are pulled open by humanoid guards and the queen enters with the sound of trumpets being played. Robert will not be denied a look at his forthcoming wife and stares open-mouthed at the beautiful sight of Queen Juliana whom is dressed in a silky pale blue wedding gown. The trumpets then stop playing, the audience is seated and Rachel who is dressed elegantly, follows Queen Juliana along the aisle towards Robert.

With his heart pounding in excitement, Robert's eyes are fixed on Juliana as his cousin accompanies Simon to join their other human companions. The Welshman notices how smart his human friends are dressed, even Bobby. He begins to feel the euphoria of this special occasion but manages to control his emotions and keeps his composure. Staring at Juliana he knows there are no doubts in his mind of the decision he has made and they both smile at one another. Simon coughs from the crowd, prompting Robert to remember to take hold of Juliana's hand and allow the ceremony to commence.

Accepting Juliana's hand they both walk up the steps towards a stage where the gracious chairs of the king and queen are placed. Upon reaching the stage the couple turns around to face their audience at which point they begin to speak their individual wedding vows. The words spoken are from the ancient humanoid language. Robert is able to translate his vows, which signify his undying love for Juliana. The queen declares that her love for him shall remain until the passing of time and she gratefully accepts him to be her husband. She then offers him the seat of the king.

Robert looks at the seat in awe of its power and of the responsibilities that will follow. Frozen to the spot through fear, Robert stares at the chair. With each eye blink the seat appears to be growing in size but he realizes this is because his legs are automatically walking him towards the chair as if he is a spectator in his own body.

Once he is seated, Robert senses a tingling sensation as he begins to realize that his destiny has been fulfilled. The queen also sits in her seat alongside Robert and the handmaidens place the hand crafted silver crowns onto the king and queen's head, at which point the audience's loud applause causes the hair on the back of Robert's neck to stand up on end.

The new humanoid king and queen both stand and walk hand in hand down the aisle towards the open doors whilst acknowledging the audience's congratulations. Robert and Juliana both share tears of joy and are followed by those who have witnessed the ceremony. Glancing out from the windows of the hallway, Robert is shocked to see thousands of gathered humanoids are waiting beyond the courtyard.

The queen's handmaidens lead the majesties outside where they are welcomed with more cheers and applause. Robert soon notices that on the courtyard a young girl is accompanied with a harpist and a group of violinists' who begin to play a tune. The young girl begins to sing a song to mark the joyous occasion, her voice is powerful and yet has the sound of an angel.

The spectators enjoy the performance and two horse-ridden carriages are then brought to a halt in front of the king and queen who are about to leave for a romantic destination. Robert turns around as his human friends bring them their gifts. Robert appreciates their gesture and whilst helping his wife to get into the carriage, turns around to thank them all when he suddenly hears the voice of a woman screaming for them to stop.

Wondering what the commotion is about the gathered spectators become silent. Bobby notices that the woman approaching is Carmen.

Since she had come back from the afterlife, the humanoids considered her to be spiritual and wise. Now Carmen is seen grasping onto all three of the magical books. Bowing before the majesties, she hastily informs the humans that she has discovered a way for them to return home but stresses to them, "We must leave immediately and travel towards a lake within the forest, otherwise the chance will be lost forever".

Robert is shocked to hear this and quickly tells Bobby, Hideki, Claire and Simon to ride in the other carriage that was meant to be for the queen's handmaidens. Carmen provides both of the riders with a route to their destination. Robert then allows Rachel and Carmen to enter the spacious royal carriage before getting in and closing the doors behind him.

The crowds understand that the Saviours of Sephire may never return and begin to show their gratitude by cheering their heroes, whose names will be remembered as legends of their history. As the horse and carriages begin to move forwards,

Robert's companions look back at the glistening towers of Valadreil. The humans hoping to return to Earth are sad this day has finally come where they will leave the humanoids to get on with their lives.

Chapter Twenty Four

The large presence of humanoids maneuver out of the way to allow the two horse ridden carriages to pass by. The number of humanoids who have come to celebrate the royal wedding is overwhelming and both carriages continue to move along the cobbled streets that are aligned with people. The horses eventually reaches past the gates of Valadreil. Robert sees his cousin take one final look of the vast capital whilst in the other carriage Simon points out a stone carving to Bobby. The teenager is amazed and gasps, "Wow I never thought I would be honoured by anyone. Look they have me holding my club".

Hideki jokes, "They carved a statue of Bobby first because he would take the quickest to complete".

Simon laughs as the older teenager raises his objections in between giggles and they continue to ride towards the eastern lands of Sephire.

A couple of hours later, the riders bring their horses to a halt along the borders of a forest. Carmen announces that they have arrived and calmly steps out of the carriage along with Rachel to join the others.

Queen Juliana asks Robert to remain with her for a moment before saying, "I can sense how saddened you are to be parting from your friends. If you are unable to say goodbye to them, I will understand should you wish to return with them back to Earth".

Robert looks to his wife and grasps gently onto her hands and tells her, "I admit I am upset to see them go but I am also happy that my friends have the chance to return to where they belong and live their lives.

For me, I know I belong here with you and would not wish to be anywhere else". Juliana is comforted by what he has told her and they both step outside to follow behind the group who are led by Carmen.

The spiritual humanoid takes them past some trees of the forest where after a short distance they find a small lake that Carmen calls by the name of Mawrllyn. Sephire's red moon is reflected against the calmness of the water to the lake. Robert and his companions wait in anticipation as Carmen places all three books on the edge of the grass before speaking phrases from ancient times.

With a few minutes having elapsed, Carmen is still talking but to no avail of anything happening. Bobby whispers to Simon, "I don't think Carmen's spell is working". The Englishman asks him to be patient and they remain fixed on the female humanoid.

Suddenly the group has to shield their eyes from a bright light, which appears with the opening from each of the three books. Robert catches sight of pages being automatically turned before they suddenly stop on one particular page. Carmen manages to see through the brightness and looks down at a phrase, which has been highlighted in each of the books.

With their hearts pounding with excitement, the gathered spectators hear Carmen speak out each phrase.

Suddenly water from the lake begins to bubble. Slowly a sparkling white platform rises above the water and an image of a closed door appears from the middle of the crossing.

Carmen has now stopped speaking, she turns around to the humans to inform them, "The time has now come for you to return to the world that you left with one day having elapsed. The quest is now over, you have completed your duty to Sephire and will be remembered as the Saviours of Sephire". Carmen then bows before them.

Beyond Carmen, the door on the crossing opens to show a picture of an island where everyone notices the golden sand of a beach and the clear blue sky. Bobby cannot believe what he can see and screams jubilantly, "It's Earth!"

Realizing that it is time to say their good-byes, one by one they approach the queen and give Juliana their warm-hearted wishes. Individually they prepare to bid a sad farewell to Robert who has decided not to return with them. Hideki shakes Robert's hand and tells him he is honoured to have fought alongside a hero. Robert thanks him and is barely able to withhold his tears.

Rachel then gives her cousin a big hug saying to him, "I will miss you but I know that you will find happiness here".

Claire thanks Robert for everything and wishes him her best, as does her younger brother. Robert looks at Bobby, amazed by how much he has grown and matured.

Simon is the last to say goodbye to Robert, they have known each other since childhood and have been through so much together. Now it seems sad that they will never see each other again. Robert can sense his close friend is too emotional to speak and decides to hug him. Whispering in his ear, Robert thanks Simon for always having been there to support him and tells him to consider himself to always be his good friend. The Welshman reaches into his pocket to retrieve a card before handing it to Simon.

The Englishman looks at the picture of San Francisco's sunset and realizes it is the postcard Robert had previously purchased from the amusement park on Earth. Robert informs his friend, "I have written down a message and ask if you would be kind enough to send it onto my parents". The Englishman nods his head and allows Claire to offer her support. Robert asks Claire to take good care of Simon. Claire promises that she will when suddenly her younger brother yells, "I can see the boat that was washed up on the beach where we left it".

Carmen warns them the gateway will not remain open forever and Robert watches his friends saying farewell to the spiritual woman before they walk across the platform. Upon reaching the open gateway the departing humans turn around and wave back to Robert, Juliana and Carmen before entering through the doorway.

A small feeling of sorrow not to join his friends remains inside Robert but he feels the enchanting presence of Juliana and knows this is where he wants to be and places his arm around her.

Accompanied by Carmen, Robert and his wife look on to see that his friends have safely returned to the beach when the image vanishes and the doorway then closes. The crossing platform lowers down into the water and Lake Mawrllyn returns to how they found it.

Carmen smiles at the happy ending and informs the majesties that she will go back and wait for them in the carriage. Before she walks away Robert asks her if she is going to take the three books back with her?

The wise humanoid responds gently, "The books no longer contain any power, they are safe for all to see". Carmen then leaves the king and queen to be alone.

Robert and Juliana take a slow walk back towards the horses. Juliana tells her husband she feels save to be here within his arms. Robert kisses her forehead in affection, happy just to be with her.

Meanwhile a shadow appears below one of the trees surrounding Lake Mawrllyn. A small creature with a tail lurks towards the water's edge. The creature is seen to be carrying a long thin pole and then suddenly stops to be certain that it has not been seen. The feline tracker called Finch had been spying on what had happened.

The opening of the gateway had not interested him, as his only desire is to learn of the location to Sephire's treasure, which is contained within the Black Book of Barmothenue. Gleaming with joy that the humanoid king and queen would be foolish enough to have left the book behind, Finch bends down and holds his prize under the moonlight to read of its contents.

Opening the book, Finch is immediately horrified to discover that it contains only blank pages. Frantically searching through the other two books he screams out in frustration upon discovering that the pages are exactly the same in those as well and are worthless to him. Annoyed to have failed, he throws all three books into the lake.

With his breath visible against the cold temperature, Finch suddenly comes up with an idea. Controlling his anger, Finch picks up the magic staff that once belonged to Peirlee and comments to himself, "Yes I know who can help me". He then begins to crawl inconspicuously towards the trees where he intends to travel towards the eastern shores.

With Carmen opening the doors, Robert and Juliana enter the royal carriage. Once the doors are closed the horses are led away to return to Valadreil. Robert stares out of the window, wondering how his life has changed and of the responsibilities now placed upon his shoulders.

As the pale green sun begins to rise, both carriages are seen to be traveling towards the distant horizon where the king and queen are both excited to be able to lead the humanoids in a world that has finally restored peace.

About the Author

Owen Butler is thirty years old and was born and raised near Windsor. He works as an assistant accountant and relocated to Wiltshire where he now lives with his wife and their dominating cat.

Printed in the United Kingdom
by Lightning Source UK Ltd.
124656UK00001B/25/A

9 781425 998158